UNDER ATTACK!

Through the hotel's open windows, manhunters Asa Cain and Cemetery John quickly sized up the situation. Outside were half a dozen armed and cursing men. "I'm beginning to get a real dislike for this town," Cemetery John said as they both took cover.

A heavy boot smashed open the door. "There they are boys," a fat man with a bloody bandanna tied across the right side of his face growled. "Them's are the bastards that did this to me. Now let's have some fun and kill both of 'em."

Cemetery John's shotgun boomed loudly as the man was blasted back through the door in a spray of crimson.

"Damn, they up an' kilt Uncle Wesley," a shrill voice cried out before Asa silenced him with two slugs through the chest.

"Charge the son's a bitches," another thug bellowed. "They's only two of them an' four of usn's."

Cemetery John slid a fresh cartridge into his ten-gauge and fired both barrels at the first two attackers. The red-hot buckshot tore through their middles. Asa's Henry barked once, and the third man's forehead exploded. Two slugs slammed into the heart of the last man.

"You okay?" Cemetery John asked.

"One of those bastards was luckier than I expected," Asa said as blood ran down his arm.

BOOK YOUR PLACE ON OUR WEBSITE AND MAKE THE READING CONNECTION!

We've created a customized website just for our very special readers, where you can get the inside scoop on everything that's going on with Zebra, Pinnacle and Kensington books.

When you come online, you'll have the exciting opportunity to:

- View covers of upcoming books
- Read sample chapters
- Learn about our future publishing schedule (listed by publication month *and author*)
- Find out when your favorite authors will be visiting a city near you
- Search for and order backlist books from our online catalog
- Check out author bios and background information
- Send e-mail to your favorite authors
- Meet the Kensington staff online
- Join us in weekly chats with authors, readers and other guests
- Get writing guidelines
- AND MUCH MORE!

**Visit our website at
http://www.kensingtonbooks.com**

HARD BOUNTY

KEN HODGSON

PINNACLE BOOKS
Kensington Publishing Corp.
http://www.kensingtonbooks.com

*In memory of
Fred Bean*

*Non omnis moriar.
I shall not wholly die.*

Then out spake brave Horatius,
the captain of the gate:
"To every man upon this earth
Death cometh soon or late.
And how can man die better
Than facing fearful odds,
For the ashes of his fathers
And the temples of his gods?"

—*Macaulay*

Do unto the other feller the way he'd like to
do unto you an' do it fust.

—*Edward Noyes Westcott*

PART ONE

BITTER HOMECOMING

ONE

Raz Pendragon had just plopped several strips of moldy bacon into a blackened skillet when a heavy-caliber lead slug came screaming across the rolling, cactus-studded West Texas countryside and blew out his heart.

Jake Freeman, Raz's longtime partner on the owlhoot trail, winced in shock as his friend was swatted away from the campfire in a spray of crimson, but he did not allow his surprise to linger. Jake had not survived for years as a bank robber and highwayman by allowing himself to become rattled by something so trivial as having a partner killed.

He dove from the rock he was sitting on to the dry earth, grabbing up his Winchester with a fluid motion before flattening out like a horned toad behind a scrawny mesquite bush.

The outlaw squinted into the red glare of a dying sun where the shot had come from. Whoever was out there, he had to give them some grudging credit. Making your adversary stare into the sun was a great advantage, one he had used many times himself.

"Who in the hell are you?" Jake yelled at the

top of his lungs. He had quickly dismissed the idea that a lawman had killed his partner in cold blood; lawmen had the admirable tendency to yell out a warning before shooting. He was likely dealing with a fellow outlaw, the type of person he could do business with. "We're just cowboys on our way to Mexico. What do you want?"

Only the wind sighing across the prairie answered his call.

He kept stone still for a long while, blinking watery eyes into the lowering sun, looking for any movement to shoot at. Jake kept a steady finger on the trigger and collected his thoughts. He was most assuredly dealing with a lone man. Indians or a posse from Wolf Springs, where Raz had plugged a skinny bank teller who'd had the temerity to pull a gun while they were making a withdrawal, would certainly have kicked up some type of disturbance by now. A group of men always worked themselves into a fever pitch and did something rash. At least, Jake decided, the odds were even.

But where in the hell *was* this gun-toting phantom? Nothing except mesquite leaves and dry grass moved against the bloody sun. His patience exhausted, Jake removed the sweat-stained flop hat that had somehow remained on his head, stuck it over the barrel of his Winchester, and began waving it like a flag.

"You can drop that rifle and live to hang, or I can take care of the matter here and now—your call."

Jake froze. The voice came from his back side and its calm, coldly unemotional tone, along with the surprise of having someone sneak up on him totally unheard, gave the outlaw sufficient encouragement to unhand his Winchester and allow it to fall onto the dusty earth.

"Smart move," the voice behind him intoned. "Keep your hands out where I can see them and get to your feet nice and slow. If you so much as twitch, I'll blow a hole in you big enough for a bird to fly through."

Jake Freeman did as he was told. His left leg had gone to sleep during his time on the ground, but he didn't dare try to shake life back into the thing. It was an effort to get to his feet.

"Turn around."

The desperado gingerly placed his weight on his good leg and turned to face the man who had killed Raz Pendragon. He winced when he recognized the thin, clean-shaven young man who had shoulder-length blond hair and piercing blue eyes that never seemed to blink. Every outlaw in Kansas and Texas knew of and feared this unassuming man.

"You're that bounty hunter, Asa Cain," Jake said. "I've heard tell folks call you the undertaker's friend. I reckon they were right."

"I don't pay any mind to saloon talk. But keep in mind the governor's office will pay me a thousand dollars for you whether you're breathing or draped over a saddle." Cain nodded to the bloodied corpse lying sprawled against a scrawny greasewood bush. "Pendragon there's worth five hundred more than you are. I figured he might make for the most trouble, so I decided to take him back the easy way."

"You didn't even give him a chance," Jake said bitterly.

"I gave him as much chance as he did that whore he killed over in Sulphur Springs. I can't abide any outlaw that'll kill a woman." Asa kept his .44-caliber Henry rifle pointed squarely at the outlaw's chest as he slipped a pair of handcuffs from his belt and tossed them over. "Put 'em on, nice and tight."

Jake gritted his teeth in anger when he picked up the steel cuffs. "What I'd like to know is how in hell you got behind me without makin' a sound. I've heard tell that you was part Indian, but with those eyes an' hair I reckon it ain't so."

"I'm not Indian, but I was raised by the Comanche for six years. It made for good training. Now snap on those cuffs and I'll give Sheriff Wilburn Deevers of Wolf Springs, Texas, reason to hold a hanging. That banker your pardner went an' shot was a friend of his."

"I ain't never kilt nobody." Freeman's voice had turned desperate.

"Don't matter to the law. You were there an' you'll hang same as if you pulled the trigger."

Jake's hand began trembling so that he dropped the handcuffs. "Don't go gettin' upset none, Cain. I'll pick 'em up nice and easy, an' put 'em on. I promise I ain't gonna cause you no trouble."

The bounty hunter simply nodded.

Freeman knew that getting his boot gun out before Cain sent a bullet through him was a long shot, but it sure beat his chances if he tarried. He had watched a hanging once in the Indian Territory. The man had died slow and hard. It was sufficient motivation to cause him to put on his best act at being scared and give the task his best effort. He had carried the Butterfield .41-caliber pocket pistol in a leather holster sewn inside his right boot for years as insurance against this type of happening. It was time to see if he was good enough to kill the famous bounty hunter.

"My leg went to sleep while I was waitin' on you," Freeman said shakily. "I'll likely have a bit of trouble gettin' those cuffs. Don't go an' get an itchy trigger finger."

Asa Cain clucked his tongue and nodded again.

Jake groaned as he bent down, then quickly dropped and rolled behind a huge cholla cactus and extracted the Butterfield. When the outlaw spun to fire, a slug of hot lead hit him square in the Adam's apple, almost blowing his head off his shoulders. Freeman was dead before his body slumped to the earth.

Asa sidestepped and jacked another round into the Henry. He knew the fugitive had been fatally wounded, but like a man who handled dynamite, his first mistake would likely be his last. He had seen a lot of people soak up lethal doses of lead and still be able to shoot a gun before actually cashing in their final chip.

Keeping the rifle pointed at the bloody figure on the ground, Asa used the toe of his boot to kick away the pocket pistol. Patiently he waited several moments to make certain life had fled the outlaw; then he lowered the hammer on his rifle and shook his head sadly.

"Blasted idiots. Just once I'd like to chase a bandit who wasn't dumb enough to put his boots on the wrong feet and wonder why they hurt."

Twilight began to settle across the trackless plains. Before darkness claimed the remains of the day, Asa walked a mile to the ravine where he had left his roan tied when he had spied the telltale wisp of smoke from the fugitives' fire, and led it back to camp.

He grabbed up the dead man's slouch hat and using water from their canteens, gave all three horses a hearty drink before hobbling them to find whatever grazing they could in this hard country.

Asa dragged $2500 worth of dead outlaws into the nearby brush, where he wouldn't have to look at them yet would be close enough to keep the coyotes at bay. Then he turned his attention to the smoldering campfire, poked it back to life, and began adding a few sticks of dry mesquite from a pile the men he had killed had thoughtfully provided.

The skillet full of bacon hadn't spilled, which made him grateful. Asa set the black frying pan on glowing coals, which started the bacon to sizzling, and he relished the delightful aroma. It had been days since he'd had anything hot to eat.

Cain felt no remorse for his actions. He never did. The men he had hunted down for money under the blessing of Texas State Governor Edmund J. Davis were undeserving of mercy. They were all hard-boiled criminals of the worst sort. Every single one of them he had killed would have been hung anyway. And it was always a lot less trouble to bring them back dead. A man could at least get a good night's sleep when he was packing bodies instead of fugitives, who were always looking for a way to kill him and escape.

He chuckled when he remembered Freeman had called him "The Undertaker's Friend." From the talk he'd overheard in saloons from Buffalo

City, Kansas, to Mexico, he'd killed well over a hundred men. The true total was twenty-eight, including the two lying in the brush. Cain had no intention of ever correcting anyone; his reputation gave him a much-needed edge. Even hardened gunmen got nervous when faced by a legend, and nervous people made mistakes.

Tomorrow, he would drape the dead outlaws over their saddles, tie them firmly, and head for Wolf Springs. After apologizing to Deevers for depriving him of a public hanging, he planned to collect his reward and take a much-needed break.

If the legendary bounty hunter Asa Cain had had any inkling at the turn of events that was to come his way when he arrived at Wolf Springs and home, he would not have slept as peacefully as he did that night beneath the star-studded West Texas sky.

TWO

Sheriff Wilburn Deevers wore a frown on his leathery face when he walked over to the second dead outlaw that was draped over the saddle of a horse. He grabbed a handful of greasy, shaggy black hair and lifted up the dangling head, causing a horde of flies to take wing.

"Yep," the sheriff said dryly. "This one's Jake Freeman all right. An' he's just as ripe as Pendragon." He pinched his nose shut and scowled at the bounty hunter. "Dang it all, Asa, it's things like this that would make me consider takin' up another line of work."

Asa Cain clucked his tongue, a habit he'd had for years when he got even slightly anxious. "Wilburn, it ain't no fault of mine they made it halfway to Mexico after pluggin' your friend, and you sure can't blame me for the hot weather; it comes around ever summer whether I'm about or not."

Deevers sighed. "I know that, but it would be a delight if just once you'd bring 'em back still kicking. Hangings are good for business, and that way I could get 'em planted before they started stinkin'. Christ on a crutch, I don't know how you can stand the smell."

"Sign off on the bounty release and Cemetery John can have 'em. I reckon he'll get them in the ground before it's your dinnertime."

The sheriff snorted. "Come on over to the office an' I'll take care of the matter. Twenty-five hundred dollars is a passel of money, an' ole Cemetery will charge the county a hundred bucks for two coffins and diggin' the holes. I swan, Asa, it seems ever mother's son makes more money off'n wickedness and evildoers than a hardworking sheriff. I'm expected to work ever blasted day of the week an' get shot at on occasion for a measly hundred dollars a month."

"I can't see where you've got much choice in the matter," Asa retorted with a grin as the duo headed down the dusty main street of Wolf Springs. "If you tried making a success out of being a pimp, Mildred would kill you. And no matter how hard I work my thinker, that's the only other occupation outside of lawin' I can come up with that you might make a go of."

A rare smile washed across the sheriff's chiseled features. "Asa, you ain't changed a whit since we were in Robert E. Lee's Army of the Confederacy together. I sure never figgered back then when Colonel Reeves started sending you off to chase down deserters, you'd go an' turn it into a profitable profession."

"I'm only doing this temporary, you know that, Wil."

Deevers snorted. "The longer you keep at bounty huntin', the more likely it'll be temporary all right. Those outlaws you go chasing after are desperadoes of the worst sort an' they're damn good at what they do. So far you've been lucky, but luck's something that sure don't last forever, not even yours."

Asa glanced up and down the street before stepping onto the plank wood sidewalk in front of the sheriff's office. "Two or three more bounties is all I'll need. Then you can thin out the criminals without my help. I've got the ranch paid for and nearly enough money saved to head back East and go to college."

Wilburn spat a wad of tobacco onto the dirt before turning to go inside. "I'll give you credit for bein' hardheaded. I've known you for nigh onto nine years, an' all you've ever planned on was goin' to school an' become a sawbones. It still seems to me to be a stretch, goin' from shootin' 'em to saving 'em after the fact, but you do seem determined, I must say."

"If my father hadn't gotten killed like he did, I'd have had my shingle out long before now; the way things were, I had no choice but to take care of Mom and Sadie first."

"Cemetery," the sheriff said to the lanky, silverhaired old black man who was leaning back in a swivel chair with his boots propped up on a desk. "There's two mighty dead outlaws down at the livery stable in bad need of a quick buryin'. Go earn your keep."

"Yessir, Sheriff." Cemetery John swung his legs to the floor and stretched as he stood. He nodded at Asa. "Obliged for the business. Folks hereabouts been terrible healthy. Buryin' outlaws pays a bunch better than workin' as a deputy for Wilburn."

Deevers grinned evilly. "You'll earn every dime on those two."

Cemetery headed for the door. "Ain't no problem. In hot weather I always dust 'em down with some quicklime. After that's done, they won't even draw flies."

The sheriff watched as Cemetery strode off, then went behind the desk and sat in the recently vacated chair. "I don't know how anyone could stand bein' an undertaker. I'll say one thing for Cemetery. When it comes to workin' as a deputy there ain't no one around more reliable. He don't drink, and when he's packin' a sawed-off ten-gauge loaded with buckshot, no one gives him any sass about his being blacker than the ace of spades."

"When I was living among the Comanche, I learned it wasn't wise to judge anyone by the color of their skin. Saints, sinners, and all those in between come in every hue of the rainbow and I keep a sharp eye on all of them."

Wilburn slid open a desk drawer, extracted a pile of papers, and spread them out. He found what he was looking for, and began scribbling with a nub of pencil. "Ain't no different than all the other times. Take this over to Livermore at the bank an' he'll credit you for the bounty. I'll telegraph Governor Davis so he can start work on bankruptin' the Texas Treasury." The sheriff signed his name and handed over the paper. "Who are you chasin' after next? Jesse James an' Cole Younger are prob'ly worth more than any these days."

"Too far to travel. They're in Missouri and my family's here. Trogett Benson's still wanted for murdering that saloon keeper down in Scabtown, and if the Dolven gang hasn't been killed off lately,

I might go after them. But I plan on spending a few weeks on the ranch first. There's never been much of a drought when it comes to outlaws, especially here in West Texas."

Deevers laughed. "You ain't wrong there, and I reckon a wagon load of preachers wouldn't change things. Some folks just plain take to bein' mean. Brock Dolven an' his sons are still healthy and spry last I heard of 'em. They're hangin' out up around Tascosa, or so folks say. While you was away, Benson got his hide perforated by some saloon gal over in Fort Griffin. She led him into the back room an' took his mind off business long enough to pull a gun from under a pillow and put a bullet in his ear. Reckon it paid her a lot better than what she usually earned for her services. Cemetery said it was likely a tolerable job gettin' the grin off Trogett's face, him goin' doin' what he was at the time."

"I always figured Trogett would go out with a bang. The big galoot wasn't any brighter than a goose." Asa cocked his head. "I'd planned on bringing him in and give you a hangin' to perform. Benson wasn't smart enough to warrant the cost of a bullet."

Wilburn Deevers leaned back in the chair and laced his fingers behind his head. "I'd rather hang the Dolvens; they'd draw a bigger crowd." He bent forward and picked up a flyer. "This here just came in. Brock an' the two boys he's got left have been busy. They robbed a stage outside of Round Rock an' made off with a pile of money, but for once they didn't kill nobody. The reward's still only six hundred for each of 'em."

Asa picked up the poster and tucked it into his shirt pocket. "If they stay outta whorehouses in Fort Griffin, they'll keep for a spell. I've got a ton of trail dust that needs scrubbing off, and there's plenty of work that'll need done on the ranch. I darn near got the whole gang when I killed Slim Dolven last fall. I don't expect Brock's forgotten about me."

Deevers shook his head. "Nope, word is he's still tolerable upset with you over the matter."

Asa clucked his tongue, spun around, and headed outside. "I'll let him tell me about it when I come to call on him."

The sheriff hollered, "Could you just for once bring at least one of 'em back alive for a hangin'? The saloon trade pays my salary."

His only answer was the fading scuff of leather boots on the wood sidewalk as the bounty hunter left to go about his business.

Asa Cain noticed a thin spiral of smoke from the direction of his sprawling ranch house on the banks of the Concho River, and hoped Pablo Rodriguez had butchered a fat hog. His rotund wife, Lupe, was likely roasting it over a spit. He was famished for a good home-cooked meal. The genial Mexican family he'd hired to look after the Turkey Tree Ranch were not only dependable, they were excellent cooks to boot.

A sudden whirring sound from a towering live oak tree caused him such a start that he had the Henry rifle out of its scabbard and the hammer cocked before he realized what the commotion was; a wild turkey, the abundance of which had given birth to the name of his nine-thousand-acre spread.

He breathed a sigh of relief and returned the rifle to its usual place alongside the saddle. "You're getting jumpy, old scout," he said to himself. "You're home now."

Asa reined the roan to a stop and surveyed the serene beauty of his surroundings. Here, along a row of lush green pecan and oak trees that stretched as far as his eyes could see, the Concho River bubbled cheerfully along giving life to a harsh desert country.

This was prime and rare land, a place a man could be proud of. He had garnered a herd of well over a thousand Texas longhorns, and they had flourished, thanks to the abundant supply of good water.

Early this fall he expected to add many of his cattle to a drive his friend and neighbor, Albert Miller, was organizing for Buffalo City up in the jayhawker state of Kansas.

Briefly, Asa wished he could accompany them on the long trek northward, but it would not be possible. With any decent luck he would be back East by then, beginning his longtime goal of attending medical school at Harvard University.

He knew it was a strange dream, but one that had he not wavered from since childhood. His father had been a doctor. His mother had always told him that it had been his father's wish to have a son to follow in his footsteps.

In 1850 they were part of a wagon train heading for the goldfields of California. Then the Comanche had struck. . . .

Asa whipped his head from side to side in an unsuccessful attempt to throw off bitter memories.

He spurred the roan into a gallop, forcing himself to watch out for low-hanging branches.

Concentrating on dangers present helped him to forget the trials and heartaches of his past. He had been but a mere boy of four when he watched his father, Hezekiah, be scalped alive by the renegade warrior he later came to know as Lame Bear. Asa Cain could never think back to that time without wanting to run as he had done then. And now, just like on that terrible day, he found that it was impossible to outrun a nightmare.

He reined the horse to a stop in a clearing. The brief burst of speed had done the trick once again. His mother and younger sister, Sadie, would run to see him the moment he rode in. They relied on his strength, and it would never be prudent to allow anyone to see him as made of anything but iron, not his enemies or his family.

Asa Cain breathed deeply of the sultry air that clung to the Concho River. Then, circling black specks against billowy white clouds caught his attention. Vultures, at least three dozen of them, were lazily floating about the column of smoke that marked the ranch house.

The bounty hunter was well aware these scavengers could smell death from a long ways away. The stench of death was what had drawn them there. They were obviously landing, feeding.

And vultures only fed on dead flesh.

His heart pounded in his chest like a hammer striking an anvil when Asa spurred bloody gouges into his horse's sides in a desperate dash towards the homestead.

THREE

The moment Asa rode crashing from a thicket of trees, the first thing he realized was that the column of smoke he had seen earlier wasn't coming from any cookfire or chimney. The once-proud log home and barn on a rise overlooking the river was now a blackened mass of charred wood and dying embers.

Then he saw the first body. It lay sprawled in the garden plot between the Concho River and where the house had stood. Asa watched a pair of vultures as they stretched their necks skyward to swallow bites of flesh torn from the bloated form that was wrapped in a blue and white print dress.

Whoever had done this terrible thing was likely long gone, but he could not take that chance. Asa lunged from his horse, extracting the Henry from its scabbard as he did so. He knelt in the shadow of the roan, reins in one hand, the rifle in the other, and surveyed the countryside with a trained eye.

Only the multitude of buzzards and smoke from the remains of his ranch moved in the still heat of late day. Birds twittered happy songs from towering trees. He watched as a pair of red squirrels scampered playfully from a pecan tree and began poking around on the ground for food. If any gunman was hiding to ambush him, the wildlife would be conspicuous by their absence and silence.

Asa stood, led the roan to a small peach tree he had planted a couple of years ago, and tied the reins to it. Now, the task he dreaded most could be postponed no longer.

A half-dozen vultures took flight when he approached the body that lay facedown in the garden. From the paired circling of the buzzards, he knew at least two others were on the far side of what had been his home.

"Oh, my God, it's Lupe," he muttered to himself. Asa had had a lot of experience with death, yet he forced down the urge to gag. Even after the damage the scavengers had wrought, he could make out where bullets had riddled Lupe's back, and her throat had been cut so deeply her head lay askew, nearly severed from her shoulders.

The evidence was plain. She had tried to run away, only to be cut down by a hail of large-caliber rifle shots. To make certain the bloody deed was done, someone had pulled a huge knife and nearly decapitated the hapless woman, who, to his best memory, had always had a smile on her dusky face. Her clothes were mostly intact. Lupe had at least been spared the indignity of rape.

After a moment to collect himself, he turned and strode up the slight hill on leaden feet, steeling his emotions for the worst. The vicious animals who had done this butchery, be they Indians or white, would not have granted his lovely flaxen-haired sister a quick and merciful death. Attractive girls such as Sadie were a commodity more valuable than gold—for a while anyway.

Asa did not want to even think of what they had surely done to his mother, Jenny. He felt it strange trying to picture her as the object of other men's lust. In spite of all that she had endured, at forty-one years of age she was youthful of appearance, wasp-waisted, with sparkling azure eyes. She also sported the same long, glowing straw-colored hair as her daughter Sadie. Asa remembered that on occasion he had had to wait until he could get a look at the face before he knew if it was his mother or sister he was approaching. There was little doubt that his mother had not been granted a quick death.

The next body he encountered was on the grassy slope of hill behind the smoldering ruins of his house. It was that of Pablo Rodriguez. From the entrance wounds bullets had made in his chest and belly, it was obvious Pablo had met his attackers face-on.

"I hope you got at least one of the bastards before they did this to you," Asa said. He chewed on his lower lip for a moment, then clucked his tongue and forced himself to walk the several yards to where vultures had been picking over a third corpse.

"Oh, Lord, please don't let it be my mom," he muttered softly to himself. The buzzards had done considerable damage to the body, more so than to the others because this one was farther from the smoking rubble than the other two had been. Even though the carrion eaters had stripped away much of the flesh, it was obvious the remains were those of a man.

"Thank God," Asa said aloud as he rolled the dead man over to study what was left of his face.

"I reckon it's up to the devil to know who you were; there's not enough left for me to figure it out. From the looks of things, I see you took a shotgun blast up mighty close. I only hope Pablo was the one who did the honors."

Asa stood, and resisted the temptation to kick the outlaw's carcass. At least one of them had paid the supreme price for what had happened here. It was painfully apparent that his sister and mother had been abducted by the ruthless gang of cold-blooded killers that had laid waste to his ranch.

The bounty hunter gritted his teeth and began to study the signs left behind in the dusty ground. From the marks of steel-shod hooves he quickly ruled out Indians as the culprits; they always rode unshod mounts. Carefully and meticulously, Asa began comparing the size of the different hoof marks and noted the small imperfections that set them apart.

By making increasingly larger circles around the ranch, he determined that five horsemen had slowly crept in from across the plain to the west. Six mounted horses along with one being led had left hurriedly, heading south along the Concho River. A galloping horse always left deeper marks than one that was walking easily. A horse burdened with a rider made an even deeper impression.

At least now he knew in which direction his family had been taken, but there were many possibilities. The outlaws could have circled back toward Wolf Springs, headed northwest to Tascosa, or per-

haps even be going to the outlaw settlement of
Titusville.

But tracking was something Asa Cain knew how
to do. He joked to his friends that he could follow
a snake's track across a flat rock. Six shod horses
made this a much easier task.

A sudden roll of thunder shook the dimming
day. A drop of cold rain slapped him on the cheek.
It seldom rained in West Texas, but when the
event occurred it could be a torrential downpour.
Asa studied the black clouds while increasing rain
began to soak through his clothes. He had been
so distraught over what had happened that he had
not noticed the building thunderheads that now
covered the land.

Asa Cain raised a clenched fist to the darkened
heavens, then choked back his anger toward the
Almighty. With the rains already beginning to
obliterate all traces of the killers' path, he would
likely need to call on God for some assistance in
the future; therefore, it didn't seem prudent to
rile the Big Man.

Heavy sheets of rain accompanied by howling
gusts of wind swept across the countryside for what
seemed to Asa to be hours. He made no attempt
to seek shelter from the storm. The house and
barn were burned to the ground, and trees at-
tracted lightning. Asa sat on a rock with the Henry
rifle in his lap and hunkered over it to keep the
ammunition dry. A long while could pass before
he had need to shoot it, but shoot it he would.

As do all storms, this one eventually blew itself
out. By the warm glow of a red and dying sun,
Asa, using a shovel he had found leaning against
the garden fence, began to dig two graves. Pablo

and Lupe Rodriguez were good people and deserved a decent burial. The dead outlaw he would leave to feed the buzzards.

FOUR

Soak Malone swatted a fly with a dingy bar towel, then draped it over his pudgy arm and went to greet Asa Cain when he saw him stride through the batwing doors of his Rara Avis Saloon. "Folks said you was back in town, but I sure didn't expect to see you show up here fer a spell. What can I fetch you to drink?"

Asa ignored the barkeep's entreaty and headed straight for the end of the long plank counter, where Cemetery John was standing with one boot on the brass rail. Alongside him rested his huge double-barreled ten-gauge shotgun. The deputy spent most of his evenings here sipping on a cup of hot chocolate while keeping an eye out for trouble.

Cemetery turned and squinted as he surveyed Asa by the flickering yellow light of coal-oil lamps. "You got worry draped all over you like ugly on an ape. What's gone an' happened?"

Asa nodded to Soak on his way to belly up to the bar alongside Cemetery John. "Bring me a whiskey. And leave the bottle."

The lanky deputy took a moment to study Asa before asking anything more. A man of Asa's ilk did not get as distraught as he appeared to be without darn good reason. "The sheriff's gone up to Finster Rahn's ranch at Phantom Hill to check out some missin' goats," said John. "That hard-headed German came in here claimin' the Comanche took 'em, but more'n likely it was coyotes or wildcats. In any case, he'll be gone three days or so. Until then, I reckon I'm all the law there is in these parts. I'll do my best to help out if you'll tell me about it."

Soak set a freshly opened bottle of Old Gideon along with one glass on the bar, and quickly headed off to attend to the needs of other patrons. It wouldn't be prudent to upset a man who was reputed to have killed nearly two hundred men by sticking around without being invited to do so.

Asa poured the shot glass full of whiskey and belted it down. He poured himself a refill, then hollered loudly at the corpulent bartender. "Soak, come on down and the rest of you folks in here listen up. I don't think I care to repeat this again."

Sam Shankle quit trying to pound out a tune on the piano, and Lulu Debo postponed hustling a drunken cowboy. The Rara Avis Saloon grew silent as night in the desert.

"The ranch was burned down when I got there," Asa said, turning his head to survey the crowd. "Pablo and his wife were murdered. My mom and sister are missing, the outlaws took them. From the looks of things, Pablo got one of them before they killed him. These killers weren't Indians and the horses they ride are shod. From the tracks, I figure there's four of them left alive. Five rode into the ranch and Pablo blew one to hell. Six horses left along with Mom and Sadie. I was going to track them down, but the rain washed away all signs. There's nothing I can do now but wait for word of where they might have gone. I'd appreciate any help I can get."

"Damn," Cemetery John swore, using the first curse word anyone had ever heard him utter. "Lupe an' Pablo were plumb decent people. Lord knows we'd better find those poor women folks mighty soon. . . ." He turned to Asa and studied his worn boots. "Dang, I'm sorry to have brought that up."

"It's all right," Asa said softly. "You didn't say anything that isn't the truth. I've been chasing after men like whoever did this for a lot of years. I know all too well the type we're dealing with. The problem is, until some lead turns up, there's not a damn thing I or anyone else can do but wait."

"The whiskey's on the house," Soak said to Asa. He fished a key from out of his vest pocket and laid it on the bar. "Room six ain't had nobody in it since Silver Tooth Sally left town. You can stay there long as you need to."

"Thanks, Soak," Asa said. "I do appreciate it."

Tate Webster, the telegraph operator, came over. "I'll go an' get this out on the wire right away. I'll notify every sheriff in West Texas along with some in Kansas and New Mexico Territory for good measure. Then I'll send a wire to the Texas Rangers over in Austin. They'll likely get a posse together mighty quick."

Asa took another shot of whiskey. "Those bastards had better hope the Rangers get to them before I do. The Rangers will just shoot them or hang them. I learned a few things from the Indians that'll give me a lot more satisfaction and make those men beg to die for days."

Cemetery John worried the handle on his cup. "Whenever you leave to go after 'em, Asa, I'm comin' with you. Nothin' you can say will change that fact. When I pinned on a badge I swore to uphold the law. Animals that'll kill sweet ladies like Lupe an' abduct others need to be hung legal as an example for others who might do the same."

Asa glowered at him; then his features softened slightly. "I'd appreciate your help, but when the shooting starts, don't get in my way. That wouldn't be a healthy thing to do. I like you, Cemetery, but if you come between me and those bastards I *will* kill you."

The deputy grinned broadly and took a sip of his tepid chocolate. "I'm glad we got that out of the way. I *always* hate misunderstandings."

Asa bolted upright from the narrow bed; his breath came in sharp, shallow gasps. He had the pistol out from underneath his pillow and cocked before he realized where he was and the fact that he had suffered another of his frequent nightmares.

A haze of wan light from a half-moon peering through an open window gave a ghostly illumination to the pitifully squalid crib he occupied above the Rara Avis. The silence from the saloon told him it was likely early morning.

Soak Malone never closed his doors to business, but by this time the piano player had quit and the soiled doves had retired to their rooms, with or without the luck of having a paying customer for the night. Fridley Newlin, a stove-up old cowboy with a wooden leg, tended bar from two in the morning until noon every day for ten dollars a month and a room to sleep in.

Asa lowered the hammer on his Whitney Eagle .36-caliber revolver and laid it on the nightstand. A few deep breaths. Better now. The incubus had once again been tucked away into some dark crevice of his mind—for a while anyway.

He bent down, found his pants, and pulled out the gold pocket watch that had belonged to his father. Even by the dim light he could make out the caduceus of two snakes intertwined around a staff that had been engraved into the cover. The watch, a set of medical books, and faded memories were all Asa had left to remember him by. It was sufficient, especially when coupled with Asa's never-ending dream of leaving the violence and killing behind and becoming a doctor himself. Asa felt driven to become a man like his father, a man who saved lives rather than take them.

He flipped open the watch cover, and winced when he saw his mother's smiling countenance framed in yellow moonlight. She was still as beautiful as when she had sat for the daguerrotype back in New Orleans just before they had joined a wagon train headed for the newly discovered gold fields of distant California.

Asa could remember the leader of the wagon train, Victor Green Fields, whom everyone referred to simply as "Green." What he could never forget about Green was his long black beard that he wore in two neat braids. Then, as they crossed West Texas, the appearance of a Comanche raiding party led by Lame Bear had changed his life forever.

Now, unnamed and unforeseen monsters had once again conspired to take his family and loved ones from him. Rage boiled in the pit of his stomach like acid bile. He forced himself to breathe deeply once again and exhale slowly. When he moved the open watch into a shaft of light to where he could see the hour, his hand was rock steady.

It was five A.M., his usual time to rise. Asa clicked the cover closed and lovingly laid the watch on the nightstand alongside his revolver. He filled the porcelain washbasin with water from a pitcher and shaved. Then he bathed as best he could using the small cloth, toweled dry, pulled on the clothes he had worn yesterday, and went downstairs to meet the day.

"Mornin' Mr. Cain, good to see you up an' about." The lanky white-haired saloon keeper waved his arm along the bar to where two patrons were draped over it snoring. "All my business has done gone an' passed out on me. Be dang nice to have someone to talk to that ain't gonna see spiders an' spooks afore the day's out."

Fridley Newlin jumped down from the stool he'd been sitting on and hobbled into the back room. After a short time he returned carrying two steaming mugs of black coffee. The old man kept one close, and scooted the other across the bar to Asa. "Ain't no one in these parts but me knows how to brew a decent cup. I got me some secret ingredients that'll make ya live longer than Methuselah an' keep a smile on the lady's face to boot." He pointed proudly to the dark scar where his right ear used to be. "I got a whore up in Fort Worth so blame excited that she bit the thing plumb off. Yes, sir, my coffee'll keep yer horse at a gallop, but don't go an' lose an' ear. Makes it difficult as hell to wear a hat."

In spite of everything that had transpired, a grin crept across Asa's leathery face. He knew old Fridley was simply trying to buck up his spirits. It was common knowledge the old cowboy had gotten drunk on tequila down in Mexico and passed out behind a cantina where rats had gnawed his ear off.

"You ought to consider bottling some of that secret ingredient of yours and selling it," said Asa. "Seems to me that would pay better than tending bar for Soak Malone."

Fridley blew on his coffee. "Won't work. An' since yer a friend of mine, I'll tell ya why. One of the things I need is rattlesnake milk. It's dang hard to collect much of the stuff, an' even harder to find a stool short enough so's I can scoot under 'em."

For the first time in a long while, Asa Cain laughed. After taking a sip of coffee, he reached into his pocket, fished out a gold double eagle, and plunked it down on the bar.

"There ain't never no charge for my coffee, Mr. Cain."

"My name's Asa, if you would. The money is to hire you to do some work for me."

Fridley thumped on his wooden leg. "I'll be right proud to do what I can, Mr.—Asa."

"The first thing I want you to do is look up the Hanson boys. They're the ones who built my ranch house and barn." His gaze grew cold. "I suppose you know about what happened out there?"

"Yes, sir, I 'spect near everyone does. Terrible thing, Mr. Asa, that was plumb terrible."

"Tell the Hansons to get cracking on building the place back. I want them to stop whatever they're doing and start work posthaste. I'll make arrangements with Sam Livermore at the bank to pay them what they need."

"I'll be right happy to do that for you, sir."

"Then drop by and see Minnie Simpson at the general store. She's a good friend of my mother's and has been to the ranch several times. Have her order in all of the furniture and household items that we had—before. She'll likely know what they were better than anyone. I want the place to look just like it did, and I want it all done quick as they can."

"I'll see to it, Mr. Asa. What else do ya need done?"

"Just take care of making certain Mother and Sadie's home gets put back like it was. It'll be a great comfort to them when they return. The rest of the matter will be handled by myself and Judge Henry."

A look of puzzlement came to Fridley's stubble-bearded face. "The only judge I've heard tell about in these parts is that circuit feller who rides through here on occasion, Issac Weatherwax. Has he been replaced?"

Asa grinned, reached down, and patted the heavy, lever-action rifle resting against the bar that seldom left his side. "This Judge Henry holds fifteen decisions of the forty-four variety that no one gets to appeal."

The old saloon keeper's hand trembled as he reached for his cup of coffee. "No, sir, Mr. Asa, I'll bet fer sure they don't get to appeal any verdicts of that caliber."

FIVE

At the first glimmering of dawn the Comanche had risen to begin the day. Even after all the years since he had returned to the white man's civilization, Asa Cain still kept time by the same inner clock that guided the Indians.

Early every morning, while the town still slumbered peacefully, he would leave the room he had taken at the Paisano Hotel and spend a few hours drinking coffee with the broken-down old cowboy.

Asa knew Fridley was surely in constant pain from his numerous maladies and injuries, yet the wizened fellow maintained a buoyant spirit and wonderful sense of humor, both of which Asa needed at this time.

It also felt refreshing to be away from people who were continually offering condolences, or trying to get him to drop down on his knees and pray for God's help, like Preacher Sweet had done.

"If you're dead set on praying for someone's salvation, Reverend," Asa had told him, "go to that church of yours and pipe away for whoever killed the Rodriguez family and kidnapped my family. Right now, *my* god is a bullet, and I intend for him to condemn those bastards straight to hell before Saint Peter even gets the news." This tirade effectively ended Preacher Sweet's entreaty.

Asa had moved from the whore's crib into the hotel, where he could take his meals in a decent dining room and be able to enjoy a bath in a deep copper tub filled with hot, soapy water. It cost a dollar for the first tub (second users paid four bits; all those who came later could wallow in the same dirty water for a mere quarter) but after weeks on the trail, he felt the extravagance of taking the first tub was warranted.

Moving into the Paisano also gave him good reason to avoid spending too much time in the Rara Avis Saloon. Mornings spent sipping coffee and listening to Fridley's windies didn't cloud his mind and judgment. Nights were a different matter entirely.

All men have their own private demons. Asa Cain knew this well. The secret to getting through life was to recognize these demons and deal with them before they snatched your soul.

Whiskey warmed a man's blood and gave a false sense of comfort and invincibility. In his troubled state of mind, it would have been very easy to crawl into a bottle. A lot of men Asa had known had done just that. Not all of them had crawled out again. He had to be ready to leave at a moment's notice when word came, any word, of where his family was. This could be by telegraph, stage, or the chugging steam train that had just come to town last fall. Having whiskey-clouded judgment or a hangover was something he could not afford.

The waiting was the hardest part of all. He was all too aware of the terrible indignities his mother and innocent sister were most certainly suffering.

There simply wasn't a damn thing he could do about it without some direction. Running off on a wild-goose chase wouldn't accomplish anything, and would possibly cost lives he couldn't bear to see lost.

With any manhunt, waiting was always the worst. Just a little whiskey would make time pass much faster, but with Asa Cain, a little whiskey was too much and a case was not nearly enough. The bottle he'd drunk that first night would have to last him for a long while.

"When I was jus' a whippersnapper I could rope a twister an' ride it into the ground. Yes, sir, I had a durn good body afore the blame thing up and went bad on me. Say, did I ever tell you the story of how I lost my leg?"

"Only three different versions so far," Asa said with a grin. He sipped some of Fridley's terrible coffee. "One of these mornings I reckon we might at least spook the truth."

Fridley Newlin looked put out. "Well, dang, that's a fine thing to say. I'll have you know that ever thing I've told you up to now's been nuthin' but the truth. It's just that I didn't go and lose my blame leg in one big hoorah. No, sir, the thing sorta got whacked off in episodes, not all at once."

Asa started to reply when in the huge mirror behind the bar he saw Wilburn Deevers come through the batwing doors. He kept his gaze focused ahead. "Morning, Sheriff, good to see you back in town."

Deevers bellied up to the bar alongside Asa. "I

sure wish I had come back to better news. Damn it all, I'm sorry about what happened."

"Your being out of town didn't cause it."

"I know, but the goats I went to save from rustlers weren't even stolen. The durn things come back on their own while I was there. I could of shot the stinkin' things myself, I was so mad."

Fridley hobbled up and set a steaming cup of coffee on the bar in front of the sheriff. "It must be hell havin' to get elected ever four years."

Deevers stared at the coffee and cocked his head. "Hell comes in a lot of different varieties."

Asa said, "I reckon you just got back, but I really need to know if you've heard anything I can use."

"Nope, nothin' like you're hopin' for." The sheriff sipped at his cup and frowned. "Cemetery John got a telegraph from Governor Edmund Jeremiah Davis himself yesterday. He's comin' to Wolf Springs in his own private rail car. The wire said he'll be arrivin' around noon tomorrow."

Fridley Newlin was aghast. "Well, I'll be a monkey's uncle. The governor of Texas is comin' all the way out here? I declare, that potbellied ol' grafter leavin' his rockin' chair an' comin' to visit is a miracle to pale the partin' of the Red Sea. I wonder what put that bee in his bonnet."

Sheriff Deevers worried his lower lip. "I surely don't know why he's headed for Wolf Springs, but the last part of his message was even more mysterious."

"Why's that?" Asa Cain asked.

"It was about you. The telegraph *ordered* me to detain you here until the governor's arrival."

Asa bolted upright, nearly spilling his coffee. "What the hell!"

For the first time either could remember, Fridley Newlin was at a loss for words.

SIX

"Windbag politicians are only long on words when they're runnin' for office or trying to talk good, innocent, hardworkin' folks outta money," Cemetery John said to Asa and Wilburn. He was leaning back in the sheriff's rocking chair, feet propped on the desk, cleaning his huge ten-gauge shotgun. He nodded at a piece of paper on the edge of the desk. "The governor's telegraph was economical, but he made a point of making it plain he didn't want Asa to go wanderin' off."

The sheriff cocked his head at Asa. "You've been to Austin and met him. Any good ideas what's afoot?"

Asa Cain stepped over and picked up the telegraph. He had insisted on seeing it with his own eyes. The message was short, and only took a few seconds to read. "I can't explain this. In the past I've taken on some 'special' jobs the governor asked me to do. The best I can say is that we'll all find out tomorrow when his train gets here."

Cemetery John looked up at Asa from oiling the trigger mechanism. "I reckon that's a fact. It's just the use of the word 'detain' that's a bother."

"I'm sure it's nothing," Asa said. A wagon creaking along outside, accompanied by a dozen or so yelling and shouting men, caught his attention. "Looks like word's already out about the governor coming to visit."

"Yep," Wilburn Deevers said. "Ole Fridley's better at spreading gossip than a whole herd of churchwomen. I reckon Sam's already working himself into an apoplexy over the event."

The sheriff's assessment was correct. Sam Livermore, the corpulent bank president, was also the self-proclaimed mayor of Wolf Springs, and an aspiring politician to boot. He viewed the governor's visit as political manna come straight from a heaven called Austin. A few well-placed words from Edmund Davis could work wonders for his future aspirations of being elected to Congress. A stopover by President Ulysses S. Grant himself would not have goaded Sam into a more opulent, festive occasion than the one he envisioned.

The mayor dipped into the meager city treasury and then his own pocket to hire a score of men to clean up the town. In short order, wagon loads of empty whiskey bottles, horse apples, and dried dog turds, along with anything else that slightly resembled trash, were being carried a half mile away from the railroad station and unceremoniously dumped into a shallow ravine. The locals hoped a roaring gully-washer would carry the whole shebang into Mexico someday and save them the bother of burying the mess.

The rumor that Sam held more than secondhand knowledge of Fannie Fay and her sporting girls was borne out when he hired the redhead

herself to sew a huge banner. He had the madam
cut two-foot-high raised letters from the girls'
skimpy working clothes and spell out *Welcome Governor* on white bedsheets. He wanted to include
the governor's name, but there were not enough
red dresses to be found, so he was forced to cut
back on words.

By the middle of the afternoon the banner was
flapping away on ropes strung across Main Street
between Sam's Paisano Hotel and the bank, allowing him to pursue a speaker's platform that he
wanted to set up at the depot.

Fridley Newlin, who had taken residence on a
bench in front of the hotel to watch the goings-on,
commented to Soak Malone, "If'n ole Sam really
wants to get the gov'nor's attention, he oughtta
take them whores he's gone an' defrocked an'
stand 'em nekkid under that banner. All politicians take to whores like a duck to water."

Sheriff Wilburn Deevers went into a futile tirade
when a bunch of Sam's hired help began jacking
up the gallows behind the jail and placing it on
log rollers so it could be dragged to the train station.

"Consarn it all," Wilburn shouted as he ran out
the back door to stop them. "Leave it be; we're
supposed to give the governor a decent greetin',
not hang the man."

"Sam told us to fetch it," George Cheatham,
the town barber, said without slowing his work
with a pry bar. "I can't see why you're so blamed
upset over the matter. The thing ain't never been
used for nothing 'cept a bird roost."

"Well, it's gonna be," the sheriff growled. "What's Livermore got in mind for it anyway?"

The barber quit work, arched his back, and said, "Sam's gonna have us whack off the scary part and use the bottom as a perch for the windbags to stand on while they tell us how lucky we are to have them takin' our money. Nothin' to get in a dither over; we can patch it back together and it'll work just fine. These things ain't known for bein' delicate."

Wilburn Deevers let his shoulders sag, and he took on a hangdog expression. "Politicians are a royal pain in the seat of your jeans."

"Yep," Cheatham agreed with a nod before returning to work. "That's a natural fact."

SEVEN

While the denizens of Wolf Springs were busily preparing for Governor Davis's visit, or as many chose to do, simply going about their own business, Asa Cain retreated to his hotel room. He fluffed the pillow, plopped down on the bed, and stared at an unopened bottle of White Mule whiskey that sat on an oak dresser across from the footboard.

Asa had stopped by the Rara Avis Saloon and bought it only moments ago. In the peace and solitude of his own private space, he realized the folly of uncorking that flask of temptation and letting its amber contents temporarily burn away trouble from his soul.

It was just that he couldn't fathom why the governor had sent such a cryptic telegraph message and was personally coming to town. His home had been burned, good people horribly murdered, and his only family kidnapped. Now, for some inexplicable reason he had been *ordered* not to leave Wolf Springs.

There had to be a connection, but no matter how hard Asa studied on the matter, he could not fathom what it might be.

Yes, in the past he had undertaken some rather unsavory and bloody tasks for Edmund J. Davis. The governor had, years ago, taken note of Asa's success at tracking down criminals and summoned him to the state capital in Austin.

"Texas is still in a state of turmoil from the war," Davis had said, puffing away on a long black cigar behind a massive walnut desk. "There are certain—elements—that need to be removed for the public good. These are outlaws of the worst sort that I am referring to, only you will not find their names on any sheriff's flyer."

At this point the governor had offered him a cigar. Asa had accepted, lit it from an ornate gold lighter, and listened with interest as Davis continued.

"These men are not wanted by the State of Texas, yet I assure you they are criminals of the vilest sort. I have at my disposal some rather discreet funds to pay for their, uh—removal. I propose to give you a list of names. As these offenders are, shall I say, *dealt* with, I will personally wire you the sum of one thousand dollars for each and every one of them.

"You have a proven ability to handle matters of this sort. Should anything go awry, let me assure you that I shall see to it the problem goes away. You will be working directly for me and I *always* take care of my friends. I assume you understand the discreetness that must be maintained and that I require absolute silence as to my involvement."

Asa nodded. "Yes, sir. Where shall I deliver the bodies?"

"You are a true patriot, my good man. The State of Texas shall be eternally grateful to you and shall become a safer place for women and children to live because of you. As to the, ah—*proof* of your accomplishments, simply leave them for the buzzards. I have my way of finding out these things."

There had been five names on that list. Within three months all had either gone missing under mysterious circumstances or been found dead.

Asa had collected his money with a clear conscience. The governor was his commander in chief. He had been given an order and had followed it to the letter. A soldier does not question his leader, especially a notable one like Edmund Jeremiah Davis. Besides, he had been assured the men on that list were criminals of the worst sort.

It was not reasonable to expect that his earlier dealings with the head of state had anything at all to do with the governor's cryptic telegram and his impending visit. No, it was not reasonable at all.

Asa Cain sighed, got up from his bed, and placed the whiskey bottle in a drawer. He picked up a dime novel and lay down to read it. Tomorrow his questions would be answered. The problem was, that would be many hours hence. The book he held open, but in his mind voices whispering from the past held his attentions.

It was going to be a long and trying night.

Noontime came and passed without any sign of the governor's special train. Tate Webster fired off telegraph messages to stations down the tracks, and received assurances that Edmund J. Davis was actually heading for Wolf Springs.

"The train's likely been attacked by Injuns," Fridley Newlin commented to Sam Livermore, who was dressed to the nines in a gray pinstripe suit and bowler hat. "If'n the train's all decked out with banners an' flags, they'll think the Great White Father's come from Washington to give 'em a new treaty. Considerin' how the old deals turned out, can't say that I'd blame 'em any."

Fermin James, who was standing on the raised platform with a fiddle to welcome the governor with a rousing rendition of *"The Battle Hymn of the Republic,"* squinted to the east along the glistening steel rails. "She's a-comin' boys," he shouted. "I can see her smoke plain as day."

A building murmur of voices grew in intensity like an approaching thunderstorm as the assemblage became swept away by the magnificence of the occasion. All except Asa Cain, that is. He kept to the shade in front of the Paisano Hotel, and surveyed the event with what he knew was an unreasonable dread.

He had slept but little the past night, spending many hours with his fingers laced behind his head, staring at the plank wood ceiling, playing out endless scenarios in his mind as to what Davis could want of him.

It was likely another "special" assignment. This would be one that he could not accept. When he explained to the governor what had happened at his ranch and the facts of his mother and sister being kidnapped, the man surely would understand. Possibly Edmund Davis would even assist him, but Asa doubted it. Lately there had been articles in the newspapers about the governor's plan to disband the Texas Rangers. This was of no consequence. When it came to killing, Asa Cain required no help.

EIGHT

The hissing locomotive chugged and sputtered its way past the crowd, showering them with a cloud of hot cinders. Aside from the engine and tender car stacked high with mesquite wood, a lone black Pullman car with drawn shades was the sole accompaniment to the creaking processional.

The engineer engaged the brakes and the train groaned to a stop, leaving the Pullman alongside the depot platform a good hundred feet farther down the tracks than Livermore's gaily bedecked welcoming platform. Sam had wrapped the bottom part of the gallows with a huge Texas flag the banker had bought earlier in hopes of using it in a career-building event such as this one.

Fermin commenced playing his fiddle anyway. The mayor had paid him an entire dollar for his services, and Fermin James was a man who believed in giving his money's worth.

The milling crowd moved to the depot, all of them expecting the governor of Texas to make a grand appearance. But this did not happen. The blinds of the Pullman car remained down. A rhythmic puffing of smoke, followed by a hissing of steam from the locomotive, was the only activity.

After several long and suspenseful moments, the back door to the private car swung open. A great cheering from the townspeople erupted, to quickly fade away as two burly, unsmiling men wearing pinstripe suits identical to Sam Livermore's slammed the door closed behind them and strode onto the deck of the depot.

"Gentlemen, gentlemen," the corpulent banker wheezed, sticking out his hand. The short run and being forced to climb a few stairs had left him winded. "On behalf of the good citizens of Wolf Springs, I bid you welcome—"

"Stow it, Chubby," the big man with a pockmarked face growled. "We're here to fetch Asa Cain."

Sam Livermore was taken aback. "But we have prepared a grand welcome for the governor. We even have three pigs roasting—"

"Asa Cain," Pock Mark repeated, sliding his hand inside his suit coat. "Davis wants to talk with him—now!"

Wilburn Deevers stepped close and put his face directly into Pock Mark's. "Folks hereabouts went to a passel of work to make the governor welcome. A little respect might be in order here."

The other man in Edmund Davis's retinue, who had beady eyes and sported a long, pointed goatee, spoke. "We ain't here for no party. The governor's brother-in-law's been killed. This is a business call."

Sam Livermore began to sputter as loudly as the locomotive. The sheriff felt a hand on his shoulder, urging him aside. It was Asa Cain, who stepped in front of him.

"I'm the man you're looking for," Asa said

coldly. "Take me to Davis and let's see what the trouble's about."

Without another word the two bodyguards flanked Asa and escorted him inside the darkened coach. Silently as a snake glides through wet grass, the duo of ruffians disappeared into a side compartment, leaving the bounty hunter facing the governor of Texas.

The office had obviously been good to Edmund J. Davis. Asa figured he now weighed nearly three hundred pounds. A few short years ago when Asa had first set eyes on the governor, he'd been at least seventy five pounds lighter. The big man sat in a plush leather chair behind a huge desk nearly as big as the one in the state house. He was puffing away on a black cigar, a crystal glass of amber liquid spotted with real ice on the desk in front of him.

"Have a seat, Mr. Cain," Davis said blandly. "May I offer you some refreshment?"

"A glass of tea with some of that ice in it would be good."

"Balderdash!" the governor snorted. "By the time you leave my car you'll be damn glad you had a *real* drink." He turned to face a red-curtained doorway. "Ebony, bring my guest a whiskey on ice and while you're at it, a plate of oysters would be delightful."

Asa could barely contain a gasp as one of the most beautiful girls he had ever set eyes on parted the curtain and carried in a silver tray with silent grace. She was a cream-colored mulatto girl, possibly nineteen years old, wasp-waisted, with extraordinary physical attributes that showed magnificently above her low-cut blue dress.

"Anything else, sir?" Ebony asked with a sweet cooing voice.

"Not for a while," Davis said. "I'll call when I need you."

After Ebony floated from the room and closed the curtain behind her, Asa was aghast to find the silver tray was full of plump oysters on the half shell nested in a bed of ice. Here in West Texas ice was only a dreamed-of luxury in the long, hot months of summer.

The governor grinned slightly. "The whiskey is Kentucky bourbon, there simply is none finer. Help yourself to an oyster. I find them to be both delicious"—he glanced toward the red curtain—"and beneficial."

Asa nodded, picked an oyster from its incredibly cold and icy bed, and plopped the delicacy into his mouth. He washed it down with a drink of what admittedly was the smoothest whiskey he had ever tasted. "Thank you, sir; now I believe we should get down to business."

"I admire a man who does not beat around the bush. My time is quite valuable."

"I'm certain it is, Governor. One of your hired help mentioned that your brother-in-law has been killed. I assume that's why you wish to see me. This isn't a good time for me . . ."

Edmund J. Davis sat upright and fixed Asa in a predatory gaze and barked, "I know all about *your* problems, Mr. Cain. I am telling you that they are intertwined with my own, so forgo any insipid whining."

"Yes, sir."

"Bertha Anne, my wife, is beside herself with grief over the loss of her brother, though I am not. Herman Dits was ineffective as a lawyer or anything else he tried to accomplish. At my wife's urging I bought a bank in Battle Flats, which, as you are aware, is only a short distance north of here, and placed Herman in charge of it. Even an idiot can make a successful bank president. Unfortunately, the bank was robbed by the Dolven gang, and my unarmed brother-in-law was cut down in a hail of bullets for attempting to protect the money."

"I'm sorry for your loss, sir, I truly am. The Dolven gang will be taken care of—"

Davis interrupted again. "You don't realize yet just how sorry you actually are. Herman being killed was trivial. Having my money stolen and Bertha Anne harping away at me is not. The Dolven gang—all of them—must be killed outright or caught and publicly hung without delay."

"Sir, you said you knew about my family."

Edmund Davis sighed; then with a slim smile, he said, "Have a cigar, I get them shipped in from Havana. I believe you will find them of excellent quality." The governor slid a cherry wood cigar box across the desk. "And do enjoy your drink, for now I am going to tell you the *real* reason for my coming to this godforsaken wasteland."

Asa extracted a cigar, bit the end off, and lit the stogie with Davis's solid-gold lighter. "Go ahead," he said sharply; the governor's arrogance was becoming vexing.

"Before I continue, Cain, I understand you are well acquainted with a rancher by the name of Albert Miller?"

"He owns the spread next to mine. He's a good

man; we're planning on a cattle drive up to Buffalo City later this year."

"Then Miller has met your mother?"

Asa cocked his head in puzzlement. "Why, yes, many times, but what's this got—"

"It's got *everything* to do with it." Davis's eyes narrowed, and he slammed a ham-sized fist onto the desk. "Miller was in my bank on business when the Dolven gang came in and robbed the place. He gave sworn testimony to the sheriff that Brock Dolven now has a bloodthirsty female outlaw in his gang of thieves. Brock even had his arm wrapped abound her when they *both* shot and killed Herman. Dammit, Asa, that woman was Jenny Cain—your mother!"

NINE

Asa Cain had an understanding now of what it must feel like to have a red-hot slug of lead tear through your heart. He bolted back from the desk as if he had been shot.

"No—this can't be. My mother and sister have been kidnapped and the ranch burned to the ground. Pablo and Lupe Rodriguez were murdered. Good God, man, if you think my sweet mother had anything to do with a bank robbery, you are terribly mistaken."

"Please do not use the Lord's name in vain, Mr. Cain. I can sympathize with your plight, but there is never any justification for blasphemy against the Almighty."

Asa's hand trembled with barely subdued rage when he picked up the glass of whiskey and drank it dry. His mind was in too much of a turmoil to allow himself to speak.

"I *told* you that you'd need that drink," Governor Davis said flatly. "I have no explanation to offer—only facts. The situation is this. My money has been stolen and Herman Dits is dead. Reliable witnesses have stated that the Dolven gang accompanied by your mother are responsible for this dastardly crime. I need not add that Bertha Anne will give me no peace until they are all hung."

"My mother—she couldn't—it's not possible," Asa stuttered.

"The law operates on cold, hard facts, Cain. Surely you must realize that your 'business' keeps you gone from home for long periods of time, so there is no way you could know what goes on during your absence. Please understand I do not hold you responsible for the crime, only for its resolution. You are the best and highest-paid bounty hunter in the State of Texas. I simply expect you to do your job."

"You can't believe I would bring in my own mother to be hung."

"But I do," Davis barked. "And so you shall. As we speak, wanted flyers are being posted and telegraphs being sent throughout the area offering a twenty-five-hundred-dollar reward for each of the Dolvens along with Jenny Cain—dead or alive, I might add. I am hoping ten thousand dollars will be adequate incentive to bring them *all* to justice."

Asa clucked his tongue and glared at the governor through narrow slits. "No, this I refuse to do. There *has* to be another explanation."

Edmund Davis sighed and leaned back in his leather chair. He regarded Asa for a long minute, then grabbed up the whiskey bottle and refilled both of their glasses. "I must say I am saddened that it has come to this, my old friend, but either you will bring in your mother to be hung, or I shall see that you swing from the gallows yourself. The call is yours."

Asa downed his drink as if he were trying to put

out the raging fire that blazed in the pit of his stomach. "Don't threaten me, you pompous ass!"

Davis met his rage with a maddening smile. "Oh, I *never* threaten. If you recall, there were some 'special' jobs you carried out on my behalf a few years ago?"

"So?"

"You killed five innocent men who had never broken any laws. Two of them were striving to cause me political problems, the other three were the sons of men I wished to send a 'message' to. It will be a simple matter to hire a few witnesses to testify as to your terrible crimes. Your execution will be a swift one, I assure you."

Asa felt his legs turn rubbery. The governor's words burned into his wounded heart like hot coals. Adding the realization that he had been duped into killing innocent people to his mother's and sister's plight was almost more than he could comprehend. "I was working for the governor of Texas."

"And so you shall continue to do if you proceed as I ask against the robbers of my bank and the murderers of Herman Dits. Otherwise—"

"I—I'll do what I have to."

"Excellent, Mr. Cain. I knew you were an intelligent man." Davis cocked his head and looked past Asa. "Parks, you and Baltazar may escort Cain from my car now. And please place your weapons back inside their holsters. He has wisely decided to continue working for me."

Asa was further shocked to realize the two thugs had been behind him for some time, silently waiting with pistols in hand. In all of his years of bounty hunting he had never allowed such a thing to happen. If he had uttered the wrong words, the corrupt governor obviously would have carried through on his threat to hang him.

Strong hands shoved Asa Cain from the Pullman car onto the depot platform. The door slammed harshly behind him as he blinked to adjust his eyes to the bright sun.

"Well, what did our esteemed governor have to say?" Sam Livermore asked, his face livid. "He *is* coming out and gracing us with his presence, isn't he?"

The banker's question was answered by a groan and hiss of steam from the locomotive as Edmund Davis's train began slowly chugging out of Wolf Springs.

"Why, I cannot believe the audacity of that man," Livermore growled.

"*I* can," Asa spat. Then he spun and strode from the platform heading for the Rara Avis Saloon. Those who noticed the killing look in his eyes stepped quickly aside, glad to be out of the bounty hunter's way.

"You look like a man who really needs a drink," Fridley Newlin commented to Asa when he strode through the batwing doors. "Ain't no surprise to me; windbag politicians generally have that affect on folks."

"Set me up a bottle," Asa said. He scanned the nearly empty saloon. "I wasn't expecting you to be here."

"Oh, Soak Malone wanted to go hobnob with His Worship, so I told him I'd work over for a spell. I don't mind none. I'd rather be around a bunch of decent drunks any day than some sleazy grafter like Edmund J-stands-for-Jackass Davis."

Asa nodded and poured a shot glass full of amber salve for his tortured soul. "You're a better judge of character than most. Bring another glass and I'll buy you a drink."

"Don't mind if'n I do," Fridley said as he hobbled over. "I always limit myself to no more than thirty a day 'cause I don't want folks sayin' I imbibe to excess, but hell, I ain't even spookin' that number yet."

Asa filled the old cowboy's glass to the brim, then began staring into the ornately framed mirror behind the bar with a face of stone. "I've always prided myself on knowing which way the wind was blowing. Now my whole damn world's gone topsy-turvy and I don't know how to begin to straighten it out. If I don't get my bearings soon I may just spin off into oblivion."

"Never heard of a town called Oblivion before; must be in Kansas. But your ma had nothin' to do with that bank holdup in Battle Flats. Hell's bells, only an idiot would believe that she's gone an' turned killer an' robber."

Asa's muscles tightened. "How do you know about that?"

"Why, I reckon ever soul fer a thousand miles will be chasin' after her an' that big reward. It's a real passel of money." Fridley reached under the counter and pulled out a handful of wanted flyers. "The gov'nor's pet thugs plastered 'em all over town while you two was jawin'."

The bounty hunter grabbed up one of the handbills and studied it with wide shocked eyes. His mother's picture on the flyer was the same one he carried in the cover of his watch. He could only shake his head in angry wonderment as to how Davis could have obtained it, and in such a short time. Jenny Cain's beauty would cause her to stand out anywhere. With a huge price on her head dead or alive, she could not help but attract bullets the way a flower does bees. His mother's only hope would be if Asa found her first.

Fridley shook him from thought. "Leastwise, that cute little sister of yours might've gotten away from the Dolvens. Ain't no one said nothin' about her an' accordin' to the flyer, all three of them crooks were present at the bank robbery."

"That doesn't add up. Five of the horses that left the ranch were mounted. The Dolvens have likely got a hired gun to help them out. That man was keeping her hostage, I'm certain of it."

"There ain't no reward for anybody but the Dolvens an'—"

"No matter," Asa said matter-of-factly. "Whoever he is, I'll kill him for free."

Fridley Newlin downed his whiskey. "Yep, I don't doubt that you will at that. The problem, as I see it, is figgerin' out which hole them bastards is hidin' in."

"That's *always* the hard part, and it's the only reason I've hung around Wolf Springs as long as I have."

"Lots of folks move through here at night. Tell ya what I'll do. When Soak takes over in a bit, I'll go grab me a nap, then come back later an' visit with ever one I can. Just might be I'll learn somethin' that a lot of folks would be afraid to tell you."

"Obliged," Asa said, and plunked down a gold double eagle on the bar. "I'm buying."

Fridley grinned and stuck the coin into his shirt pocket. "An' I'm broke enough to let you."

TEN

Asa Cain stood bellied-up to the bar, staring at his untouched whiskey for a long while after Fridley Newlin had retired for his nap. The earlier drinks with the governor now coursed warmly through his veins, prodding him to empty the golden contents of this one glass. Then the bottle. Then another.

It would be a perfect way to forget his troubles, but the demons would still be there when he sobered up. His mother's and sister's only chance at survival depended on him. He couldn't allow himself to crawl inside a whiskey bottle when the only family he still had in this world needed him so badly.

"That Old Crow'll eventually evaporate if you stare at it long enough," Soak Malone commented with a conspicuous grin.

"Cork it," Asa replied, dashing the contents of the shot glass into a nearby spittoon. "And give the bottle to Fridley when he runs dry. I've got too much to do to drink any more of the stuff."

Soak Malone shook his head sadly, slammed the cork into the whiskey bottle, and said, "I'd reckon you've got one helluva bad situation on your hands all right." The bartender nodded to the crowd in the now-packed saloon. "Ain't a soul in here that ain't talkin' about your maw bein' on the wanted poster. It just beats all about Gov'nor Davis doin' what he done. Postin' that big reward will most likely get her killed. Hell, everyone hereabouts know the Dolvens were behind the whole thing."

"Albert Miller saw her help rob that bank. I know she was being forced to do what she did, but it'll be hell proving it without a confession in front of a judge by at least one of the Dolvens."

Wilburn Deevers stepped close. "Well, this time you've got an incentive not to go killin' ever one of 'em and give me the opportunity to hang at least one of the bastards."

Asa had been so lost in thought that he had not noticed either the sheriff or Cemetery John approach, a fact that startled and shook him. He couldn't afford to lose his edge just when it was needed the most.

Damned whiskey, he thought. *That stuff can be deadly as a bullet.*

Cemetery John leaned his massive shotgun alongside Asa's Henry. "Don't you go frettin' about your ma. We'll see she gets out of this mess. I give you my word on it."

Asa spun around and fixed Cemetery John then the sheriff with his gaze. When he spoke, his voice was cold as wind blowing off blue ice. "There's going to be a lot of people wind up dead before this is over. I don't want it being family—or friends. Whenever I get a good lead on the Dolvens, I'll go do what has to be done. And you two will stay right here in Wolf Springs while I take care of the matter."

Wilburn Deevers set his chin in a stubborn line. "We've been friends for a lot of years, Asa, but you have a tendency of forgettin' that you ain't the law. Cemetery's a sworn deputy. He's determined to go with you an' by God he's a goin'. If you're gonna save your family, you'll need all the help you can get. Besides that, any confession to a lawman will carry a lot more weight with the courts than your say-so."

Asa sighed deeply. "I know that and I appreciate your intentions. There will be more than the Dolvens to fight now. That reward will cause a lot of folks to turn mighty mean. I've been bounty hunting long enough to have seen it happen. Men will kill anyone who even resembles the picture on a poster and try to sell the body. Once I even had to run off two cowboys who were trying to steal a dead outlaw I'd shot in New Mexico Territory. Big money causes mighty bloody things to happen. I don't want Cemetery John or anyone else involved. And I damn well mean it."

"I swan, Asa," Deevers said shaking his head. "You're more contrary than a pen full of Missouri mules, and sometimes not much smarter. I'm not givin' you any choice about Cemetery John goin' along. Jenny and Sadie are like family to us too. If you can't understand the fact that you've got a passel of friends that *are* goin' to help you, I'm gonna lock you up on the charge of bein' plain dumb."

Cemetery John stepped to the bar and rapped his knuckles on the well-worn oak. "Give us all something to drink here, Malone. I'll have my usual. Jawin' with hardheads is dry work."

"Amen," Deevers said. "I'll have a whiskey to verify that truth."

"Coffee, black," Asa said. "And I'll be drinking it with idiots."

"Wilburn can't go off and leave a town that's elected him unprotected," Cemetery John said, keeping his eyes fixed on the mirror behind the bar. "It took me a good hour of yellin' to convince him of the fact. If I have to stay here until the cows come home to hammer some sense into you, I'm prepared to do it." He snorted. "White folks beat all I ever seen when it comes to bein' hardheaded."

Asa put his elbows on the bar and joined Cemetery John in staring into the huge back mirror. "Who's going to do the job of undertaker if you're gone for a long spell?"

"When you're not about, the town generally don't have need of one."

"You likely will get killed."

"I've drunk Fridley Newlin's coffee an' I'm still here."

"If I head out on my own, I figure you'll follow anyway."

"Sure as God made little green apples."

"I've always been of the opinion that buffalo soldiers—like you were for a spell after the war— are plenty smart."

"That's a truth, and it's also a fact that once we set our mind on doin' something, it gets done even if the creeks do rise."

Asa gave a sigh of resignation. "Just remember

it's *my* family that's at stake and I make all the decisions."

Cemetery John studied the steaming cup of hot chocolate Soak Malone had just set in front of him, then fixed his gray eyes on Asa. "I reckon that's exactly the reason you shouldn't be callin' all the shots. You're too damn close to the problem. Even a doctor will send his own family to see another doc. When a person thinks with their heart instead of their head, they lose that edge that keeps other folks and themselves from getting killed."

Asa's face was a mask of stone when he nodded grudging acceptance of Cemetery John's statement. He knew all too well everything the undertaker had said was true. He had allowed the governor's thugs to sneak up behind him totally unnoticed. Even Wilburn Deevers had been by his side before he realized the fact. He could blame the effects of alcohol, but he'd certainly not drunk enough to cause such carelessness on his part.

"Just remember," Asa said, grabbing his coffee cup. "I've been chasing outlaws for a lot of years and I've always brought back everyone I set after."

"No, sir," Cemetery John said. "I sure won't forget how good you are at killin'."

A full moon was shooting rays of ochre light through the open hotel window when a sharp rapping on the door took Asa from a fitful sleep.

"I'm coming," the bounty hunter shouted loudly to mask the sounds of his sliding off the bed and the cocking of the .36-caliber Whitney Eagle revolver that he always kept dangling in its holster from a bedpost. He went into a crouch and pointed the gun at the center of the door. "It's not locked, come on in."

"Now it plain an' simple ain't polite to go an' take potshots at folks comin' to visit," Fridley Newlin's raspy voice grumbled. "If'n you'll put that hogleg away, I've brought someone you'll want to talk to fer sure."

Asa lowered the hammer of the Whitney, but kept it pointed at the door. "Get on in here, Fridley."

The door swung open, and the wan light outlined Fridley along with an ashen-faced Tate Webster clinging behind him in the shadows. The old cowboy hobbled into the room with the telegraph operator in tow.

Fridley clucked his tongue and shook his head sadly. "There's two things a man never fergets the sound of: one's a rattlesnake's buzz an' the other's a hammer bein' cocked. Hell's bells, Asa, I've only got one ear an' I knowed what you was up to."

Tate Webster pleaded into Fridley's good ear, "Don't go and rile him any more than he already is."

Asa Cain came to his feet and reholstered the Whitney. "I only shoot people who are desperately in need of it. Neither of you two fit that bill." He lit the lamp on the nightstand, blew out the sulphur match, and stared at the duo through curling smoke. "What have you got?"

Fridley Newlin stepped into the light; Tate Webster followed him like a shadow. "I was sure right about the gov'nor's big reward startin' tongues to waggin'. Every mother's son's rackin' what brains they got tryin' to figger out where Brock Dolven an' his gang's got yer maw and sister stashed."

"That's not news," Asa grumbled, causing Tate to move a step back into the darkness.

"Nope, it ain't," Fridley said. "But ol' Webster here's got access to ever telegraph goin' down the wire no matter where it was sent from."

"Oh, goodness gracious," the telegraph operator whined. "I simply knew this was a terrible idea coming here. All messages are private and I just know I'll be fired for this."

Fridley snorted. "Well, you're here now, an' if'n Asa don't plug you fer not helpin' him, I will. Gettin' shot is kinda worse than gettin' fired in my opinion. Spit it out just like you done after I bought you that tenth beer."

The telegraph operator's teeth chattered as he told of several messages he had intercepted between the governor's office, the sheriff of Tascosa and the town marshal of Canan, which was on the Canadian River in the Texas Panhandle.

"Sheriff Reed over in Tascosa's friends of the Dolvens," Tate said shakily. "That marshal, Emil Quackenbush, in Canan is working with him to collect the reward." He hesitated. "*All* of it."

"How?" Asa asked calmly.

"Sheldon Reed and Quackenbush, well, they've sent a bunch of messages to each other and to the governor to stake out the reward money for themselves. The sheriff, who says he's Brock Dolven's friend, is more fond of money than Brock, apparently. He's described a ranch the Dolvens have that's just over into Indian Territory on the Canadian River. That's where your mother and sister are being held."

"What are their plans?" Asa's voice was cold and distant.

"The two of them have hired a gunman, a man by the name of Sand Drawhorn, to help them out. Sheriff Reed's on his way to Canan already. Once Reed and Drawhorn get there, they're going to simply raid the ranch and kill everyone. Governor Davis said in a telegraph that he didn't want to know the details, but that he'd be happy to pay the reward once the bodies were identified."

Fridley turned to the quaking telegrapher and pressed some silver dollars into his sweaty hand. "Go have some more drinks an' consider yourself a shiny beacon of humanity."

Asa and the old cowboy listened as Tate Webster's footsteps drifted off into the dark.

"He ain't a bad fellow," Fridley said. "He's just scared is all."

"That's not important. I've got to get packed and going. You've been a great help, Fridley, and I'll remember that. Could you drop by the livery and have Larson saddle my horse and ready a couple of others for me to take along?"

"Ain't no need. Cemetery John's been over there since this afternoon. He's got horses, grub, an' ever thing you'll need right down to handcuffs an' bullets."

"Damn it all," Asa growled. "I planned to be long gone before he got the news."

"Reckon this might not be his first time at man-huntin', and it's plain certain that's what you've finally got—a manhunt."

"Yes, it is," Asa commented as he slid into his pants and strapped on the Whitney Eagle. "And when the hunt's over, the killing begins."

ELEVEN

The West Texas sun was rising bloody on the eastern horizon when Asa Cain and Cemetery John halted to allow their horses to drink from the swirling muddy waters of the Colorado River.

Asa motioned toward a low range of hills to the north that shone purple from the still-clinging remains of night. "There's a small town up there between two groups of hills. Folks who live there call the place Buffalo Gap. We should make it by the shank of the afternoon. If they've got a hotel we'll spend the night, rest ourselves, and stable the horses. From Buffalo Gap north, we'll be camping out and the going will be dry and rough."

Cemetery John kept his gaze on the water. "I've spent too much time already up north in that Canadian River country. Back in '64 I was in the Union Army under Kit Carson's command."

Asa turned from staring at the distant hills and cocked an eye at his companion. "I didn't know you were in the Army back when the war was still going."

"That was ten years ago, but sometimes it feels like only the other day. I came to Wolf Springs back in '67, a year before you did. The war was only a few months old when I joined Grant's Army. Hell, Asa, you didn't think I was a grayback. There's a bunch of slave lovers down South that I wanted to kill mighty bad. Then I was shipped out west and had some time to cool off. I found not all Southerners need killing an' some Northerners really deserve a good hanging."

"I've made the same observation. Come to think on the matter, I've never even heard of a bounty being posted on a black man. But tell me a little more about the time you spent in the Panhandle under Kit. If you can remember any water holes or landmarks, it'll be a help."

Cemetery John grinned. "Well, sir, if Colonel Carson hadn't brought along some big cannons, mountain howitzers he called them, my scalp would be dangling from some Comanche's war lance. There were a passel more Indians camped about Adobe Walls than ol' Kit or anyone suspected. Luckily, those redskins had never seen thunder that could rain down death on a clear day. Their medicine just wasn't up to the task and they let us retreat with dignity."

"Kit Carson claimed in the papers that his campaign was a success."

"Reckon his biggest success was rattling all those Comanche and Kiowa Indians long enough to get his hide, along with everyone else's, the hell out of there before they got filled with arrows. He did lay on enough crap to confuse the Army into making him a general. Hell, Asa, there was a good twenty Indians to each one of us back then."

"I'd imagine a lot of those same Indians are still about."

"Yessir, I'd reckon that's a truth because that country *is* where they call home."

"We'll avoid them if at all possible. What about those water holes?"

"Mule Springs and Adobe Walls have the only water outside of the liquid mud that oozes down the Canadian. Before a person drinks any water in that neck of the woods, they'd darn well better boil it first. Still, the gyp taste is enough to stampede a herd of thirsty goats and the stuff will clean out your innards quicker than castor oil."

"Sounds like just the kind of country the Dolvens would call home."

"We'll fill up plenty of canteens and do just fine. The reason I came along was to save your ma's and sister's life. Let's quit lollygaggin' and head for Buffalo Gap. If I can remember correctly, the main Indian camps were off to the west. We'll stay east from there."

"I hope like hell you've got a good memory."

"Reckon we'll both find out soon enough. Let's ride."

"When they put the definition of a town into the dictionary, I'd venture none of them responsible had ever set eyes on Buffalo Gap, Texas, before."

Asa couldn't contain a grin. "It's a safe bet they didn't. I've seen towns after they've been shot up and sacked by bandits that still looked a lot more prosperous than this place."

The duo rode side by side down the dirt lane that passed for Main Street. The clacking of their horses' hooves kicking up little clouds of white dust was the only sound to echo in the still air of late day. A mongrel dog ventured a bark from the shade of a pecan tree, but decided that an all-out assault wasn't warranted in the stifling heat and lay back down. A few frame one-story buildings had signs out proclaiming the existence of various stores and enterprises. Only not a soul was in evidence. Not even a saddled horse could be seen tied to the hitching rail in front of the unimaginatively named Buffalo Gap Saloon.

Cemetery John reined his horse to a stop. "In most towns the local watering hole's the place to ask about findin' a livery stable and hotel room." He stared into the dark maw of the batwing doors. "Here, I ain't certain."

"Let's tie the horses and go visit. They might have some sarsaparilla or lemonade."

"They could," Cemetery John said, swinging his lean body to the dusty earth. "Perhaps we'll order a bottle of fine French champagne and dine on pheasant under glass this evening too."

"Come on, the joint can't be as bad as it looks."

A cloud of green flies billowed outward when the batwing doors swung open. The stench of stale sweat mixed with piles of rotting buffalo hides in the unmoving air was nearly overpowering. A lone window to one side barely illuminated a long plank bar that rested on empty whiskey barrels.

At one end of the bar a fat man sat perched on a stack of fresh hides, a double-barreled shotgun rested across his lap. Myriads of flies hovered about the man, crawling on his arms and among his bushy black beard.

"Evenin'," the ponderous barkeep slurred drunkenly as he struggled to his feet. "You got hides to sell, I'm a payin' two dollars. If'n it's whiskey you want, set out two bits silver in advance fer each shot. Other than that, get the hell out." He shot a red-eyed angry glance at Cemetery John. "An' I don't serve no niggers in here either."

Asa Cain's face turned bland and unreadable as he approached the bar. "I can see that you run a respectable establishment." He fished a quarter from his jeans and laid it on the plank. "I'll take a whiskey, please."

Cemetery John stood by the door and watched. He desperately wished he had not left his shotgun lodged in its scabbard, still on the horse that was tied outside the saloon.

The barkeep waddled over, picked up the money, and studied it. "Jus' checkin' to make sure this ain't counterfeit. It's a shame what some thieves'll try to pull on an honest shopkeeper."

"Isn't that the truth," Asa said disarmingly, then clucked his tongue. "I really worry about what this world's coming to."

The fat bartender nodded his approval, leaned his double-barrel against the bar, and turned to grab a shot glass and bottle. When he rotated back, his eyes didn't have time to widen before Asa pulled the Whitney Eagle from its holster. With a lightning-quick upward thrust the bounty hunter sliced a deep crimson gash along the fat man's right cheek and eye with the sharp front sight. Then he brought the gun barrel down hard above his ear. The portly bar owner crumpled to the floor with a dull thud.

"The way this day's goin'," Cemetery John commented from the doorway, "he's deader than a mackerel and his brother's the sheriff."

"Nope," Asa said with an unconcerned shrug. "I just buffaloed him. I learned the trick from a marshal up in Wichita by the odd name of Wyatt Earp. Not too many people take having a pistol barrel wacked over their heads serious enough to die from the procedure. This big galoot will live to look at that scar across his eye every day in the mirror. Maybe it'll remind him to watch his manners."

"I wouldn't place any money on that happening. Be easier to teach a mule to dance, most likely. Too bad you didn't ask about a place to eat an' a hotel before puttin' him to sleep. My belly's beginning to rub on my backbone."

Asa reached across the heavy plank bar, plucked away his quarter, which was still in the barkeeper's hand, and returned it to his pocket. Quickly he grabbed the double-barreled shotgun, opened the breech, and shook out two red and brass shells onto the filthy floor. He then brought the weapon up over his shoulder and smashed it down hard on the bar several times, shattering the stock and ruining the hammers.

Asa held the wreckage up to the lone window and nodded approval of his handiwork. "It's never wise to leave a man anything he can shoot at you with later. Now, let's go see if all of Buffalo Gap is as low-down as this joint."

Cemetery John stood in the doorway staring at the bleeding saloon keeper as Asa approached. "Reckon I oughtta go wake him so he can thank you proper," said John.

Asa cocked his head in amazement. "Why in the world would that man thank *me*?"

"Oh, he really should." Cemetery John's eyes

were cold. "The last man that called me a nigger,
I cut his throat open and grinned while he bled
to death."

Asa looked over his shoulder and shrugged.
"He looks plenty grateful. Let's go and leave him
to nap in peace."

"Yessir, I'm gettin' hungrier by the minute,"
Cemetery John said as he pushed open the doors,
letting out a fresh horde of flies. "And that fool
ain't smart enough to worry over."

Cemetery John dabbed at the remains of a plate
of stew with a biscuit. "Considering the first impression this town gives, I reckon that I'm favor-
ably impressed with this supper, though I can't say
I'm anxious to know what variety of meat went
into its fixin'."

"When you're on a manhunt, any chow you
don't have to cook yourself is a blessing." Asa Cain
eyed his meal. "I'd guess it's rabbit, but it may be
cat. Some folks eat lots of cats when meat's scarce,
dogs too. The Indians always keep a lot of dogs
around their camps. The things yap whenever in-
truders are about, and are mighty good to eat to
boot. I never figured you for being a finicky eater."

"Bein' curious ain't the same as bein' finicky.
Leastwise we've got a roof over our heads for the
night and full bellies. I plan on having some hot
chocolate, then I'm gonna buy a handful of long-
nine cigars for the trip."

Asa finished the last of his stew and leaned back
to study the main street through the front windows
of the Anson Hotel. "Remember to pack that shotgun of yours wherever you go. Forgetting it when

we went into that saloon could've gotten us both killed."

Cemetery John's reply was halted by the return of their waitress, a rotund German woman with a face of granite.

The lady, who they guessed was either the owner or married to him, surveyed the two men with angry eyes and snarled, "I haf heard of your talking and I vill not listen to such lies. Rabbit stew iss vat you haf ate." She slammed down a handwritten bill on the table. "Vun dollar, you men pay me now and no more food here for you!"

Asa came up with a silver dollar and placed it on the bill. "We're sorry to upset you, ma'am. No offense meant."

The German snatched up the money quick as a snake striking a mouse. "The rooms you haf paid for, my husband says. I cook plenty good food here. But for you ungrateful peoples I vill not serve. You go hungry, then your manners maybe improve."

Cemetery John leaned back and grinned broadly. "I've been tryin' my best to train this man to behave, ma'am. Perhaps this lesson will sink in and help his shabby soul." He rolled his eyes mischievously. "If I could get a cup of hot chocolate, I'll read to him from the Good Book while I sip it."

"Nein," the waitress snapped. "You are also no good and my ears tell me truth—" She focused wide eyes toward the front windows and color drained from her face. *"Gott in Himmel,"* the German sputtered, then spun around and ran into the kitchen. *"Gott in Himmel."*

"Reckon this means I can forget about that hot

chocolate," Cemetery John said, grabbing the ten gauge he'd leaned against the wall.

"Sure looks like it'll get postponed anyway." Asa reached over and jacked the lever of his Henry. "I'm beginning to get a real dislike for this town."

Through the open windows of the Anson Hotel the two manhunters quickly sized up the situation and scurried to take cover. Outside on the dusty main street of Buffalo Gap a half-dozen armed and cursing men clambered onto the boardwalk. A heavy boot smashed open the door.

"There they are, boys," a filthily dressed fat man with a bloody bandanna tied across the right side of his face growled. "Them's are the bastards that did this to me. Now let's have some fun and kill both of 'em."

From the shadows of the kitchen door Cemetery John's shotgun boomed loudly as the fleshy saloon owner was blasted back through the door in a spray of crimson.

"Damn, they up an' kilt Uncle Wesley," a shrill voice cried out from the west window before Asa silenced him with two slugs through his chest.

"Charge the sons a bitches," another obviously drunken thug bellowed from the boardwalk. "They's only two of them an' four of usn's."

Cemetery John opened his ten-gauge, plucked out the spent shell, slid a fresh cartridge home alongside the unused one, and slammed the breech closed just before, to his utter amazement, four of the most crackbrained, idiotic gunmen he'd ever encountered came crashing through the doorway and windows shooting wildly at everything, especially the overturned oak table Asa was hiding behind.

A thunderous explosion sent two of the attackers flying back out the doorway they were charging through. Cemetery John had fired both barrels, sending red-hot buckshot tearing through their middles.

Asa's Henry barked once, and a young blond-haired man's forehead exploded. Asa rolled quickly, poked his gun from the other side of the tabletop, and sent two slugs slamming into the heart of a black-bearded burly man who kept shooting as he died.

Silence swept through the bullet-ridden building.

"You okay?" Cemetery John shouted.

"One of those bastards was luckier than I expected," Asa said. He stood shakily, blood trickling down his left arm and dripping from his fingertips onto the plank floor. "I sure as hell didn't need this," he mumbled.

Cemetery John reloaded his shotgun just in case one of the gunmen wasn't as dead as they appeared to be, and reached Asa's side just in time to ease his fall when the bounty hunter passed out from his wound.

TWELVE

"Well, look who's finally through nappin' away good daylight."

Asa Cain rolled his head toward Cemetery John's voice, and blinked his eyes several times in an effort to clear away the fog. A sharp pain stabbed at his left shoulder when he attempted to sit up in bed, causing a groan to escape his lips.

"Now just settle back an' relax a spell. I'd reckon it must hurt like hell getting shot, even though I've never had the honor myself. At least you'll be fit as a fiddle after a spell, which is sure a lot more than can be said for the Hayes clan. The local undertaker planted the last one of them idiots while I was enjoying dinner in the hotel dining room. You know that place didn't get torn up near as bad as I'd feared."

The veil of haze cleared to where Asa could clearly make out Cemetery John sitting in a rocking chair by a window leisurely smoking a cigar. From the sharp blue of the sky Asa knew it was likely past midday. "Where am I and how long was I out?" His throat felt like raw meat.

"You got plugged just last evening. Griselda Anson, the nice lady who was serving us supper, had

some laudanum. She made you swallow enough
to give you a good rest. The slug blew away a hunk
of flesh from the edge of your shoulder. Luckily,
it looks like no bones got cracked or anything vital
got in the way of the bullet. She used a sewing kit
and put in a few stitches to hold things together
until they heal, but by an' large there wasn't that
much damage done, 'specially considerin' how
much lead was flyin' in your direction."

Asa slid his legs to the floor and clenched his
jaw tight when he forced himself to a sitting position on the edge of the bed. "Cemetery," he
gasped, "you've got a real knack for understate-
ment. I reckon I should've expected that barkeep
to cause more trouble. Damn it all, I can't tolerate
any delays."

"We'll see how you're feelin' in the mornin'.
You pop loose one of those stitches Griselda put
in an' catch an infection, you can still wind up
deader than a doornail if'n you work at it hard
enough."

"Why did that woman help me? The last I heard
was she was going to run us both off."

"Oh, killin' the Hayes clan changed not only
her attitude towards us, but that of most folks in
Buffalo Gap."

"How did all this come about?"

"Seems the whole Hayes family moved in here
about four years ago. They was from Arkansas,
which explains why they acted like they did, bein'
both mean an' idiots. Well, sir, it seems like the
first thing Wesley Hayes accomplished here—he
was the gentleman you tried to educate—was to
kill the local marshal. Then he and his family simply took over the town. They charged every busi-

ness twenty-five dollars a month for 'fire' protection, and never paid for a single thing they took from a store or for a meal in a restaurant."

"Nice folks to have for neighbors. I'm surprised the law wasn't called."

"They were, but all that showed up had 'accidents,' or so it was reported back to Austin. Seems one Ranger got snakebit an' another got scalped by Indians a few miles from town, nothing to get any suspicions riled. The Ansons and others hired a so-called gunslinger—paid him five hundred dollars—but the Hayes bunch came at him from all sides and fatally perforated him with rifle balls before he got off a single shot."

Asa nodded. "Then we came along."

Cemetery sent a puff of smoke to the ceiling. "Yessir, and we were kind enough to get rid of that whole den of vipers at no cost to the hotel owners other than what a few dollars of patchin' work will take care of. That's why the room's free, an' when you're up to it, so's supper."

"I should have been smart enough to skirt this place. You know that sheriff and the gunfighter I've told you about are on their way to join up with the marshal in Canan. My mother and sister can't afford the time for me to heal."

"You're gonna rest the afternoon. Then we'll take supper and see how well you're movin' about. You won't count for much in Canan if you show up there dead from a blood poison."

"Early tomorrow morning we head north. That's the last I'll tolerate of hanging around Buffalo Gap."

Cemetery John took a long drag on his long-nine and stared out the window. "It's a real scorcher out there, an' I can tell you from past experience that the devil would feel right at home in the country where we're headin'. I'll fetch us an extra canteen or two. Reckon we'll have need of them shortly."

Asa Cain lay back down stiffly and carefully. After a long minute he said, "I want to thank you for what you did last night. Those men would have killed me if you hadn't been there."

"You won't tolerate Buffalo Gap and I won't tolerate that kind of talk. I didn't do one single thing for you that you wouldn't have done for me. That don't deserve no hurrahs in my book."

Asa nodded his understanding and studied the ceiling for a few moments before the laudanum in his system claimed him once again and he slept.

"For you, my brave man," Griselda Anson said to Asa as she set a heaping plate of food in front of him. The German wore the closest thing to a smile he figured she was capable of mustering. "I haf fried up the livers of calf buffalos along with much turnips. This vill very quick build up the blood you lost ven that awful outlaw shot you and keep away the infections."

"Thank you, ma'am," Asa said, attempting to mask his trepidation. "But my appetite isn't up to much this evening."

"I'll see to it that he finishes ever little speck of your good cookin', Missus Anson," Cemetery John said firmly as he ladled cream gravy over a mountain of mashed potatoes that rested alongside golden brown pieces of fried chicken and a heap of steaming fresh green snap beans. "Asa's like a lot of folks when they get hurt. He's just going to have to be prodded into doing what's best for his recovery. We both know he's going to need all the strength he can muster to be able to hit the trail in the mornin'."

"*Ja,*" Griselda agreed with a nod. "Und liver with turnips ist just vat the doctor ordered."

"Dig in," Cemetery John said, focusing a wry grin at Asa. "Startin' tomorrow you'll be eatin' my cooking, so enjoy fine food while you've got the opportunity."

Asa grabbed up a knife and winced with pain as he began sawing at a slice of liver. He opined to himself that cutting a chunk of leather out of the sole of one of his boots would be an easier task, but decided that saying so would likely cause him more problems. He had started to thank the German lady to get her to leave, so he could pilfer a piece of fried chicken, when a rifle shot split the air from down the street.

"Mighty interestin' town to live in," Cemetery John said, reaching for his huge shotgun. "I might oughtta move my undertaking business up here. Seems to me there's considerable more need of my services here than in Wolf Springs."

Asa jumped up, sending the chair flying. He pulled the Whitney Eagle from its holster, cocking the hammer with his thumb. The stabbing pain in his shoulder reminded him it would be some time before he could again fire the Henry rifle that he had depended on for many years. A pistol was a close-in weapon. The bounty hunter preferred to take care of problems while they were still in the distance.

"It ist from at the mail office," Griselda Anson shouted, making a dash to the kitchen.

"Well, let's go find out who needs shootin' this time," Cemetery John said, heading for the front door followed by Asa.

"It's the stage," a burly freighter yelled at them the second they came onto the boardwalk. "Everybody's been kilt 'cept the driver. He's the one who fired the gun to draw attention."

Asa shook his head to clear away the wavy lines that shimmered across his eyes as the freighter and some kid joined them in the dash to the stage.

"That's the Wheeler an' Hawkins Line," the young boy squawked excitedly. "They run from Fort Worth through here on the way to New Mexico Territory."

"Well, this one didn't make it," the freighter said when they got close enough to make out a profusion of arrows impaled in the sides of the stagecoach. "Them durn redskins have been threatenin' to go on the warpath. Looks like they've gone an' done it."

The kid ran up, gawking with wide eyes at a young flaxen-haired woman not much older than he was whose head dangled listlessly from an open window. He reached out and gently placed his hands on her cheeks. He then paled when he saw where an arrow had entered the hollow of her throat to protrude several inches from the back of her neck. "Sweet Jesus," he gasped as he spun to run away, losing his supper.

A milling crowd began to build around the coach. One man, a tall, beanpole-thin older fellow with leathery features, pushed the gathering aside and headed straight toward Cemetery John, his narrowed eyes fixed on the tin badge. "I'm the driver of that stage. Are you the law hereabouts?"

"Nope," Cemetery John said. "I'm only a deputy from Wolf Springs." He nodded sideways toward Asa. "We're only passin' through on a manhunt."

The stage driver silently sized up the duo for a long moment before he thrust out a hand to Cemetery John. "My name's Homer Penbrook an' I'm plumb happy to be makin' y'all's acquaintance. There ain't no one but me outta the eight of us that started this trip can say the same. I didn't even get a scratch while ever one else, even that purty little lady, got themselves dead. Sure a shame about losin' the whore. This here's hard country an' we need all of them we got."

Cemetery John nodded. "Indians generally kill everyone they can and sort it out later. When I was here in this neck of the woods back in '64, folks hereabouts were havin' similar problems."

"Well, soaplock my hair an' call me a rowdy," Homer said with the vestige of a grin. "You must've been a buff soldier with ol' Kit Carson. Damn good men, you buffs. The problem was there weren't near enough of y'all. A passel more Injuns anyway. An' things ain't changed a whit since."

Asa made his introduction, skipping the likely painful handshake. "This Indian attack, Mr. Penbrook, just where did it occur?"

The driver stared at him, his brow wrinkled in thought. "I've heard tell of you before. Reckon you're that bounty hunter folks are always jawin' about. Makes no never mind to me 'cause my carcass is already owned by the Wheeler an' Hawkins

Line. An' I've done tol' you my name's Homer; it ain't 'Mister' or 'Penbrook,' gol durn it. I'd reckon you to be from back East somewhar. May God have mercy on your scrawny soul."

"He's gettin' improved," Cemetery John said. "But Asa's right about us likin' to know where you found all of those Indians."

Homer Penbrook spat a wad of tobacco into the dirt alongside his boots. "The fact of the matter is *they* found *us*. I've been on this run fer nigh onto three years an' had nothin' but an occasional holdup to slow me down. Folks have been talkin' about an' Injun uprising." He looked back toward the stagecoach. "I'd venture that we've done passed the jawin' part."

Asa's eyes darkened dangerously. His wounded shoulder throbbed mercilessly and his head was spinning. "Tell us exactly *where* the attack happened, Penbrook."

"I declare, you young'uns are always in such a dither. Now back in my day folks had patience. Since you're so jo-fired up, I'll tell you. We was about halfway down here from Canan when the ruckus struck."

"Canan," Cemetery John sputtered.

"Yep, that's where they came at us," the stagecoach driver said. "We began pickin' up arrows 'bout ten minutes after we'd changed horses at Adobe Walls. Danged if I know how even I made it through with Quanah Parker hisself leadin' all them warriors. Must of been nigh onto a few hundred of them painted-up redskins a-hoopin' an' hollerin'."

"You say you recognized Quanah Parker?" a man wearing a suit asked from behind Asa. "Why, that just can't be. He's not been about since he was made Chief of the Staked Plains."

"Tell that to those dead folks in my stage," Homer Penbrook growled. "I know Quanah Parker when I set eyes on him. He had his ol' friend ridin' with him too. Lame Bear, that murderin', sneakin' scalawag who loves to attack travelers an' helpless wagon trains, was ridin' alongside Quanah Parker, plain as the nose on yer ugly face."

Asa Cain staggered as if he'd been shot. "Oh, shit," he mumbled. "Oh, shit!"

THIRTEEN

"Oh, shit," Asa Cain repeated. He stepped close to the stage driver and grabbed onto his shirt collar with his good arm. The soreness and pain of his wound had been subdued by burning rage. "Lame Bear! Tell me *exactly* how you know it was him."

"Take it easy, my friend," Cemetery John said. He fixed the startled Homer Penbrook in a steely gaze. "This renegade they call Lame Bear killed Asa's father, then kidnapped Asa and sold him to be raised by the Comanche. I'd reckon he's got a tolerable good reason for gettin' upset."

"I'd heard tell you was on ol' Green's wagon train," the stage driver said softly, and Asa released his grip. "That was a terrible thing that happened. But to answer your question, Lame Bear had his noggin creased by a bullet back in the forties. The wound healed up leavin' a big streak of white hair across the left edge of his greasy black mop. He stands out like a skunk at a church social."

"My God," Asa said. His eyes had become mere slits. "That's him all right. I've dreamed of getting that bastard in my sights for a lot of years. Now he's plundering and killing right where my poor mother and sister are. It's just not possible Lame Bear could get to them. No God who is righteous would allow that to happen."

"The Lord moves in mysterious ways that we often cannot understand at the time," the suit-wearing man behind Asa said loudly to be overheard by the crowd. "I am the Reverend Jedediah Green, and I have seen the terrible works these savages have wrought. Come join me at the hotel this evening for a prayer meeting."

Asa spun to face the clergyman. "And just what will you be praying for, Preacher?"

"Retribution. Divine retribution as is described in the Good Book. Psalm 147 says: 'The wicked shall be casteth down to the ground.' I'm fixing to send up a sturdy prayer that you'll be successful in casting those red demons straight to hell."

"Thank you, Preacher," Asa replied sincerely. "I'd venture we'll need all the help we can get before this is over."

Cemetery John tugged gently at Asa's sleeve. "Let's be getting back to the hotel. You need your rest and we've both left our dinners on the table."

Asa sighed deeply. "Lame Bear, Quanah Parker, and thousands of Indians are on the warpath. Crooked lawmen and a gunslinger are on their way to kill my mother for reward money, and I've been shot. If that isn't enough hell for a man to endure, there's a plate of liver and turnips waiting for me."

"I'll smuggle you a chicken leg," Cemetery John whispered cheerfully in Asa's ear as the pair walked back to the Anson Hotel in the fading light.

* * *

Cemetery John squinted his eyes against the glare as he surveyed the flat, distant horizon. Only a lone dust devil winding its way across the prairie broke the monotony. "This country is even worse than I remember it bein', and I remember it bein' somewhat worse than hell. By this afternoon it's gonna be hot enough to blister lizards an' cause heatstroke to buzzards."

"There's sure no trees for any Indians to hide behind," Asa said. "That's the only good thing I can come up with."

"And that means no shade for us to rest or camp under."

"We can't afford to lollygag anyway, Cemetery. That incident in Buffalo Gap cost us way too much time already."

The deputy had been surreptitiously eyeing his friend for some time now. It was obvious that the blood Asa had lost from his wound was taking a toll. While he sat tall in the saddle, his shoulders were slumped, and a few times his eyelids had dropped closed as his body fought for some more healing sleep. The rhythmic jogging from the horse, coupled with the oppressive heat, was not conducive to Asa's recovery, yet Cemetery realized there was no way he could talk Asa into stopping or even slowing their pace. Asa Cain, though wounded, was a driven man who would tolerate no delay. Should their situations be reversed, Cemetery John decided that he would be just as stubborn himself.

"We'll keep movin', but the horses can't be pushed. If we lose one of them, things'll get worse in a hurry."

Asa shot a glance at the four packhorses Cemetery John was leading with a head-and-tail string. They carried the only water the two men would find for quite a few days, along with food, sleeping blankets, and extra ammunition. He felt a burning lump form in his throat when he realized two of those horses were meant to be ridden back by his mother and sister. *But back to where?* he thought bitterly. *The governor of Texas is determined to see Jenny Cain hang. Only a miracle will spare her from the gallows, and miracles always come mighty dear when a person needs one.*

"They call this country the *Llano Estacado* or Staked Plains." Cemetery John's voice jerked Asa from his troubled thoughts. "All of this wonderfully level desolation extends for hundreds of miles and reaches clear over to the Pecos River in New Mexico Territory."

"Never had any call to come up here before. The Indians who attacked our wagon train on the Pecos in Texas and the tribe that I was sold to didn't venture north. I've spent most of my time east and south."

"Consider yourself as bein' plumb lucky up till now. You know why they call this the Staked Plains?"

"No, but I've a feeling you're going to tell me."

"Yep, I am. There ain't much to do out here but talk or kill buffalo. So we might as well jaw. The hide hunters are doin' a good job of killin' off the buffs, which is what the Indians depend on for their livelihood. Reckon that's why they've got a bee in their bonnet. But to go on with what I started to say in the first place, there simply ain't no way to navigate out here. Most places have a high point of some kind to aim for or a river to follow. Out here it's only flat land with waving grass that's usually lookin' dead for as far as a person can see. The first travelers through here drove stakes in the ground for others to follow an' not get lost. That's how it came to be known as the Staked Plains."

"If you ever get tired of being a deputy or undertaker, you might make a go of teaching school."

"That couldn't happen." Cemetery John lowered his gaze to the ground and watched as a horned toad scurried from their path, its legs kicking up little puffs of white dust as it ran. "I can barely read a wanted poster, an' cipherin' is a strain."

"I didn't know."

"Ain't no real problem. I've taught myself enough to get along. At least out here in West Texas."

"You come across so well, I thought you'd had a decent education."

"I don't hold any grudge 'cause you fought for the South, but that war was mighty personal for me. There's a lot you don't understand about what it was like bein' raised a slave. My owners weren't any different than most; they just looked on us the same way we look on cattle an' horses—as a commodity. An educated nigger was nothing but problems, so they never let us have any schoolin' at all."

After a moment Asa said, "For as long as I've known you, I've never heard anybody call you by your last name."

"Don't have one and never did. When you're raised as livestock there ain't much need of one. Most of us slaves took the names of our masters, if anyone asked. I was owned by a judge in South Carolina by the name of Elijah Witherspoon. He wasn't a bad sort, leastwise far as masters went. There was a lot worse, that's for sure. Hell, I was even happy up till the time my wife and little boy got sold by him and shipped off to where I never could find 'em again. Reckon calling myself Witherspoon ain't anything that I'd care to do."

Asa Cain chewed on his lower lip for a long while before speaking. "I can surely see why you would never use that man's name. Here I'm faced with losing my own family and you had yours *sold*. And there wasn't a damn thing you could do about it. That was a terrible injustice."

"It was called slavery and thank God it's over, at least for the most part anyway. But losing one's family is something a body never gets over. That's the reason I'm here. You're Wilburn Deevers' friend and he's treated me better than I can remember anyone else ever doin'. He asked me to keep you from gettin' dead an' to help save your mom and sister. I gave him my word on the matter. And even if'n I have to shoot you in the other shoulder, by gum I'm gonna get the job done."

"Thank you," Asa said simply. His eyes were tired from want of sleep, and the relentless hot wind had burned them raw. This explained the stinging wetness through which he stared as he and Cemetery John rode side by side across the wavering brown expanse of the Staked Plains of West Texas.

FOURTEEN

Cemetery John fed some thumb-sized sticks of dead sagebrush to a fledgling fire and frowned at Asa, who sat on a large flat rock watching.

"For a man who's spent years chasing down outlaws and the sort," Cemetery grumbled, "you've sure become mighty finicky about your eats. I can see where you might've had some slight call to complain about the quality of grub back in Buffalo Gap, but there's no good reason to fuss up a storm about me roastin' us a rattlesnake for supper."

"I'm not fussing. Rattlers aren't called desert lobsters without good reason. I've eaten a lot of them and they're plenty tasty. It's just that I'm really hungry and one little diamondback, not even three feet long, doesn't stretch very far."

A grin passed across Cemetery John's face. "Bein' hungry is a sure sign you're healing up. To celebrate the occasion I'll fry up a skillet full of bacon and then add a heap of taters to the grease. I'll take them biscuits I brought along, slice 'em open, and stuff in some of the bacon slices. Before the grease gets cold I'll fill them biscuits full of pig lard and wrap 'em in muslin. That way we'll have some fillin' meals to take on the trail with us." He stared across the darkening trackless plain. "Reckon it wouldn't be wise to build any more fires."

Asa kept his attention toward the campfire. "You're right about that. Not too many people realize from how far away an Indian can smell smoke or meat cooking. A lot of folks, who later paid for their ignorance with their lives, believed that if they simply kept the smoke down they couldn't be detected. All Indians share the senses of wolves. They have to to survive out here."

Cemetery John shook his head, and turned his attention to threading the freshly skinned and still-writhing snake onto a sharpened green stick he had hacked from a low-growing bush. "I sure can't see no problem with lettin' the Comanche have this country. The only seep of water I seen all day smelled like burnin' sulphur and had so much black tar mixed with it even a coyote would leave it be. This here's likely the most worthless country that there is anyplace."

Asa bent down stiffly, picked up a dried buffalo chip, and slid it into the fire. "Buffalo migrate through here by the hundreds of thousands every year, and some folks say they even gain weight. The Indians who live in this country get everything they need to survive but water from those buffalo. I know the Comanche far better than most white men. There's some good water holes around here, there has to be. When Indians want something hidden, no people on earth are better at the task than they are."

"Could be we'll get in trouble before too long. If we do, I'll reckon to find out just how much teachin' you managed to pick up from the Comanche."

"That was a long time ago, Cemetery. I hope to make it straight through to Canan without us setting eyes on a feather that doesn't still have a bird attached to it."

"We'll hang to the east and hope for the best. That stage driver said the Comanche struck him just outta Adobe Walls, which about says it all for the joint; leastwise it pretty well described the place when I saw it. There sure ain't nothin' there to cause a visit. We've got water enough for ourselves and the horses until we reach the Red River. Besides bein' safer, Adobe Walls is a lot of miles out of our way if'n we take a straight line north."

"Canan is where we're heading, and the sooner we get there the better. . . ." Asa's voice trailed off to join the incessant wind.

"Toss some more chips on that fire an' we'll soon have us a heapin' tasty platter of snake and taters." Cemetery John's voice was cheerful. "After supper I'll give the horses a bait of grain and water 'em so we can get an early start come sunup. I'm anxious as you are to get out of the Staked Plains and into Canan. Hell, the place can't be any worse than Buffalo Gap."

Asa grimaced when he added fuel to the campfire. "I know, and that's got me worried."

Three days later, on a cloudless and blistering hot afternoon, Asa Cain and Cemetery John reined their horses to a halt on a low rise overlooking the sandy, tree-lined banks of the Red River.

Other than losing a few hours a day ago when they were forced to skirt a large herd of buffalo, they had made good time and, thankfully, had encountered no fresh Indian sign.

Cemetery John motioned to the swirling murky water. "This here's a mighty popular river. A few hours north we'll strike the Salt Fork of the Red River, which is aptly named, I might add. Then, after a hard day, we come to the North Fork of the same darn stream. This one's got most of the water, however."

Asa raised up in the saddle and carefully surveyed both up and down the river with his keen blue eyes. The movement caused him only a little pain. The wound to his shoulder had healed to an angry red welt and his strength was nearly back to normal. "I don't see anything out of the ordinary, but we'd best be on our guard."

"With Comanche about I generally am. Folks say a nice curly scalp like mine would be a real prize for some warrior."

"They're right. When I was among the Comanche a good buffalo soldier's scalp was worth a decent horse. I'd guess yours would be worth maybe two skinny dogs, considering the market's still the same."

Cemetery John feigned a snort of anger, glad that his companion had recovered to the point of being able to poke fun. "If'n the thing's only worth two mangy dogs, reckon I'd best keep it." He nodded toward the river. "Let the horses water but don't drink none yourself, too big a chance to take unless it's boiled first, which might be fatal all by its self. We'll play it safe and stick with what's in the canteens."

"We have plenty left to make Canan," Asa said, giving his anxious mount slack to head for the water. "If we push hard, I think we'll be there by sundown tomorrow."

"Possibly. I've never been to Canan before so I ain't certain. Kit Carson wouldn't let any of his troops visit there. Too much sin, shootings, and corruption going on there for him to stomach, or so it was said. Fort Griffin was where we all went to blow off steam. If Canan's a meaner town than that one, I reckon we oughtta take extra care. Killings in Fort Griffin were so blame common nobody bothered to call the law, probably 'cause there weren't none anyway. We just stepped around any bodies that were left lying in the way, and ignored anyone who wasn't shootin' at us."

"Canan sounds like far too many places I've been, where life is cheap and the pleasures expensive. The Dolvens have a ranch up there for good cause, and you can bet it's not lush grazing land that drew them."

"No," Cemetery John said with a sigh as he dropped the reins to allow his roan to drink its fill of the questionable-looking water. "Lack of law and a suitable place to hide stolen cattle, and sell bad whiskey to Indians from, most likely came way ahead of raising cattle. Now your Turkey Tree Ranch back in Wolf Springs could be right profitable without risking any law-breakin'."

"It could have—" Asa stiffened and cocked his head. The plaintive trill of a quail down river caught his attention.

Cemetery John grabbed up the reins and stared at Asa with dead silence.

Again and again the bobwhites sounded. After

a moment Asa relaxed. "It's okay. Those are real quail. I just had to be certain."

"You take all the time you need. A man who used to haul nitroglycerine once told me that in his profession he was allowed one mistake, his first an' his last. I'd reckon we're kind of riding in the same wagon he did."

"There's no Indians, but we'd best move away from the water when the horses are through drinking. I'd like to make some more miles before dark, and any Comanche will likely follow the river."

Cemetery John whacked his horse's side with the heel of his boot. "Come on and drink up, you nag. We're not here for you to enjoy the scenery." He surveyed the riverbed. "Reckon any place that's shallow will work for a crossing as long as there ain't no quicksand. I can't abide the stuff. I heard tell a whole company of soldiers once got swallowed up on the Canadian. The trouble is, I ain't never found anyone believable who could tell quicksand by lookin' at it."

"Tall tales are mostly what you've heard. I've never known first-hand of a single person actually getting sucked under by quicksand."

Cemetery John cast a jaundiced eye at the river. "Let's just not go and make that first and last mistake I was telling you about."

Asa joined in looking worried. "One thing that has me a lot more concerned than quicksand is the total lack of Indians."

"Why's that a matter to fret over, for Pete's sake? I thought we was tryin' to *avoid* redskins."

"This is the Comanche and Kiowa homeland. We both know the buffalo are here because we had to ride around at least five thousand of them.

We should have seen at least fresh signs of a hunting party. Instead, every Indian track I saw was at least several weeks old."

"And this is a problem?"

Asa nodded worriedly. "It is, if what I think might have happened caused the Indians to change from their usual ways. That stage getting attacked is also a bad sign."

"And just what might this latest situation be that's liable to get us scalped?"

"A war gathering against the whites. Even when I was among the Comanche there was talk of such a thing. A lot of the Plains Indians believe that if the tribes band together they will be sufficiently strong to rub out every white person west of the Big Water, which is what they call the Mississippi. This has been what Quanah Parker's been asking for for a lot of years."

Cemetery John sighed and stared forlornly at the swirling waters. "Outlaws are one thing, an Indian war party is another. Now you're tellin' me all of the Plains Indian tribes have joined together to kill us. Shucks, Asa, this makes the quicksand-infested river we're fixin' to cross seem almost as safe as going to church."

Asa grinned wickedly at Cemetery John as he spurred his horse into the murky water. "I'm heading for Canan. Follow me and if I sink out of sight, you'll know I made that mistake you were talking about. By the way, what did happen to your friend that hauled the nitro?"

"He blew himself up. What the hell did you think happened to him? Lead the way and I hope to heaven your luck's better'n his was."

FIFTEEN

Through shimmering heat waves rising from the broad expanse of tawny grass, they could plainly make out a long dark line snaking across the horizon.

"That's one mighty strange-lookin' herd of buffalo," Cemetery John remarked when Asa and he reined to a stop.

Asa Cain's features were stony as he reached into his saddlebag and extracted a leather-covered brass telescope.

"Lordy, I do hope that ain't what I'm fearin'," Cemetery John said. "Yesterday I had to survive quicksand, and now this."

"That's why I brought along a telescope, to find out for certain from a nice safe distance."

Asa extended the spyglass, brought it up to his eye, and slowly clicked it into focus. "We've got ourselves a big problem. Those are all mounted warriors. I can make out at least a thousand or more Comanche, Kiowa, and Kwahadi. All are wearing war paint and riding together."

"Dang it all, Asa. I wisht you weren't right about so many blasted things. There weren't any quicksand, and now that big Indian war against white folks has become real as a bullet."

"It appears so. I wouldn't have thought Quanah Parker could have pulled it off, but the son of a gun did. Those tribes out there have been raiding and killing each other for centuries. Parker must be a real diplomat getting them to bury the hatchet and band together like this."

"If you're through congratulatin' that half-breed for bein' smart enough to likely kill us, I would appreciate it if'n you'd put a tad of thought into how we might get out of this fix with our hair still intact."

"We're just so close to Canan. If I'd had the good sense to skirt Buffalo Gap, we could have been there a day ago. Saving my mother and sister is why we're here in the first place, not to get involved in an Indian war."

"I know that an' you know that. The problem, as I see it, is about a thousand really wrathy an' worked-up redskins that don't care we're just tryin' to get someplace else."

Asa kept the telescope to his eye, occasionally clicking it a notch one way or the other to keep it in focus. "Damn it all!" he swore. "That stage driver was right about Lame Bear. I'm looking straight at the son of a bitch who killed my father."

"Perhaps there might be a better time to get even, like when he's got less friends about."

Asa brought down the telescope, folded it closed, and replaced it in his saddlebag without taking his gaze from the horizon. "You said that you've been to Adobe Walls? This is a good time to see if you find the place."

Cemetery John looked at him, aghast. "I did,

but I remember plain as day you saying you didn't care to visit the joint. If we just stay put right here, I figger those Indians'll keep moving onto wherever the heck it is they're headin' an' we can go on to Canan once they're outta sight."

Asa clucked his tongue. "It's no wonder so blame many people get scalped. They don't understand Indians. Anytime you can see them, they can see you. And an Indian learns to see with more than their eyes. Lame Bear felt my spirit reaching out and hating him. At this very moment he and at least a few hundred braves are riding hard straight for us."

"You mentioned that this might be a good time to visit Adobe Walls." Cemetery John calmly took out a long-nine cigar, bit the end off, and lit it with a sulphur match. He noticed Asa's impatient looks. "The place is on the Canadian River maybe fifty miles to the northwest. Right now the wind is blowing toward the direction those redskins are comin' from."

Asa cast a surprised nod of approval at his companion when Cemetery John tossed the still-burning match into the tinder dry, grass-covered prairie.

"Shame to waste a lucifer match," the undertaker said seriously. "Those things cost money. Let's ride hard for Adobe Walls and give the folks there the splendid news that there'll be some singed and mighty upset company comin' their way."

"That's the trouble with settin' fires," Cemetery John complained as they rode hard and fast along the south bank of the Canadian River. "The blasted things never go and burn up what you want 'em to."

Asa ventured a glance over his shoulder at the distant dust cloud being kicked up by a horde of pursuing Indians. "Well, it seemed like a good idea at the time, and likely bought us a few minutes. The wind was blowing so blamed strong, it sent the flames east too fast to do us any good. Lame Bear and his warriors stayed to the north and probably didn't even get smoke in their eyes, and wound up with our pack horses to boot."

"Dad blast the luck. I was hoping to give 'em a decent scorchin' at the very least. How far back are those savages anyway? I hate to ruin this day any worse than it already has been by turning and lookin'."

"We've been holding about ten minutes ahead of them ever since you tried to burn up the Staked Plains. If one of our horses don't step in a prairie-dog hole and break a leg, we'll hold this lead. Comanche horses don't run any faster than what we're riding, no matter what you might have heard."

The deputy stared into the setting sun, which was sending dying red rays across the plains. "We're near to Adobe Walls. I surely hope there's some folks there. Back about ten years ago it was just some fallin'-down old adobe shacks with a water hole where people could lay over and rest for a spell. Most of the time no one was there."

Asa shouted, "Why didn't you tell me this before?"

"I informed you plain as day that you wouldn't like the place. The way things turned out, I'd venture there weren't no other choice 'cept to go see if things might've improved some of late and hope like hell that they had."

The bounty hunter shook his head, then reached up and pulled the brim of his hat down to shield his eyes. "Whatever Adobe Walls amounts to, we're about there." He pointed into the red glare.

Cemetery John squinted at a staggered row of buildings, and shortly made out roofs that hadn't been there before, along with a high gray wall that now surrounded the settlement. He breathed a sigh of relief when he saw scores of horses and cattle penned inside and smoke drifting upward from several chimneys. "Looks like my career of buryin' folks and bein' a deputy ain't over yet."

"If there's a company of cavalry inside that compound, I'll agree with you. A few dozen buffalo hunters, which I'm guessing is all that's there, won't hold off Lame Bear's warriors for long."

"That's the trouble with you lately, Asa, you fail to see the good side of not gettin' killed. Long as we're alive, your ma and sister's got a decent chance."

"Our chance of saving them gets slimmer the longer it takes us to reach them."

"Reckon I know that. Right now the best we can do is let the good citizens of Adobe Walls know they've got callers and to break out their rifles."

PART TWO

BATTLE AT ADOBE WALLS

SIXTEEN

"You two look like you're fleeing either the devil or the law," a thin, black-bearded man with deep-set cadaverous eyes growled as he sauntered over to meet Asa and Cemetery John. He kept the twin barrels of a sawed-off ten-gauge shotgun trained square at their middles. "I mean to find out here and now which it is."

Cemetery John turned and motioned to the silver star pinned on his shirt with his chin. The man with the shotgun was obviously anxious for a reason to use it. "Simmer down and save your ammo. You're likely to have more need for it shortly rather than blowing us outta our saddles for no cause."

"You could have stole that badge." The shotgun-wielding man kept both his aim and his scowl.

"Oh for Pete's sake, George, put that gun away and behave yourself. I swear, somebody's gonna shoot you someday just to improve the country-side." The melodious voice belonged to a trim and beautiful lady with short, curly blond hair who had just stepped through the batwing doors of what a crudely lettered sign proclaimed to be "The Sunday School Saloon."

"Only looking after your welfare, ma'am." The man named George lowered the hammers on the Stevens. "There's a passel of bad men about who need to be sent back to their maker."

"Get down, gentlemen," the lovely lady said cheerfully. "George Maledon's just an out-of-work hangman and a sorehead, to boot. He thinks he might get paid to become sheriff here someday, but if he keeps pointing guns at customers, I'll see him run off." She motioned toward the batwings. "Come in and have a drink. The first one's on the house, and remember your upbringing. Going to Sunday school will make your mother proud."

Asa Cain winced and remained in the saddle. "Ma'am, Mr. Maledon was more right than he realized when he asked if we were fleeing the devil, because at least a close relative of Satan by the name of Lame Bear along with a few hundred fired-up warriors that follow Quanah Parker will be along in a few short minutes. They've been chasing us for hours."

"Oh, my God!" George Maledon sputtered. "Why didn't you say so earlier."

"You seemed plenty happy listenin' to your own gums rattlin'," Cemetery John said. "Now that you're convinced we ain't your biggest problem, perhaps this might be a good time to go fetch some men with rifles."

Before the self-appointed lawman of Adobe Walls could answer, the blonde had grasped a rope dangling from the roof of the saloon, and began yanking it. A brass ship's bell began clanging out an alarm.

A few grizzled buffalo hunters came slowly outside, blinking their eyes to adjust to the dying bright light of a bloody Texas sunset.

"Are them savages back again, Missus Olds?" A fellow not much older than Asa, but who had likely not encountered a barber or a bathtub for a long while, sized up the two strangers on horseback. "I swan, will you gents get down an' quit making a target of yourselves? We'll go blow a few of them savages outta their moccasins an' they'll go away. This ain't nothin' new in these parts. Don't go gettin' dithered up."

Asa and Cemetery John swung down to the dusty main street and made their introductions.

"My name's Billy Dixon," The man who seemed to be in charge wiped his hand on a filthy wool shirt and offered it. "Reckon I've heard tell of a bounty hunter by the name of Asa Cain. You one an' the same?"

"I've brought in a few outlaws," Asa said simply.

"Round about two hundred, an' all of them deader than a politician's thinkin'," Billy Dixon said firmly. He spat a wad of tobacco juice at a lizard and turned to the lady. "You best go back inside an' see to your husband, ma'am. If he decides to take a stroll right about now, reckon that'd be too durn bad."

Asa and Cemetery John made note of nearly twenty men casually taking up positions behind the thick adobe wall that surrounded the town. These were buffalo hunters and all packed heavy Sharps big fifty rifles, a few of which had a small brass telescope attached. From the wooden platforms of varying heights that the men stood on, it was obvious this had happened before.

Billy Dixon waited until the young blond lady

had gone through the batwings before he turned to Asa. "Shame about her havin' to care for a man that can't even go to the outhouse without gettin' lost. Hibb's his name, hers is Willow. They bought this place half a dozen years ago an' done right good. This is where we buffalo hunters come for supplies an' a rest up."

"What happened to this Hibb fellow?" Cemetery John asked.

"He caught a fever from drinkin' the water. This was 'bout a year ago. He'd been better off if'n it'd kilt him. Poor li'l wife of his has to do bartendin', cookin', and everything else these days. Hibb ain't done nothin' but sit and stare or wander about. He's not said a word anybody can understand since he got sick."

Cemetery John shot a knowing glance at Asa. "See, I told you what the water's like up here. Boil it first or pay the consequences."

Billy Dixon spat another wad of tobacco. "Whiskey's safer an' tastes better." He turned to notice the cloud of dust approaching from the east. "Hell, let's go kill us some savages."

Asa pulled the Henry from its scabbard and grabbed his telescope along with an extra box of shells from his saddlebags. Cemetery John had brought along a Winchester Model 1866 repeating rifle in a scabbard opposite the one that carried his familiar ten-gauge shotgun. As this fight was hopefully going to be done over some distance, he chose the Winchester.

The pair took up positions on a section of the wall with Billy Dixon and George Maledon, who still packed his shotgun, to their right. On their left, next to the gate, stood a skinny kid who was still young enough to be fighting pimples. Asa nodded to the boy, and was surprised at the steely calmness he saw in the lad's eyes.

"Folks call me Bartholomew," the young fellow said unexcitedly, keeping his eyes fixed on the approaching Indians. "Bartholomew Masterson, late of Kansas. From the number of redskins a-comin', I'd say they're really riled at y'all. We never had half this many attack us before."

Cemetery John motioned toward his companion with the stock of his rifle. "Asa here has that effect on a lot of folks, not just Indians."

"Asa Cain, the famous bounty hunter?" Bartholomew said with obvious awe. "I'm honored to be by your side, sir."

"We'll get better acquainted later on. Right now let's see if you can send a few braves to their happy hunting ground."

"Yes, sir," Bartholomew said. "I'm looking forward to it."

"Damn, but there's a passel of Indians out there," Billy Dixon said.

Cemetery John worried a stub of cigar between his teeth. "Shucks, what's comin' at us is just a small fraction of what we run across. There was Comanche, Kiowa, an' Kwahadi, with likely some Cheyenne mixed in for fun, all ridin' together."

Billy Dixon spat tobacco juice on the gray wall and sighted through the telescope on his rifle. "Never is a good idea to count Injuns or buffaloes. You can only shoot one at a time anyway."

The heavy Sharps boomed and the recoil knocked Billy Dixon back a good two feet. From all along the wall rifles began firing.

Asa slid open his brass telescope and began to

watch the carnage. Every time one of the heavy-caliber buffalo rifles fired and sent out a slug of hot lead singing across the prairie, a warrior would be propelled backward from his horse in a spray of crimson. A few puffs of dirt erupting hundreds of feet in the distance indicated that the Indians were shooting at them from far out of range of their weapons.

"Them Injuns with holes bein' blown in 'em must be at least a thousand feet away," Cemetery John shouted to be heard over the fusillade. "I never seen shootin' like this in all my born days."

"Nah," Billy Dixon commented. "They're better'n a quarter mile distant. It wouldn't be sportin' if'n they were closer than that."

"They're runnin'," a man to the north yelled.

Asa clicked the telescope into focus and saw Lame Bear sitting on an Appaloosa, well behind the front line of attacking braves that were being decimated. The white streak in the warrior's long black hair waved in a red ray of sunset when he held up a lance. Asa could only make out his mouth moving, but the charge stopped and the Indians began retreating, carrying off as many of their dead as possible. A few of the buffalo hunters stayed at the wall to use the few braves, who had the courage to come back and retrieve their dead, for target practice. An occasional boom of a rifle never failed to give the Indians one more reason to return.

"Dang savages," Billy Dixon said. "Reckon they'll leave us be for the night anyway. All we want to do is hunt buffalo. I can't see why they're so blame set on killin' us."

Asa surveyed the thousands of buffalo hides that

had been bundled together for shipment back East. "When the buffaloes are all gone, so will be the Indians."

"Reckon I can't see no objection to that happenin', but it won't," said Dixon. "Hell's bells, we could shoot a thousand buffs a day for a hundred years an' not make a difference. I've seen herds that stretched so far you couldn't see to the other side."

Bartholomew Masterson spoke up. "I've heard stories of herds that big, but I've never seen one. By my observation there's a lot less buffs this year than there was last."

Billy Dixon ignored the boy. "Let's go have a drink an' get acquainted. There's a few of the boys that jus' love to kill Injuns. They'll hang around till dark pickin' off those that come back fer their dead."

Cemetery John stared across the broad expanse and winced when a Sharps boomed. "Seems kind of cold-blooded, killin' those that only want their dead for proper buryin'."

George Maledon hopped down from the platform where he had been standing. He was quite a bit shorter than either Asa or Cemetery John had first assumed. "My good man, just retribution against bloodthirsty savages should be encouraged, not criticized. Any one of those barbarians out there would gladly cut off your eyelids so you can't shut out the sun and stake you face-up over an ant bed. You simply have no knowledge of Indians if you believe otherwise."

Asa clucked his tongue.

Cemetery John quickly reached over and placed a firm hand on his shoulder. "It's been a heck of a long day an' a tolerable bad one. I feel we'd both benefit from spendin' time in Sunday school."

"Yes, sir," Billy Dixon added happily. "School's in session."

Asa Cain followed the men toward the beckoning batwing doors, but his eyes stayed fixed with hate on George Maledon.

SEVENTEEN

Billy Dixon smiled upon a tumbler full of whiskey that Willow Olds had just filled to the brim from one of a dozen oak barrels that lined the wall behind the crude plank bar. He smacked his lips, drank a mouthful, wheezed loudly, and turned to Asa Cain.

"This Taos Dynamite is some punkin's, bounty hunter." He bit off a chew of tobacco and continued. "Had me a pardner once up in New Mexico Territory that took a dozen Injun arrows in one leg and got a blood poison. Hell, he drunk a few snorts of this here giggle juice and whacked that bad leg plumb off. Ol' Jeb never even lost his smile when he done it."

Willow Olds came gliding over. "Billy, we've all heard that story more times than I care to remember, and I'm certain Mr. Cain here isn't interested in hearing any of your tall tales. There's some mighty real trouble outside that we all should be more concerned about."

Billy Dixon looked shocked. "Why, Willow, I was simply commentin' on the quality of the whiskey you serve. Jeb's still drinkin' a quart of Taos Dynamite ever day, an' the last time I saw him he'd even growed a new leg that was better'n the one he chopped off."

"Here is your coffee, Mr. Cain," the blonde said, setting down a steaming cup in front of him while making a point of ignoring Billy Dixon. "It's a real pleasure to have a gentleman here for a change."

Willow Olds spun around and strode off into the kitchen, giving Asa good cause to know how she had gotten her name. The lady was graceful, lithe, and supple as a green willow sapling.

"There goes one mighty pretty woman." Billy Dixon's voice turned serious as he pointed with the stem of his stone-cold corncob pipe toward a cane rocking chair beside the kitchen door. A blank-faced young man sat in it, drooling onto a towel. Strips of heavy cloth tied his wrists to the chair arms, and a thick rope was draped underneath his shoulders from the high back holding the helpless man upright. "Too bad she's stuck takin' care of him. It's gotta be a hardship that most wouldn't endure."

Cemetery John had been outside keeping his eyes on the situation with the Indians and assessing the fortifications. He picked up the gist of the conversation when he came over and leaned the ten-gauge against the bar. "Reckon she must be in tolerable love with the poor fellow." He turned to Billy Dixon. "Why does she keep him tied up like that?"

"The fever lasted for days and got so blamed hot, it fried up his brain. Hibb Olds don't know if'n he's in Texas or holdin' court with the Queen Mother in jolly old England. But he's developed a real itch to wander. He's left for some other place a lot of times, only he goes in a straight line so he's plenty easy to track down. If he ever took a stroll at the wrong time, like now, I'd reckon the Injuns would finish what the fever didn't."

Asa took a sip of the coffee, and was gratified when he found it to be some of the best he'd ever tasted. "Indians will never kill a crazy person. They consider them to be possessed by spirits. To harm a man such as Mr. Olds would be bad medicine, *very* bad medicine."

Billy Dixon worried his glass of whiskey. "Reckon a bullet fired from a long ways off wouldn't recognize the fact that it was fixin' to kill a lunatic. And for Missus Olds' sake, I'd say that medicine wouldn't be all bad."

Hibb Olds let out a loud screech and lurched against his bonds. Willow came quickly from the kitchen carrying a dish towel. She daubed spittle from her husband's chin and checked the tightness of the knots. Satisfied there was nothing else to be done, she returned to her cooking without saying a word.

Asa shook his head sadly and turned to Cemetery John. Before he could speak, an obviously nervous Bartholomew Masterson stepped close and thrust out his right hand.

"I just want to say how honored I am to make your acquaintance, Mr. Cain." Masterson was so overwhelmed he kept pumping away at Asa's arm. "I've heard a lot about you and all of those hundreds of bloodthirsty outlaws you've brought back dead. Why, you're the most famous man I've ever met."

Cemetery John grinned at the young man. "Don't go and wear his gun arm out shakin' it.

Asa might have need of it, the way things are lookin'."

Bartholomew Masterson jerked back like he'd touched a red-hot stove. "I'm sorry, sir, it's just that I've never before met an honest-to-goodness gunfighter who's killed over two hundred desperadoes."

Asa liked the boy and considered telling him the truth, but knew that wouldn't be wise. He was on a manhunt to save his family and needed all the edge he could get. A blown-out-of-proportion reputation could be an asset, for now anyway. Once this was over, Asa acknowledged to himself, he would come out with the facts to a newspaper reporter and hopefully keep youngsters like Bartholomew from believing a lot of ballyhoo and getting themselves killed trying to be as tough as they thought he was.

"I've only done what I had to do," Asa said coldly. "I go after the worst civilization has to offer, but don't think for one minute that I enjoy killing. That would make me as bad as those outlaws I bring in to face justice."

Billy Dixon took another slug of Taos Dynamite. "From what I've heard, about all justice has to do when Asa Cain brings 'em in is dig a deep hole an' fetch a preacher, if'n one's about."

George Maledon had been standing at the far end of the bar sipping whiskey while listening to the conversations. His expression was as cold and unemotional as his deep-set, coal-black eyes. He swigged his drink and came to face Asa Cain.

"I didn't know who you were earlier." Maledon's voice was gravelly and harsh as hail on a tin roof. "We're both doing the work of the Lord, removing evildoers from the face of this blighted world. Perhaps you could help a fellow enforcer of the law to find employment as a hangman. I seem to find myself at a disadvantage of late."

"I've seen you hang a man over in Kansas." Bartholomew Masterson's nervousness had fled. "This was two years ago in Abilene. It was a terrible sight. It took the poor man a good fifteen minutes to strangle to death. If a deputy hadn't grabbed on to the man's legs and pulled down to add weight, I don't know how long he'd have hung there kicking."

"He was a sinner who had broken God's good laws, son," Maledon said firmly. "You are too young to understand that lessons, public lessons, must be given to keep sinners from losing their souls to Satan's wiles. I do only as I am called on to do by the Good Book, which clearly states, in many passages, that I am just in my actions."

Masterson glared at Maledon. " 'I must be cruel, only to be kind.' Shakespeare put that quote in *Hamlet*. I suppose he had someone just like you in mind when he wrote that line."

Billy Dixon snorted, grabbed his glass of Taos Dynamite, and headed outside. "I'm an atheist, thank the Good Lord. This way I don't have to put up with phillysophical discussions or listen to rantin' stump preachers that decided to start stretchin' necks for a livin'."

Asa Cain also wanted the sinister-looking hangman gone. "There's a judge in Arkansas by the name of Isaac Parker. You can find him at the federal court building in Fort Smith. He's been trying to hire me for his chief deputy. Judge Parker has jurisdiction over the most lawless piece of land there is, Indian Territory. Look him up and tell him I recommended you. I've a feeling you and the judge will get along splendidly."

George Maledon was obviously taken aback. "Why, thank you, sir. Once we are removed from our present predicament, I shall proceed straightway to Fort Smith and offer my services to Judge Parker. I assure you that he will not regret employing me, if he so chooses."

After the diminutive hangman had left their presence, Cemetery John leaned close to Asa. "I thought Judge Parker was the fellow who not only refused to pay a bounty you had coming, but threatened to hang you if you ever set foot in Arkansas again."

Asa gave out a sly grin and reached for his coffee. "I told the truth when I said I thought those two would get along just fine. Besides, Maledon will fit in well in Arkansas, likely even improve the place."

Cemetery John chuckled softly; then his expression turned serious. "Including the two of us, I count thirty armed men. From what I'm told, Missus Olds is the only woman in Adobe Walls. A quick scan with your spyglass showed me over two hundred Indians, but it was gettin' dark and I likely missed some."

Bartholomew Masterson spoke up. "The Indians have had their dander up for some time. A lot of us figured they'd band together, so we stockpiled plenty of ammo. Billy Dixon told me there's a good five thousand rounds for each of us."

Asa Cain gave a gesture of disbelief.

"It's true, sir," young Masterson assured him. "We're buffalo hunters. I've personally shot over five hundred buffs in one day. This business takes a lot of ammunition just for normal times. It didn't seem an extravagance to order in a good supply in case the Indians went on the warpath. We'd use it up anyway."

"The biggest thing on our side," Cemetery John said, "is most of the rifles are long-range Sharps. The guns I've seen the redskins packin' are all shorter-range Winchesters an' the like. The men here are all tolerable good at long-distance shooting too. We've already seen how much damage they can do."

"The Comanche are going to attack and try to rub us out," Asa said. "I know of Lame Bear's hatred and Quanah Parker is burning for vengeance. It's well known that he has a consuming hatred for the men who are killing off their buffalo herds. No, here is where the Indians will make their strike to remove the white scourge from their land. I can feel it."

"You talk like you're Indian," Masterson said.

"Let's just say I'm acquainted with their ways." Asa focused on Cemetery John. "Round up at least three or four men to stand guard tonight."

Bartholomew Masterson regarded Asa with obvious dismay. "I never heard tell of Indians attacking at night."

"Nor have I. Remember that Quanah Parker's mother was white, and if he decides to adopt some of our ways to rub us out, I wouldn't be surprised."

"Quanah Parker ain't here," Cemetery John said.

"He will be." Asa's eyes had become dark slits that reflected yellow lantern light like broken glass. "He *will* be here."

EIGHTEEN

"Hell's fire and tarnation, it's rainin' Injuns!" Billy Dixon was one of the first to recover his wits. It was close to midnight when a center support pole that held up the flat roof of the Sunday School Saloon cracked like a rifle shot and collapsed with a thud onto the ground.

The resulting hole slanted steeply inward like the sides of a funnel, causing over a dozen startled warriors, who had been massing on the roof, to be deposited into a crashing heap on the floor of the saloon.

"Well, don't ever body stand around starin' at 'em," Cemetery John yelled. "Shoot 'em!" He dashed aside the cup of hot chocolate he was holding and grabbed his shotgun. A split second later the windows rattled when the big ten-gauge boomed and a heavy charge of buckshot sent a Comanche flying backward in a spray of crimson.

Asa rolled to one side, jacked the lever on his Henry, and began carefully selecting and shooting the hapless savages as they began picking themselves up out of the wreckage. At least a dozen others joined him in the fusillade.

One warrior, whose war paint was that of a

Kiowa, ducked Asa's fire, grabbed up a repeating Winchester rifle, and dashed for cover behind the bar shooting wildly as he ran. A scream of pain from across the room said that at least one of his bullets had found flesh.

Willow Olds quickly sized up the situation. She grabbed the shotgun that Hibb had given her for protection when they bought the establishment, a Colt 20-gauge five-shot revolver. Cautiously she peeked around the door opening into the saloon. A warrior had his back to her and was occupied with shooting at her customers. The blonde stepped close to the Indian, stuck the cold barrel of the shotgun at the base of his neck, and fired. The Indian's head ceased to exist.

Bartholomew Masterson pulled a .44 from his belt, cocked the pistol, and calmly aimed it, by the flickering light of a coal-oil lantern, at a brave who was drawing back a huge bowie knife to throw at him. A slug of lead smashed into the Indian's forehead square between his eyes. "That's what you get for having the bad manners to drop in uninvited," Masterson said.

The shooting stopped. By the wan light of a half-moon that was showing through the hole made by the collapsed roof, and by the light of the flickering yellow coal-oil lamps, not a single Indian moved. Acrid smoke drifted upward into the sultry night.

"No doubt there's more outside," Asa Cain said.

Billy Dixon poked fresh shells into his Bacon pocket revolver. "Let's go an' give 'em a lesson about messin' with our Sunday School time. Dang savages comin' at us at night ain't right. This squabble would have been a lot easier to take in the daylight."

"They'll be expectin' us to come chargin' out the front door," Cemetery John said. He motioned with the barrel of his ten-gauge to the opening in the roof. "Let's not be too predictable."

"You're right, Mr. John," Masterson agreed. "My guess is if we band together and charge up on the roof shooting, we'll catch them unawares." The young man's brow creased with worry. "I thought you had some guards posted. It'd be a shame to plug one of our own."

Asa said, "Those guards are beyond our worrying. An Indian can sneak up on you quiet as a shadow."

George Maledon spoke from behind an overturned table where he had been ever since the fracas started. "This seems to me to be mighty strange, savages coming out to fight at night. And it's tolerable odd that these Indians are Comanche, the very ones Asa Cain lived with for many years. They never did anything like this before he showed up here."

"I'm going to let you get by with talk like that just once"—Asa Cain's voice was devoid of emotion—"and only because we're going to need every gun we've got to get out of this alive. To answer your questions about tonight, Quanah Parker's here or at least his medicine man, Moon Fox, is. Moon Fox has claimed for years that he has a spell to make the Indian warriors bulletproof if they attack at night."

"Reckon this Moon Fox could use tolerable more practice with bullet-proofin'," Billy Dixon said, looking at a pile of bleeding dead Indians.

Asa Cain clucked his tongue. "They just didn't

believe hard enough in the spell. Moon Fox's magic only works when the warrior's heart is one with the Great Spirit. Now, let's get on this roof and secure the town."

A roar of gunfire erupted when the men reached the roof. A spray of bullets swept to all directions of the compass, then raked the court-yard along with the tops and sides of adjoining buildings. Silence then reigned when the shooting stopped and the stunned beleaguered denizens of Adobe Walls surveyed the town in the stillness of the night.

"They're gone," Bartholomew Masterson said simply.

Cemetery John slid two fresh charges of buck-shot into the breech of his shotgun. "I sure didn't expect this. I'd reckoned on a town full of redskins to thin out."

Asa Cain sighed and stared off across the prairie. "You can depend on the fact there were at least a hundred warriors here. In the morning you can count moccasin tracks if you want to get a number. Moon Fox's medicine just didn't work. A few Indi-ans saw the bullets killing the braves in the saloon and they took off. Don't feel too lucky, because that shifty medicine man will come up with a good rea-son why this magic didn't work and will cast a new spell that's guaranteed to do the trick."

Cemetery John shook his head sadly. "Indians have got their spellbindin' spook promoters, an' we're stuck with politicians. I don't know which is worse to be plagued by."

"Oh, my God, look at that!" Bartholomew Mas-terson pointed toward the east wall, where the bat-tle had raged earlier. The men blinked to focus their eyes in the pale moonlight. Then all saw what the boy was pointing at. Three severed heads were impaled on sharpened sticks a few feet from the adobe barricade. The guards that Cemetery John had left on watch now stared open-eyed toward the settlement they were supposed to protect.

"Wonder where their bodies wound up," Billy Dixon mumbled.

"We had best leave that task until morning," Asa said. "A few warriors still might believe they're bullet-proof."

"Morning sounds good," Billy Dixon said.

A wail of agony and sadness ripped the quiet of night in the desert. The men knew who was screaming. It was Willow Olds.

Asa Cain clucked his tongue and joined the exodus back into the saloon, only he did not rush. His eyes were better trained than most. Through the powder smoke and pale light he had seen the Kiowa with the Winchester inexplicably fire a slug into the chest of the only man there who offered him no threat: Hibb Olds.

NINETEEN

"A couple of men are digging a grave for your husband some distance away from the hole the Indians are going in." Asa Cain sat in the kitchen of the saloon across a rude plank table from Willow Olds. Two untouched cups of coffee between them were growing tepid. "It's the heat, ma'am. I'm sure you understand that's why the burying can't be put off."

Willow regarded him with reddened eyes that had long since been dry of tears. "When Hibb took sick with the fever and became an invalid, I knew this time would come. It was just so sudden and his death so hollow and meaningless."

"I'm truly sorry about your loss, but if it helps at all, I'm certain his getting shot was a pure accident. The smoke was so thick in there anyone could have gotten killed."

"I know. I still find it hard to believe those savages were grouping on the roof. I simply don't understand why they were there."

"When those braves had gotten into position, some kind of disturbance would have drawn most of us outside. We'd have had our backs to the saloon and been cut down like weeds by a scythe."

"Just like you men did to them."

"And just like they did to your poor husband, Missus Olds. War never does make sense. It just seems to happen upon average people."

"I surely wish there was a preacher here to say some words over him. Hibb was a believer, you know. The nearest man of God is in Buffalo Gap."

Asa worried the handle of his coffee cup. "There's probably a thousand or more Indians out there, Missus Olds. No one is coming to Adobe Walls, nor can anyone leave here without being killed. I'm sure you're aware of that."

The young lady dabbed at an eye with a dish towel. "Just have them nail him into a sturdy wood box. I intend to take his body back East—when I can. This country is so evil that I doubt God even pays attention to what goes on out here. I'll give Hibb a Christian burial back in Chicago. That's where we were married. Then we moved to this awful place."

Asa stood and nodded. "I'll see to it personally, ma'am. I noticed there were some heavy oak boards in the blacksmith shop where they put him. They'll make a fitting traveling box."

"That's lumber Hibb had freighted in to frame a room for our baby." Willow Olds's words came with no emotion. "Use them, they will do fine for a coffin. My husband is dead, and a few months ago my baby boy was stillborn. I can bury both Hibb and my dreams in one coffin. How convenient."

A chorus of yelling and cursing from the barroom spared Asa from having to say more. A group of burly buffalo hunters were moving poles upright and lifting up the collapsed portion of the roof.

"By damn, we'll have our saloon back in shape for tonight," a shabbily dressed man said.

"Yep," another chimed in. "Them savages didn't hardly do no damage at all."

Asa Cain clucked his tongue and strode past the workmen. The sunlight might revive his spirits. He surely hoped so.

Cemetery John took off his slouch hat and wiped sweat from his brow with the back of his hand. "If Missus Olds is dead set on cartin' ol' Hibb clear back to Chicago, I'd best dust him down plenty heavy with quicklime. It's the only thing that'll kill the smell, and Lord knows those freighters love to complain."

"I know that, and I've gone through every building here and not found any," Asa said with a shrug.

"Dang it all. In that case I'll use picklin' salt along with lots of stove ash. It's a poor substitute, but with any decent luck, we'll both be back in Wolf Springs before any freighters gets a whiff of him."

"Willow Olds is a strong and decent lady. I admire her for that."

Cemetery John stuck his hat back on, surveyed the hole he was digging, and looked at his helper. "Reckon since he's gonna be dug right back up shortly, there ain't no reason for us to go any deeper. Besides, it's tolerable hot out." He turned to Asa. "Missus Olds is a tough one all right. Holding on to a business and having to spoon-feed a husband for nigh onto a year in this godless land would be a mighty test."

Asa nodded. "Make Hibb Olds a good box," he said. Then he was gone.

"This fine kettle of fish just keeps gettin' more and more interestin'." Billy Dixon carefully focused Asa's brass telescope to get a clear picture. A trickle of tobacco juice leaked onto his beard. "If that ain't Quanah Parker sittin' on that Appaloosa yonder, I'll eat Cemetery John's hat an' allow an hour to draw a crowd to watch."

"Take a peek yourself," Cemetery John said to Asa. "You know that half-breed, but no matter what, Dixon ain't eatin' my hat."

"He's just funning you." Asa walked up to the wall and took the proffered telescope. After a moment he said, "Your hat's safe, Cemetery. That's Chief Quanah Parker himself. The skinny one wearing a wolf headpiece is Moon Fox. I reckon the Indian with a white stripe in his black hair doesn't need introducing."

"Lame Bear," Bartholomew Masterson said. "He's the worst of the lot. I hear even other Indians don't trust him."

Asa folded the spyglass closed. "Lame Bear brings in many slaves and scalps. He may not be liked or trusted, but he *is* feared. Nearly every warrior out there will do what he tells them to. Quanah Parker's plenty of trouble, only he's not insane with bloodlust like Lame Bear."

"You must know them well," Masterson said casually.

"I know Lame Bear *too* well," Asa Cain replied

in a tone that sent icicles down the young buffalo hunter's back. "He killed my father and now that I have him cornered, I *will* kill him."

Billy Dixon snorted. "First, let's convince those thousand or so redskins out there that *they're* the ones cornered. Shucks, with any good luck maybe they'll all kill themselves outta the fact they're so blamed scared of us."

Asa turned to him. His voice was calm. "Only the head of a rattlesnake is dangerous. Lame Bear and Quanah Parker are the head. Once they're dead the danger will be over."

"Yep," Billy Dixon said. "But for the present, not only are those two sidewinders safely a mile away, they're also still in grand possession of their heads. And if my peepers don't deceive me, they've just started a few hundred warriors charging at us hell-bent for leather."

"Ready your weapons, boys," a skinny young man by the name of Red Magruder yelled from down the wall. "This outta be more fun than yesterday 'cause we got more targets."

Asa opened the spyglass and rested it on the adobe wall. "This is going to be a slaughter. That red paint dotted in the middle if their chests is undoubtedly the work of Moon Fox to ward off bullets."

"I thought his magic was only supposed to work at night," Billy Dixon said, clicking the vernier sight on his Sharps. "Oh, well, I reckon they figgered out last night *that* spell didn't hold water."

"Medicine men are shrewd and very much feared," Asa said. "Moon Fox has been around for many years. He has an explanation for everything. When something works out well, he takes the credit. When things go sour, the spirits are to blame."

"Look at that, boys," Magruder yelled. "This time them redskins are nice enough to have gone an' painted a bull's-eye square over their vitals."

Asa winced when Billy Dixon's rifle boomed in his ear. He didn't need the telescope to see the brave blown out of his saddle. A chorus of gunshots began singing a deadly song as scores of Indian warriors were quickly rubbed out a quarter mile distant.

Over the din of heavy-caliber rifle fire, Asa could hear the Comanches' death chants. The Indians plainly knew Moon Fox was a fraud, yet they continued to charge as if they were bullet-proof. This was not a war and there was no glory in watching good men slaughtered like buffalo. He slid the telescope into its case and left. No one noticed his leaving. They were too engrossed in the killing.

Willow Olds wordlessly set a cup of coffee on the bar for Asa and a tumbler full of Taos Dynamite in front of Billy Dixon. When she retreated to the kitchen, Billy said softly, "I'm tolerable surprised to see Missus Olds waitin' on folks tonight and cookin' supper to boot. God ain't had time to hear the news about Hibb getting shot."

Asa blew on his steaming coffee. "She's become an automaton. It's not an unusual way for a person to deal with a severe shock."

"An otto—what?"

"The word automaton means a person who continues doing as they're accustomed to, no matter what. Like a clock or a machine, by keeping doing something familiar and repetitive, they're able to cling to reality, at least for a while."

Billy Dixon checked to make certain Willow Olds was still out of earshot. "I get it. Kinda like a sawbones sayin' someone's insane instead of comin' straight out and callin' 'em a lunatic. This word aw-tommyton's a good one. I'll remember to use it on occasions when I want to insult someone and not risk getting shot."

Asa stared at his coffee and decided to drop that line of conversation. "Quanah Parker and Lame Bear are not about to give up this fight."

Billy Dixon took a healthy swallow of whiskey and wheezed loudly. "They plain ain't puttin' much of a kick in this stuff these days." He wiped a tear from his eye. "I know what you mean about them Indians. We killed nearly two hundred of Parker's braves this afternoon, and from the looks of things, all we done was chafe his hinder. There's more campfires out there tonight than last. I'm bettin' more replacements has come in than was necessary to fill the moccasins of those we laid out."

"The chief has no choice but to do everything to win. He's waging a war to save his people."

Billy Dixon shrugged his shoulders. "Damn shame, there's lots of buffalo to go around. Reckon it's too late for anything but us tryin' to kill each other off."

"I've a terrible feeling you're correct in your assessment."

"Hell, Cain, reckon we can fight them Indians later. I was wondering about something. There ain't no doubt that you're here for some other reason than to kill Lame Bear or outrun a war party. Adobe Walls and ever place for hundreds of miles around ain't exactly resort country. Who is it you're after?"

Asa spooned his coffee. "I make a point never to talk about business until the job's done."

"Yep, I reckon doing what you do for a living, that'd be smart. But some of the boys and me have a bet going that it's the Dolven gang you're pursuin'."

"What caused people here to think of that bunch of outlaws?"

"Well, sir, they was through here only a few days ago. Surprisingly, all of 'em were in a mighty friendly mood and spending money like it was water. I can't say that anyone could blame 'em for bein' in a lively mood, however."

Asa cocked an eye at Dixon. "And why was that?"

Billy Dixon grinned evilly. "They was traveling with a couple of the prettiest women any man's ever set eyes on is why. Old Brock told me his gal's name was Jenny and that she was the mother of Link's new wife, Sadie. Gol-durn if I know how that bunch of ruffians ever managed to corral such a pair of cute fillies outside of a whorehouse—"

Billy Dixon grew silent. He realized with a chill that the narrow-eyed, flinty gaze Asa Cain had focused on him was likely the last thing a lot of men ever glimpsed in this world.

TWENTY

"You are correct, Mr. Dixon, in your observation that the two women accompanying the Dolvens are not whores." Asa's words came out even and measured, which only added to Billy Dixon's trepidation. "In fact, those ladies are why we came to be here. My ranch near Wolf Springs was burned and the hired help killed. The raiders also kidnapped my mother, Jenny, and my younger sister, Sadie. Cemetery John and I know for a fact the Dolven gang have them. This manhunt isn't business, it's personal."

The buffalo hunter spun his glass between his thumb and forefinger several times. Then he looked over at Asa. "Reckon I oughtta have sense enough to drink up and go make myself an Injun target. But dad gum it, I like you, Cain. Did what I told you about Sadie being married up with Link Dolven take, or did it just wander in one ear and float out the other?"

"I heard you."

"The truth is, that little gal was hangin' all over that outlaw from the moment they hit here until they rode away two days later. If she was kidnapped, she sure wasn't showin' it any."

Asa squeezed the handle of his coffee cup until his knuckles whitened. "I find it hard to believe my mother just watched this going on. She had to have been heartbroken."

Billy Dixon's forehead wrinkled in thought. "Come to think on it, I hardly ever seen the two women in here together. It was the young'un that sat in on the poker games and such. Your ma an' Brock Dolven spent most of their time in a room together, drinkin' whiskey."

"I don't believe any of this," Asa hissed through clenched teeth.

"Reckon there's no percentage in me telling you a pack of lies. Those are the facts straighter than a stump preacher would give 'em to you. Quanah Parker's likely gonna have all of our scalps hanging off lances before long anyway. Looking back on the matter, the whole blasted Dolven gang could have rode square into that passel of redskins, considerin' when they left and the direction they took when they did."

"The Dolvens told you where they were going?"

"Why, hell, yes. That bunch didn't seem scared of the very Devil. Besides Old Man Brock and his two boys, there was another man ridin' with 'em by the name of Bull Grossman. Ever single one kept bragging about how much they were looking forward to resting up at the ranch for a spell before going to the effort of robbing any more banks."

Asa scooted the coffee away. He needed a drink of whiskey now worse than he could ever remember. "We heard the Dolvens have a ranch on the river east of Canan. That's where Cemetery John and I were heading when we run across Quanah Parker and Lame Bear's warriors."

"Brock Dolven told everyone their place was only a day's ride from Canan headin' east. If they managed to dodge the redskins, I reckon they'll have been there a week by now."

"Something's awfully wrong here, Dixon." Asa turned and stepped close. The buffalo hunter was a head shorter than he. "I don't know what possessed my mother and sister to behave the way they did, but believe me, they had no choice in the matter. At least now I know they're both still alive—"

"Asa! Billy!" Cemetery John's voice booming from the open door sounded serious. "You two had better come. We finally found the bodies of those three guards that had their heads stuck on lances, and we've got bad trouble."

"Dang," Billy Dixon said grabbing up his Sharps rifle. "And the day has been going so good up till now."

Bartholomew Masterson stepped from the wooden bucket by the flickering light of a coal-oil lamp. "I've got the last one tied off. Let's hoist him out. My God it smells something awful down there in that well."

Asa Cain bent over and stared down into stygian blackness. "This is Lame Bear's work. Quanah Parker would never poison a well by dumping in the bodies of men."

Cemetery John frowned. "It don't matter much whose idea it was; we gotta live with the results.

Disease caused from rotting flesh in water will kill surely as an arrow or a bullet."

Asa looked at Billy Dixon. "Is this the only well in town?"

"Nope." He shook his head worriedly. "There's a couple of really good ones down by the river and another maybe a quarter mile north. But to give you the facts, this well's the only one inside the adobe walls."

"I assumed that," Asa said. "Lame Bear wouldn't have ordered it done otherwise." He turned to Cemetery John. "Who found the bodies?"

"Willow Olds come out to draw a few buckets of water just before it got dark. She come and told me the water was coming up bloody and stinky. I took my shavin' mirror and shined some light down there. Too durn bad no one found 'em before now. It's likely enough some of that water's been drank."

Asa said "Tell everyone to make sure to strain the water through a layer of burnt charcoal from the stove that's at least a few inches thick. Use cheesecloth if any can be found. Then boil it hard for a good quarter hour before drinking it."

Billy Dixon grimaced. "I'm stickin' with whiskey. There ain't near so many surprises comes with drinkin' Taos Dynamite."

"I never seen no good use for water yet," an unkempt buffalo skinner said. "This sort of thing just goes to reinforce my beliefs."

Cemetery John untied the wood water bucket and attached the rope Masterson had handed him. "Hoist him up, boys. The sooner we get these poor fellows buried the better."

Two men began the windlass creaking upward with its grisly burden.

Asa grabbed a flickering table lamp and attempted to look into the well, but failed. He turned to Bartholomew. "I don't know how you managed to see how to fasten a rope around them."

"That's why I volunteered, sir," Masterson said. "For some reason I've always been able to see really good in the dark."

"Just like a bat," Cemetery John said. "I'm surprised you ain't called 'Bat' Masterson." He grinned through the yellow light. "It's a helluva lot easier to spell than Bartholomew. That name's a real mouthful to deal with."

Masterson cocked his head in thought. "Yes sir, Mr. John, it just might be something I'll consider, if and when we get out of this fix."

A headless apparition appeared from the well, water dripping from leather clothes stretched to breaking from bloat. The men reached out, dragged the body onto the ground, and untied it.

"A quick buryin' seems like a mighty swell idea," Billy Dixon said.

Cemetery John nodded toward the north wall. "I've already got four men shovelin' away. There's a problem, however."

George Maledon spoke from the shadows. "A man's entitled to be buried with his own head. I've been keeping them in a root cellar and they're still in good shape. All that must be done is to match each one to the rightful owner."

"Maledon," Asa Cain growled, "you've been a crank long enough to get on my bad side. I can see where hanging people is likely the only thing you're good at or enjoy in this world." He grabbed up his rifle and jacked the lever. "If you ever intend to snap another neck, you'll bring those poor fellows' heads out and match them up yourself. Then you and you alone will see to their burying."

George Maledon stepped into the lantern light. His cadaverous features and flinty eyes caused him to look like every picture anyone there had ever seen of death. He glared at Asa through the flickering light. "You have a violent temper, Asa Cain. This may very well cause us to have another, ah, much more unpleasant meeting in the future. For now, I shall see to the dead as you ask."

Maledon turned and melted soundlessly into the night. After he had gone, Cemetery John said to Asa, "That man's spooky enough to give a grizzly bear nightmares."

Asa lowered the hammer on his rifle. "I'm just glad he didn't make me have to kill him. We're in need of everyone left alive who can shoot a gun."

"You're sure right there." Cemetery John motioned toward the distant campfires that flickered on the dark horizon like a multitude of fireflies. "I'd reckon maybe a couple of thousand redskins out there are really gettin' worked up into a dither over the fact that twenty-odd of us'ns are so blamed hard to kill."

"Moon Fox will work his magic for one or two more days," Asa said. "Then, Quanah Parker and Lame Bear will send every brave out there against us. And to a warrior, each will be given a medicine pouch or symbol and told he's bullet-proof."

Billy Dixon snorted. "From the way Moon Fox's magic has worked out so far, I'd doubt many out there would believe his balderdash for another go around."

Asa Cain said grimly, "Would you deny the existence or power of *your* God and claim aloud the teachings of the Good Book are false and all preachers are charlatans?"

Dixon spat a wad of tobacco at his boots. "I reckon I'll take up watch duty for a spell." He turned to Bartholomew Masterson. "How about joining me, Bat? I'd like the company of someone that can see at night. Might cause me to live long enough to get kilt by a bullet-proof Injun."

Asa and Cemetery John turned and headed for the saloon. Before they reached the batwing doors, Cemetery said, "You seem to be a tad easier to upset than normal this evening. Pluggin' George Maledon ain't a bad idea, but usually it's a smart plan to wait until the other person's at least got a gun."

Asa stopped abruptly. "While you and Masterson were fishing those bodies out of the well, Billy Dixon filled me in on the fact that the Dolven gang was through here about a week ago." He swallowed. "From what he said, my mother spent her time drinking whiskey with Old Man Brock and Sadie's happily married to Link Dolven."

Cemetery John lit a long-nine cigar and stared at Asa through the yellow light of a lucifer match. "I can honestly say that travelin' with you ain't boring." He placed a hand on Asa's shoulder. "Let's go see how Missus Olds is holdin' up. Then I want you to fill me in on those blasted Dolvens. Lately, there's so blame many folks in desperate need of killin' that I'm having a mighty difficult time keeping track of all of 'em."

TWENTY-ONE

Cemetery John stirred sugar into his hot chocolate, licked the spoon, then shook his head in dismay. "Asa, from what you've told me Billy Dixon said about your kin, and I believe he was being truthful, it's a pure mystery why they were actin' the way they did. My guess is they're probably just doin' what they have to to stay alive."

"I'm sure that's it." Asa spoke quietly to keep from being overheard in the small saloon. "My mother's smart and tough. It's Sadie that has me worried. She's spirited and thinks she's an old maid at twenty-three. She's had suitors, but I suspect my reputation might have scared them off."

Cemetery rolled his eyes. "Why, I simply can't see how that could have happened. You're only the deadliest bounty hunter of all time. Some stories credit you with killing two hundred men. The thought of havin' you for a brother-in-law would likely put gooseflesh on any man with a pulse."

Asa blew steam from his cup of coffee and clucked his tongue. "I'm sure having me for a brother must not have been easy. But I provided well for her and was always pleasant to callers when she had them. Also, I was gone a lot of the time.

No, Sadie's only doing what she has to, like my mother. They're biding their time until we can come and rescue them."

"With over a thousand bloodthirsty redskins between us and them, that may take a while."

"Quanah Parker's undoubtedly listening to Lame Bear and Moon Fox. I've spent enough time among the Comanche to know that Adobe Walls has become a test of their strength and medicine. Once the signs are right, they'll attack and overrun this place, no matter how many braves it costs. Only a miracle of our own can stop this from happening."

"Getting up a petition to the Almighty in these parts might be a tolerable task. Not only aren't there any preachers about, the only Bible in town belongs to Missus Olds. I offered to read something from it over her husband's grave, but she said God was too far away for it to count. I sure hope she ain't right about that."

Asa took a sip of coffee. "I suspect Quanah Parker and all of us will have our questions answered in a day or two." He made a grimace. "Blast, this stuff tastes dreadful."

Cemetery John cleared his throat. "I told you early on the water in these parts was bad. It likely has gotten even worse of late."

Asa dashed the cup of brew onto the dirt floor. "I'm going to turn in early. It's been a tiring day."

Cemetery John fished a long-nine cigar from his shirt pocket and lit it. "Reckon I'll take a walk, then do the same." He looked around the Sunday School Saloon and sighed. "Whiskey and beer drinkers can be a tad smarter than I'd thought."

Asa said nothing.

When the duo stepped into the sultry night, both men noticed that the number of campfires that twinkled like jewels on the distant horizon had grown considerably.

A wicked grin passed over Cemetery John's face. "Bullet-proof Indians, desperadoes, kidnappers, cold-blooded killers, Mexican bandits, rattlesnakes, lightning, cyclones, poison water, and evil medicine men. I swan, Asa, an undertaker couldn't do any better than to hang his shingle in Texas."

The fiery orb of a dawning sun was glowing red in the east when Bartholomew Masterson rapped urgently on Asa's door. "Come quick, Mr. Cain," Masterson shouted. "It's Missus Olds, sir, she's powerful sick."

Asa opened the rude door with one hand while hoisting his suspenders with the other. "I'm not a doctor, son. That was my father."

"Yes, sir, that's what Mr. John said too. He also said you plan to be a doctor someday and already likely know more about medicine than anyone here. Mr. Cain, that poor lady's hotter than a cookstove."

The disturbing realization of what had probably occurred struck Asa like a stab to the heart. "I'll pull on my boots and follow you."

Willow Olds lay in a bed that was in a small adobe room adjoining the kitchen. A single cotton, sweat-drenched sheet covered her to the neck. Even by the poor light, Asa could see her complexion was ruddy and rivulets of perspiration trickled from her forehead to add to the spreading wetness from her pillow.

Cemetery John said, "A buffalo skinner came by for a mornin' whiskey. When he couldn't rouse anyone by bangin' on a wash pan, he got concerned enough to come and check on Missus Olds. He found her just like this, unconscious. Then he came and fetched me instead of you for some reason. She's still breathin'."

Asa shook his head sadly. "The poor lady is in for a mighty big fight for her life if this is what I'm afraid it is."

Bartholomew's eyes widened. "What would that be, sir?"

Cemetery John swallowed hard and turned to answer the young fellow. "The Good Lord knows I've seen my share of cholera, and I'm sure Asa has too. This disease has done in more folks than every Indian there ever has been rolled into one."

"Cholera!" Masterson exclaimed. "That's wiped out entire settlements. I've also heard it's caused by bad water. I reckon Missus Olds must have drunk some of that well water before anyone knew three dead men were floating around in it."

"The bigger problem," Asa said solemnly, "is just how many others will become infected. That water could have been used not only for drinking, but to wash and prepare food. Once cholera gets started, there's nothing much worse. If we don't stop this now, Quanah Parker and his braves will capture Adobe Walls by simply waiting a few days and watching us die."

"What can I do to help?" Masterson asked.

"Dump out any water you find and wash out the containers with whiskey. Draw some fresh water, strain and boil it like I said earlier. In the meanwhile I'll gather up some sugar and salt.

Once I've got good water, I'll try and get some
down her. Mixing it with sugar and salt seems to
help with recovery. Other than that, there's not
much else anyone can do except try to keep her
fever cooled down with wet—"

The loud boom of a Sharps rifle from outside
took Asa's attention. "Don't tell me the Comanche are attacking already."

"No, sir," Bartholomew said quickly. "That's
just Billy Dixon target-shooting. He mentioned
something strange about an idea you'd given him,
about chopping off the head of a snake. I honestly
don't know what he's up to except that it caused
him to spend most of the night reloading shells
for his rifle."

"Fetch us some good boiled water," Asa said.
"There's no weapon in this world that will be of
any use once a person's dead from cholera."

"I'm on my way, sir," Masterson said, spinning
to run from the room. "And I'll be quick as I
can."

Cemetery John waited until the young man had
gone to speak. "Dang it all, Asa, it's times like these
that makes me wonder whether I'm in the frying
pan or the fire. If'n I recollect correct, we set out
to simply rescue your mom and sweet sister from a
gang of average, everyday outlaws. Now look at the
fine kettle of fish we're in. When I get home I ain't
never leaving again no matter who—"

Billy Dixon's rifle boomed once again, effectively ending Cemetery John's tirade.

"That sounded more like a stick of dynamite
blowin' up or a cannon firing than a gunshot."
The undertaker cocked his head. "I reckon I'll go

outside and see what Dixon's up to. You don't need my help to care for poor Missus Olds."

Asa placed a palm against her brow. "She's burning up with fever. There's not much anyone can do. If I had some laudanum or bismuth it might help, but she's too far gone to swallow any medicine even if I had some. I'll be lucky to get some water down her when Bat's done boiling it."

"I'll be back after a while to see if you need anything." Cemetery John strode off. He stopped just outside the door, but did not turn around. "My God, Asa, I hope we're lucky enough that no one else comes down sick."

"So do I," Asa replied, but his friend had already gone.

A parching sun was hanging high in a cloudless azure sky when Asa Cain stepped outside the saloon. He blinked his eyes several times to adjust to the glare. Then he strode over to a table alongside the east wall where Billy Dixon and Bartholomew Masterson were fussing over a rifle and some reloading equipment.

"Don't be skittish, Bat," Billy said. "You need to remember that it's my head that'll get blown up instead of yours if'n this don't work. Go ahead and measure out one hundred an' twenty-five grains of gunpowder and fill that shell with it."

Asa observed the proceedings for a moment, then cocked an eyebrow at Dixon. "An average cartridge holds no more than ninety grains of powder. That Sharps of yours may just blow up from the overload."

"I've been trying to tell him that," Masterson

said. "But who ever coined the word 'hardheaded'
had Mr. Dixon in mind." He hesitated. "How's
Missus Olds holding up?"

"She's doing as well as can be expected. I've
been able to get a couple of pints of sugar and
salt water down her. Thankfully, the fever hasn't
gotten any worse. Cemetery John is keeping wet
rags on her forehead while I get a break and something to eat."

Billy Dixon said, "Glad to hear she's still
amongst the livin'. That's an awful sweet little lady.
If'n this idea of mine pans out, we might all get
out of this predicament with our hair still where
God put it."

Asa shook his head. "Standing up on that wall
and blowing yourself up with an overloaded
Sharps isn't likely to panic any Indians I'm familiar
with."

"Dag nab it, Cain." Dixon spat a wad of tobacco
at a passing horned toad. "I'm simply followin'
your advice. You said if we killed the head of the
snake we'd be fine. I intend to blow that bloodthirsty Quanah Parker clean outta his moccasins
from right here."

"He'll never come close enough to allow that,"
Asa said. "Parker is the chief. When the attack
comes, he'll be watching from a mile away along
with Moon Fox and Lame Bear."

"Yep," Dixon agreed. "That's the way I figger
it too. The knoll where he watches from is close
to a mile. I've moved the rear sight high as the
thing will go. From all the sightin' I've done, with
that bigger load an' a passel of luck I can kill that
Injun from right here."

"Or blow your own head off," Masterson said.

Billy Dixon chuckled. "Then it won't hurt when I get scalped."

Red Magruder, who had been using Asa's brass telescope to keep watch on the Indians, spoke loudly from his station on a platform above them. "Well, Dixon, I sure as hell hope you can shoot as good as you tell folks you can. Because there's a solid two thousand savages linin' up right now to attack us. If you can stop this massacre with one bullet, get to crackin' or we'll all be deader than Ole Abe Lincoln darn shortly."

TWENTY-TWO

Billy Dixon gave Asa a worried glance, then turned his attention to the table where Masterson was shaking black grains of gunpowder from a small oak keg into the pan of a balance scale. "One hundred and twenty-five grains, Bat. Not the weight of a fly turd more or less. My last shot was with a hundred an' ten. The blame bullet dropped over a foot from where I wanted it to go."

"I oughtta take that shot myself," an obviously drunk buffalo hunter slurred, swaggering over. "Ol' Dixon couldn't hit a bull's ass with a banjo."

Asa spun to face the inebriated hunter. "You'd better take up a position on that wall and hope like hell he *can* pull it off. Otherwise you and everyone else here are good as dead."

"You ain't so tough, gunslinger." The man was red-faced and obviously growing angrier by the second. He held a trembling open hand only inches from the pistol he wore. "I'll kill you first, Cain, an' then I'll kill all them Injuns. Make your play, Cain."

"Wesley, we ain't got time for this," Billy Dixon shouted. He looked at Asa. "Old Wes has been drinkin' way too much lately. Maybe three gallons a day or so. Reckon his brain's done gone and pickled itself."

"Settle down," Asa said softly, taking care that he had a clear shot. "I have nothing against you."

"Draw!" Wesley yelled, and slapped for the handle of his Colt.

Asa's gun flew up and fired in the blink of an eye. Before the drunk's hand touched metal, a black hole appeared in his forehead.

"Idiot!" Asa exclaimed.

"Yep," Billy Dixon said nonchalantly. "I reckon you've got ol' Wesley fairly well figured out." He watched as the buffalo hunter slumped to the dusty earth. Then Dixon turned and grinned at Masterson. "Well, now that some of the day's entertainment is over, let's take care to load that shell just right. It's the only one we'll have to try before we're up to our butts in Indians."

Asa watched as two men dragged the body away. "I've had a run of bad luck with idiots named Wesley lately. I hope this is the end of that trend."

Billy Dixon kept his eyes on the brass scale. "I'd say we're fresh out of Wesleys hereabouts. Now, if you was to visit Buffalo Gap, Wesley stock will increase in value there considerable."

"Cemetery John and I passed through Buffalo Gap the other day, and took care of that town's problem with the Hayes clan."

"Glad to hear it." Billy grabbed a brass cartridge and inserted a funnel into the open end. "Kill off a few hundred more like 'em an' this'll be right pleasant country to live in."

"Don't forget to add in the Indians," Bartholomew Masterson said.

"I'm fixin' to do my part, Bat. Dump in that

powder, then use the press to set the lead slug in nice and solid."

Asa watched with interest as Billy Dixon put a final drop of oil on the hammer mechanism. He noticed the sliding vernier rear sight was at its highest possible point. "No one I've ever heard of has been able to shoot with any accuracy over a few hundred yards," Asa said.

"You're just a ray of cheery sunshine today, Asa," Billy Dixon answered. "When we're shootin' buffalo, it's usual practice to set up a half mile or so away. I drive a couple of sticks into the ground to make an X to rest the barrel on. Then, from that far away, them stupid buffs don't notice their companions droppin' like flies for quite a spell. I once killed well over one hundred before the herd panicked."

Asa said, "An entire tribe of Indians won't kill fifty buffalo a year."

"Ain't no matter." Billy Dixon sliced off a chew of tobacco and plopped it into his mouth. "There's millions an millions of 'em. Hell, there ain't no way we'll never run out of buffs."

"Here's your ammunition," Masterson said, handing Dixon a glistening brass .50-caliber shell. "I surely hope you don't blow your own head off with it."

The buffalo hunter took the cartridge and studied it for a moment before sliding the shiny yellow metal cylinder into the open breech and locking the action. "Well, boys, let's play this hand."

Asa and Bartholomew followed Billy Dixon to the wall and took up positions on either side.

"Mr. Cain," Red Magruder said as he walked over. "Here's your telescope. I reckon you'll want to check out Billy's shootin'. I sure hope it's good, 'cause there's a real passel of savages out there."

Billy Dixon grinned. "You might say this is a real long shot." He spat a wad of tobacco to the ground, rested the Sharps on the wall, closed one eye, and began taking deep breaths.

"There's Lame Bear, Quanah Parker, and Moon Fox," Asa said, carefully clicking the telescope into focus. "Mounted proud on their horses right square on top of that knoll so they can watch the massacre."

"Damn fly," Billy Dixon swatted at the side of his face, but kept his open eye to the sights. "Don't get in a dither, boys. I've got the windage. I'm just waitin' until them savages get lined up better."

"Shooting just one of them will be nice," Masterson said.

"That's more like it," Dixon mumbled. "Just a couple more feet closer . . ."

Through the spyglass Asa could see Quanah Parker, Moon Fox, and Lame Bear were lined up waiting for the attack. He felt a tremendous surge of hatred for the Indian with a streak of white through his hair. Then, Lame Bear turned and stared across the barren prairie straight toward him.

A tremendous explosion cracked the air. Asa turned, and noticed Billy Dixon had nearly been knocked over from the recoil.

"Dang it, I'm fine," Dixon yelled. "Keep your peepers on them redskins!"

Asa focused on the three Indians. All had turned toward the gunshot. "You must have missed, Billy. I don't see—holy smoke!"

Clear as could be, Asa saw Lame Bear's neck

explode with a spray of crimson, and Moon Fox slapped a hand to his chest a split second before being blown from his saddle to join Lame Bear on the ground. Quanah Parker's eyes were wide with surprise and shock. The Comanche chief began yelling at his braves. Then, to everyone's relief, the Indians began fleeing to the east.

"Tell me, men," Billy Dixon boomed, "how many did I get?"

Asa laid aside the telescope and smiled. "You're the best shot in Texas. Lame Bear and Moon Fox were both likely killed by that single shot."

"But I was aimin' for Quanah Parker," Billy muttered, wearing a hangdog expression.

Asa cupped a hand to Billy Dixon's ear and said quietly, "Keep that to yourself and you'll get free drinks for a lot of years. You're a bloody hero if you'll allow it."

Billy Dixon turned, to be bathed in admiring glances from men lowering their rifles. He stared over the wall at the rapidly disappearing horde of Indians. "By damn, boys," he yelled. "I done killed me a medicine man an' that skunk of a Lame Bear."

A chorus of cheers rang out from the town of Adobe Walls.

Red Magruder patted a hand on Dixon's shoulder. "I reckon a shot like that one calls for some Sunday School time, an' I'm buyin'."

"Missus Olds is awful sick," Bartholomew said.

"Don't fret it, sonny," a burly skinner said. "We'd never cheat that little lady out of a nickel. I'll fetch a jar an' we'll all drop money in it fer the drinks, same as if she was there." He glowered at the gathering crowd. "And Asa Cain can shoot the first cheap son of a bitch that holds out."

"If Cain misses, I'll wait till they're in Kansas to blow 'em outta their saddle," Dixon said proudly. "I'm ready for that drink. It's been a tiresome day."

Masterson laid a hand on Asa's shoulder. "Come on in for a spell and join us. This is a reason to celebrate if there ever was one."

Asa stared across the prairie toward the small knoll in the distance. "I'll be along shortly. There's something I have to go do first. I would appreciate it if you'd check on Missus Olds and fill Cemetery John in on what happened."

"He'll be relieved to find out he's not going to get killed by Indians. Leastwise, not anytime soon." He looked at Asa. "Is there anything else I can do?"

"No." Asa's voice seemed to be coming from a great distance. "What has to be done is for me alone to take care of."

"Yes, sir," Masterson said. Then he was gone along with the others.

"It's about time you went an' showed up," Cemetery John said with mock anger when Asa came into the saloon. "We were about ready to form a posse."

"I had a task to perform." Asa looked around the room at the revelers. "From the looks of this bunch, they would have a hard time even finding their horses."

"That's a true fact. Not gettin' killed is a real decent incentive to blow in."

Asa cocked his head. "How's Missus Olds?"

"Bat's in feedin' her some soup I made."

"She's sitting up eating!" Asa was incredulous.

"Yep, an' complainin' about not bein' able to tend bar an' make enough money to leave here."

Billy Dixon came over, followed by a number of men.

"Asa," Billy said, "you may be plenty good at killin' folks, but ever soul here in Adobe Walls thinks you're also one hell of a good doc to boot. There ain't nobody else even feelin' poorly."

"I don't know what to say." Asa was taken aback. "I just did what I knew how."

"Ain't no one ever heard of sugar water with salt in it," Cemetery John said. "Only a doctor knows stuff like that."

Billy Dixon sidled close to Asa and whispered, "It's hell bein' a bona-fide hero, but I reckon I'll get used to it some year."

Asa smiled and turned to Cemetery John, who was at the bar nursing his usual cup of hot chocolate. "Enjoy your rest. At first light, we're riding for Canan and the Dolven gang."

PART THREE

HARD BOUNTY

TWENTY-THREE

Asa Cain and Cemetery John had left the town of Adobe Walls when the sun was merely a red glow in the east. The fiery orb was blazing down from high in an azure sky before a word passed between them.

Cemetery John understood that his friend was in a funk over his mother's and sister's unexplained behavior. Added to that were the emotions and memories that had been dredged up by the appearance and subsequent killing of his old enemy, Lame Bear. But a few hours of wallowing in gloominess was sufficient. Any more could be downright dangerous for a man who needed a sharp mind just to stay alive.

"That was quite some shot Billy Dixon made," Cemetery John said between puffs on a long-nine cigar. "From the way things turned out, ol' Moon Fox should've relied more on distance rather than magic for his own bullet-proofin'. Being nigh onto a mile away, however, I doubt the thought crossed his spook-filled mind until that slug of hot lead drove home the message."

Asa kept his eyes focused straight ahead. "Billy Dixon was aiming at Quanah Parker."

"It doesn't matter. The results kept all of us from getting an Indian haircut. And Missus Olds is comin' around mighty fine, thanks to your good doctorin'."

"Cholera is an unpredictable disease. We're just lucky that it didn't spread."

"Again, that's thanks to you making folks clean up their water an' boil it. I swan, Asa, if you don't perk up, the Dolvens will do the world a favor by shootin' you. The problem with that will be I'll have to rescue your family all by my lonesome. I'd prefer to have your help, if it ain't too gol-durn much trouble."

Asa looked over at Cemetery John and smiled slightly. "I suppose I have been in the doldrums a tad. I think what bothers me most, on top of everything else, was having to kill that drunken sot yesterday."

"Hell's bells, everybody in Adobe Walls knows you didn't have any choice. That whiskey-crazed drunk would have killed you deader than a doornail, even if it was an accident he hit you. Remember, that's how Lame Bear and Moon Fox wound up dead."

Asa sighed. "This is hard country. Maybe I've grown tired of constantly being on my guard and having to kill people."

Cemetery John took a final puff from the stub of cigar between his lips, then tossed it away. "Perhaps there will be a decent hotel in Canan. I'd venture we both could use a nice hot bath and having our clothes laundered. I know when I don't take one ever week or so, I start feelin' somewhat gamy. Perhaps that'd help uplift your ailin' spirits."

"It couldn't hurt. I suppose a night there would be a good idea. Anyway, we're going to have to spend tonight camping out. Canan's a two-day ride. I would like to be rested when I kill the Dolvens."

"There you go," Cemetery John said with satisfaction. "A man with a goal is a happy person."

"Travelin' along the Canadian River is almost enough to convince a body that God at least visited this part of Texas, but if you glance to either side, it's plenty obvious he didn't stick around long." Cemetery John was tired and hungry after a long day in the saddle. He was anxiously scouting around for a likely campsite where they could cook supper and spend the night. Asa, it seemed, was prepared to continue riding east until it got dark enough for his horse to run into a tree. "I'd reckon most anyplace hereabouts will make a good camp."

"We'll stop in a few minutes," Asa said, leaning back in the saddle and nodding his head at a spiral of buzzards working in the gathering shadows ahead. "First I want to check out what those vultures are eating."

"I'd reckon it's most likely a maverick cow that got mudded in and couldn't get out. That sort of thing happens fairly often along rivers. Whatever's holding those buzzards' interest, I'm sure it ain't feeling any pain and will still be around come mornin'. Asa, I'm so blame hungry my belly's beginning to think my throat got cut."

"Whatever it is, another few minutes will get us

there. Then you can fry up that bacon you've been thinking about all day."

"I thought it was plumb nice of Missus Olds to give us that slab. Shucks, the mold will scrape right off and we won't be able to tell it from fresh, most likely."

"She's a sweet lady. I'm glad and surprised to see her up and about so soon. I said before that she's not only pretty, but strong to boot. I only hope she can make her way back East like she wants to."

Cemetery John nodded and flicked the reins. At the pace Asa was loping along, he would be forced to gather firewood in the dusk. That was the time of day when rattlesnakes and all sorts of unsavory critters came out. Any man with good sense made camp while he could still tell the difference between a stick of wood and a diamondback.

In a few minutes the deputy came to a high point on the bank of the river where he could observe the object of the buzzards' attention. Cemetery John reined to a stop and sighed. "Dang it all, Asa, we could've been fryin' up supper by now. From the looks of things, it'll be a spell."

A man, or at least the remains of one, lay spread-eagled on a plain of grass a hundred feet of so from the river. Cemetery John noted the wood pegs driven into the ground and the rawhide strips that held the nude corpse's wrists and ankles fast. He knew a closer inspection would disclose a red ant bed beneath the hapless man, and if there was enough flesh left to tell, that his eyelids had been cut away to keep the poor fellow from being able to even shut out the blazing sunlight while he died his slow and agonizing death. This was work of the Comanche. From the ruined condition of the body, at least this had occurred a few days ago. Hopefully, with the unexpected demise of Moon Fox and Lame Bear, every Indian in the vicinity was still stampeding away from Texas Panhandle.

"Asa," Cemetery John yelled, waving his hat. "I reckon you oughtta come—"

A rifle cracked from a copse of trees ahead. A ragged hole appeared in the brim of his slouch hat, followed by a ping and the whine of a ricocheting bullet. The deputy didn't wait around for them to take another shot. He dropped low in the saddle, spurring his horse to the relative safety of a nearby draw. He was surprised when no gunfire followed his departure.

A few moments later Asa came sidling from a strand of bushes. He joined Cemetery John, who had left his horse tied in the safety of the draw to go check out who had shot at him from behind a thick cottonwood.

"I've never even come close to gettin' shot at so blame much, not even during the war," Cemetery John complained. "Travelin' with you, I can't even make a nice peaceful camp without havin' to dodge lead."

"There's at least two of them. I counted that many hats on the way here. I wonder if they were drawn here by that poor soul staked out there attracting buzzards. That's Comanche work, and whoever fired at you was likely white. Indians don't wear hats, at least not generally."

"I don't appreciate being used as target practice, no matter what's the religion of the sons of bitches doing the shootin'."

"Simmer down, Cemetery. You've still got your head and most of your hat. Take that pistol of yours and start laying in fire at that clump of trees. I'll circle around and come in on their flank. With any luck, we can ask them what their problem is, instead of killing them."

"That'll be a whole new tack for you, Asa. Let's just wrap this up quick. I'm still hungry as a bear."

Cemetery John nodded. The moment Asa melted into the shadowy bushes, the deputy pulled his revolver and began slowly firing a few rounds into the tops of the trees to keep from accidentally hitting Asa.

He was reloading for the third time when he heard the words he was waiting for. "Come on in, Cemetery John. It's safe."

When Cemetery John walked into their camp, he saw two pudgy, nattily dressed men sitting on the ground leaning back against a fallen tree. Both had hangdog expressions painted across their faces. Then he was taken aback to see a coarse-featured brunette with rouged cheeks and bee-stung ruby lips standing beside Asa.

"Well, it looks like no one got killed," Cemetery John remarked. "Leastwise, not yet."

The older of the two men, with a crop of sliver hair and long sideburns, stood and offered his hand. "I am terribly sorry about the misunderstanding. My name is Webster Mudgett." He gave the other man, who was fat enough to need it, a hand to stand. "And this gentleman is Rath Woodhall, my partner. Please accept our apology and join us for supper." Webster nodded to a low fire over which a half-dozen chickens were roasting.

Cemetery John remembered the green slab of moldy bacon tucked in his saddlebag, and decided to let bygones be bygones. He returned Webster Mudgett's handshake with a slight smile. "Well, sir, I reckon I can overlook the matter if you'll be kind enough to explain why you durn near killed me."

"We were both very disturbed by that poor fellow staked out there on the grass. None of us noticed him until we'd made our camp and Helen started complaining about a bad smell. When you rode up, we simply assumed you were responsible for killing that man. From what Mr. Cain told us and the presence of that badge pinned on your shirt, we were obviously mistaken."

Cemetery John took off his slouch hat and eyed the ragged bullet hole. "No harm done to me anyway. Reckon a chicken dinner will make up for the ventilation."

"Allow me to make amends." Webster reached in his jacket pocket and extracted a twenty-dollar gold eagle along with a white business card. "The firm of Mudgett and Woodhall, brokers of quality mining properties, always strives to satisfy. Please accept our card and allow us pay for whatever damages we may have inadvertently inflicted upon your property."

"Take our token of friendship, my good man," Rath Woodhall added. "And do join us for our repast. Your company will be most appreciated, especially if the desperadoes who did this terrible thing to that poor fellow who is staked out there as vulture bait return."

Cemetery John grinned and tucked the coin and card into his pocket. "I never heard of any gold minin' hereabouts. Reckon you boys are plumb lost. Thank you anyway for being so darn agreeable over blowing a hole in my hat."

"We're heading for Colorado Territory from our office in Kansas City," Webster Mudgett said. "Our firm has recently picked up an option on some extremely rich gold properties near Oro City." A practiced smile crossed his face. "This is a wonderful opportunity for an astute investor, sir. Perhaps you wish to hear just how rich we could make you—"

"This is Helen Pickman," Asa interrupted, leading the heavily painted lady close to the fire. "She says she has been accompanying these men since Wichita."

"Yes I have," Helen said, bunching up her dress and plopping down on the log. She grabbed a stick and jabbed at one of the roasting chickens. "A girl gets plenty tired of selling herself for one or two dollars a poke. Webster and Rath here have us a deal. I get one hundred shares of United Pike's Peak Mining Corporation stock every single time I drop my drawers." She frowned slightly. "I sure wisht those two were younger. So far, I've only got five hundred shares, and this is goin' on our second week together."

Asa swallowed to stifle a chuckle. "Cemetery, you help those gents fix supper while I go out and check on whoever that is staked out there before it gets too dark. There may be some way I can identify him."

"You go right ahead, lover," Helen said. "The stench is bad enough from here, especially when the wind's blowin' from that direction. None of us are goin' any closer, I can guarantee it."

Asa nodded and slipped away into the shadows. A few short minutes later he returned and tossed a bloody shirt and a sliver badge on the ground next to the sizzling chickens. "His clothes were in a gully. I found some letters and that badge. He was Sheldon Reed, the sheriff of Tascosa."

"That's the man you said was after your ma's reward money." Cemetery John was obviously surprised. "He was to meet up with that gunman Sand Drawhorn and the marshal of Canan."

"Only the Comanche ran across him first." Asa clucked his tongue. "I just hope we're not too late."

Webster Mudgett wrinkled his brow in surprise. "There is a reward out on Mr. Cain's mother?"

Cemetery John sighed. "It's a long story. I'll tell it to you after dinner, but I'm tellin' you right now that you likely won't believe a word of it."

Helen Pickman grinned at Cemetery John. Her teeth were snaggled and yellow. "Before you turn in, lover, come see me. For that double eagle I'll give you a night to remember me by."

"Thanks for the offer, darlin'. I've got a sweet wife an' ten kids back in Wolf Springs that needs that money worse. From the sounds of things, you might have nigh onto a thousand minin' shares by the time you reach Colorado. I'm bettin' you're gonna get to be plumb rich."

"A girl can't ever have too much money, darlin'," Helen said, batting her watery green eyes. "If you change your mind, I won't be hard to find."

"Oh, I'm sure of that," Cemetery John said. He

eyed the chicken. "Let's eat before something else happens today." He glanced about. "And the rest of you'd be advised to do the same. Whenever Asa Cain's about, it's safer."

TWENTY-FOUR

"I can't help but wonder," Cemetery John said to Asa as they rode along the Canadian River under a building sun. "Between those two old-geezer mining promoters and that plug-ugly, snaggle-toothed whore, who's giving who the biggest screwing?"

A rare grin crossed Asa's face. "That is a puzzle. I've a feeling the firm of Mudgett and Woodhall are the likely winners. At least Helen Pickman's customers get more than a worthless stock certificate."

"A lasting case of the clap, most probably."

Asa chuckled. "You could have just told her no last night rather than concoct a story about having ten hungry kids and a wife back in Wolf Springs. Any skypilot will tell you that a man can go to hell for lying, same as any other sin."

"In situations like that one, God don't count 'em as sins, just as havin' good sense. At least I got paid good for getting my hat shot." Cemetery John pulled out the twenty-dollar gold piece Webster Mudgett had given him and squinted at it in the sunlight. "Hell's fire, this here double eagle's green around the edge and the lady's head's upside down compared to the back side."

"And I would venture that shoddily made counterfeit coin is still worth more than any of those shysters' stock certificates ever will be."

Cemetery John frowned and slipped the phony double eagle back into his pocket. "I hope both Mudgett and Woodall gets the clap so bad their business drops off." He sighed and decided to change the subject. "I reckon we should've buried that sheriff fellow rather than leavin' him like we found him."

"We don't have any shovels and even if we did, it would have taken too much time. I want to make Canan by afternoon. Besides that, he was on his way to kill my mother."

"I was simply makin' conversation, not complainin'. Bein' an undertaker I get plenty of exercise grave-diggin' without doing it for practice. Come to think on the matter, I've never had the opportunity to bury a bona-fide, genuine badge-wearing sheriff before."

"From what I've heard of Sheldon Reed, he was crooked as a barrel of snakes and not nearly so likable. The one I'm concerned about is Sand Drawhorn. He's a gunman who has made a reputation of note down on the lower part of the Rio Grande. From all accounts he's faster than greased lightning with a pistol and has killed over a dozen men in fair fights."

Cemetery John bit the end off a long-nine cigar, then lit it. He blew a smoke ring into the still, sultry, air and said, "With any decent luck on our part, Quanah Parker's Comanches may have already taken care of that problem. Drawhorn would have come from the right direction to run square into them redskins."

"We can always hope something good came out of that uprising. At least Quanah Parker and all of the tribes will be mourning Moon Fox for an entire moon cycle. He was a powerful medicine man and carried a lot of respect. No Indians will go on the warpath until the ceremonies honoring him are complete."

"That gives us a break of nearly a month, dependin' on how redskins count phases. I plan on being safely back home in Wolf Springs long before then. And if I am ever bedeviled again by so blame many Indians as I was subjected to in Adobe Walls, I'm going to move to New York City where there ain't any."

Asa cocked an eye at the sun. "I judge we're about three hours of so out of Canan. I hope you're correct that Sand Drawhorn is no longer among the living. That would leave only the marshal there, Emil Quackenbush, to contend with. Then we can focus on killing the Dolven gang."

"I'm bettin' your ma's fine and that little sister of yours is only playin' along to stay alive. That would be the smart thing for 'em to do. When a bunch of desperadoes captures a pretty lady and then gets tired of her. . . ." Cemetery John let his words hang unsaid. He realized he had already said too much as it was.

"Let's ride." Asa kept his gaze fixed to the east and spurred his horse into a faster gait.

Late that afternoon the duo reined to a stop on a low hill overlooking the town of Canan. For several long moments they absorbed the devastation below in silence.

Cemetery John raised an eyebrow at Asa and tossed away a freshly lit long-nine cigar. "I reckon quitting smokin' might be a smart and healthy thing to do, considerin'."

Asa stood in his stirrups and stared intently toward the south and west. "From the looks of things, I'd say that fire you started to cut off those Indians was what burned this town down all right. I can see a few buildings that only got scorched. Maybe one of them's the hotel and we can still get a decent night's sleep and a bath. The rest of Canan looks to be pretty much of a loss, however."

"Dang it all, Asa, I feel badly about this. That fire didn't even begin to spook the Comanche. Now look what I went and done to a whole town."

"If you let out the facts, they'll hang you for sure."

"No, they won't," Cemetery John said with finality. "There ain't no trees left for 'em to toss a rope over. Let's go see about that bath."

"Hold it right there, *hombres,*" a gravely voice boomed from between two smoke-blackened buildings, one of which had a sign proclaiming it to be the marshal's office. "If either one of you so much as twitch and make me think you're goin' for a gun, I'll blow both of your hides full of buckshot."

"When newcomers happen by Wolf Springs," Cemetery John said calmly, keeping his eyes straight ahead, "Sheriff Deevers an' me strive to give 'em a cheerier greeting than the one you're givin' us."

The man kept to the shadows. "If you're tellin' me that you're Wilburn's deputy, keep your hands where I can see them and turn toward me."

Cemetery John did as asked. The metallic click of a hammer being lowered came as a welcome relief. "Sorry about the misunderstanding." A burly, red-headed man with a short, neatly trimmed beard came onto the street packing a double-barreled shotgun in the crook of his arm. "Deputy, you and Asa Cain can get down. There's not another deputy in West Texas that would fit your description."

"Why are you so edgy?" Asa asked.

"It should be fairly obvious. First the Comanche damn near burned down our town. Then—"

"Blasted savages," Cemetery John interrupted with a growl as he dismounted. "Only uncivilized barbarians would do something so evil as settin' a fire to a nice town like I'm sure this one was." He looked around forlornly. "Before it got burnt."

"Canan *was* growing," the man said. Then his voice wavered and he kicked at the scorched earth. "I'm sorry, I haven't introduced myself. I'm Emil Quackenbush, the marshal of—well, what's left of Canan, Texas." He offered his hand to Asa, who had just dismounted. "I've heard about you and know why you're here. I reckon we need to talk."

Asa grasped the marshal's hand; then Cemetery John took his turn.

"We were hoping to find a hotel," Asa said, looking around at the surviving buildings. "But if that's a problem, we can go straight and visit in your office."

The marshal shook his head sadly. "The Overland House was a grand three-story hotel. Vern Rogers thought it would attract the railroad to build here." He nodded to a heap of blackened wood at the head of the street. "That's what's left of the Overland."

Cemetery John said, "I hope this Rogers fellow had fire insurance."

Quackenbush shrugged. "I rightly don't know, and it sure don't matter none to Ol' Vern. He's still in that pile of ashes somewhere. Right up to the last he was yelling and tossing buckets of water on the place; then it collapsed on him. I've been too busy to try and dig out his bones for burying."

Asa noticed Cemetery John floundering for something to say, and decided his disconcerted friend could use some help. "We were at Adobe Walls when the Plains tribes attacked. Two days ago a buffalo hunter by the name of Billy Dixon made a terrific shot of nearly a mile. He killed a warrior by the name of Lame Bear and their medicine man, Moon Fox. The Indians won't be making war again for at least a month."

The marshal spat a wad of tobacco juice and surveyed the town. "That's good news for those who might want to rebuild, but I'd say Canan's finished. With the hotel and whorehouse burnt down, the railroad sure won't come here."

Asa nodded at the open door to the marshal's office. "You said we needed to talk. I agree. And you can start by explaining why you drew down on us with a shotgun."

Emil shot an uneasy glance to a surviving clapboard building a few hundred feet away. "The problem's there in that saloon. His name is Sand Drawhorn. I'd prefer we get inside before he sees us. That man's meaner than any Indian or prairie fire ever was. Come on in. I've got a pot of coffee on and I figure you deserve to hear the story."

Cemetery John frowned when he sipped the last of what he knew was a cup of the worst coffee in the history of Texas. The stuff was black as tar, had the consistency of molasses, and a taste that would run off rats. The vile brew only added to his melancholic mood. Burning down the town of Canan and incinerating a hotel owner was a heavy enough cross to bear. But if Marshal Quackenbush was to be believed, compared to what Asa and he had been through so far, things were about to become downright dangerous for them.

"More coffee?" Emil asked cheerfully.

"No, thank you," Asa said quickly, confirming Cemetery John's opinion of the marshal's coffee-making abilities. Asa could drink Fridley Newlin's coffee and still smile. "More than one cup keeps me awake at night."

Cemetery John set his empty cup on the oak desk they were sitting around, and cleared his throat. "Asa and I thought you and Sheriff Reed of Tascosa had hired Drawhorn to kill his mother for the reward money. Glad to find out we were mistaken."

Quackenbush refilled his cup while he measured his reply. "I never met Sheriff Reed, but that reward of twenty-five hundred dollars a head for the Dolvens' hide didn't sound bad at all. Like

I told you, the first telegrams were all about my helping kill that bunch of outlaws, which didn't cause me any bother. Then, after the gunslinger was already on his way, Reed sent me a message that we were gonna kill the lady too. I'd never hold for that, but by then there weren't no way to stop 'em until they got here."

"The sheriff from Tascosa is who Drawhorn's waiting for?" Asa inquired.

"It *was* who he's waitin' for. When the sheriff didn't show—and from what you told me, he had good reason to be delayed—Sand sent a telegraph the morning before the town caught fire for two of his brothers down in Laredo. Hell, both of 'em are wanted for murder. The reward for the pair of 'em is two thousand dollars. When you come riding in, I thought for sure you two were Drawhorn's kin. I'm surely sorry about pullin' a gun on you, but with the town being burnt, I'm out of work. That reward money would've come in mighty handy."

Asa sighed and looked out the window. "Marshal, I'm betting that the Drawhorn brothers have their scalps dangling from a Comanche lance. Sand Drawhorn is simply an annoyance. It's just too bad he's not worth anything dead. When he's out of the way, we're going for the Dolvens. You can come along and we'll share the reward for them equally. I explained that my mother and sister are hostages, so the bounty will be strictly on the Dolvens, understand?"

"Yes, sir," Emil said with a grin. "That will be fine with me. Like I said, I'd never hold for killing any woman." He nodded toward the saloon. "How do you intend to handle Sand Drawhorn? He ain't

wanted, but I hear he's killed a lot of men in gunfights."

Asa's eyes became mere slits. "I'm going to call
him out and kill him."

Emil Quackenbush looked aghast. "When do
you plan on doing this?"

"Right now," Asa said, shrugging his shoulders
as he stood. "There's no time to lollygag." Then
he spun around and was gone.

"Is he serious?" the marshal asked.

"Oh, yeah," Cemetery John said firmly. "When
it comes to killin', Asa's always *real* serious."

TWENTY-FIVE

The sign over the batwing doors of a long and low single-story saloon had been so charred by the fire that Asa had not noticed it before. He hesitated and studied the plank with the words "Cash Bar" that obviously had been painted a bright red before the conflagration.

Not a very imaginative proprietor, Asa thought. No matter. He wasn't planning on becoming a regular customer. He slid the .36-caliber Whitney Eagle in and out of its holster a couple of times to reassure himself all was in order. Then he clucked his tongue and strode inside the dark and smoke-filled saloon.

It took a few moments for his eyes to adjust from the brightness of a lowering West Texas sun to the murkiness inside. To Asa's surprise, the Cash Bar was packed with people. Then he remembered that nearly every building in Canan had been destroyed. Most of the people here simply had no place else to go.

"Well, hello there, sweetheart," a husky female voice said into his ear at the same time the over-powering scent of lilac perfume assaulted his senses. "Little Timberline would just love to have you buy her a drink."

Asa turned to the woman and blinked his eyes into focus, staring up at the cleavage of Timberline's enormous breasts, which were straining to burst free from her low-cut red dress at any moment.

"I can see where you came by your moniker," he said.

Timberline shook out her long auburn hair, bent over, and nuzzled Asa's ear. "You're lookin' at six and a half feet of pure lovin', sweetie. After a few drinks we can go to my place. I've got a tent set up out back. Since the fire, I'm the only girl in town that's got any privacy to offer a gentleman."

Asa nodded toward the bar. "Let's get that drink first."

Timberline used her elbows to clear a path. A few men gave out yelps of pain and curses, until they saw it was a woman who had jabbed their ribs, and retreated in silence. The soiled dove wrapped a ham-sized arm around Asa and bellowed at the harried-looking little barkeep, "Moe, bring me an' my man here a shot of that good stuff you've been savin' back."

The diminutive tavern keeper pawed through some bottles below the big mirror behind the bar. A smile washed across his face when he came up with a decanter of what the label declared to be Bear's Breath Whiskey.

"Welcome to the Cash Bar, stranger," he said, pouring out two full glasses. "My name's Moe Cash, an' I can see you've already met my sweet wife, Timberline."

Asa choked out, "Your *wife!*"

"Yep, Yep," Moe said, keeping his smile. "The little lady makes more money than I do." He shrugged. "So why the hell should I complain. I ain't no Bible-banger."

Timberline grabbed the shot and jolted it down. "Drink up, sweetie. Here in Canan we call the first shot of Bear's Breath a revelation. The second is a pure taste of heaven—"

"And the third is called a serious mistake," Moe interrupted. "Li'l Timberline can handle strong liquor better than any man. Once she got a drummer to drink a whole bottle of that stuff on a bet. He did it, but there weren't enough money in his pockets to pay for his coffin."

Asa tossed a five-dollar gold piece onto the bar. Then he slid his drink over to Timberline. "I'm here on business. I understand there's a scalawag by the name of Sand Drawhorn in here. I'm looking for him."

The din inside the crowded saloon gradually lowered to become as silent as night in the desert.

"Sweetie," Timberline said, unwrapping her arm from around Asa. "You shouldda taken li'l ole me to the tent. Now you'll go to hell without ever knowing what paradise is like. That Drawhorn's a mankiller if there ever was one."

The whore, her husband, and everyone else in the vicinity beat a hasty retreat to the rear of the saloon. Now only two men stood at the long walnut bar: Asa Cain, and at the far end, a tall, slender, clean-shaven fellow with waist-length silver hair who coldly surveyed him with dark, deep-set cadaverous eyes.

The long-haired gunman mustered a thin smile.

"I am Sand Drawhorn. My friends call me Sand. You can call me *Mr.* Drawhorn."

Asa's face became expressionless as he stepped away from the bar and turned toward his adversary. "I think I'd prefer to call you simply Asswipe."

The slight smile vanished, and Drawhorn very carefully reached for a glass of beer that was on the bar in front of him. "I'd reckon you to be that bounty hunter, Asa Cain?"

Asa nodded.

"Well, bounty hunter, I expected you'd show up eventually. There ain't no need for anyone to get killed here today. That reward on the Dolvens, I know it includes your ma. Considering your reputation, I would think you of all people could understand why I've set out to do what's gonna be done anyway. If it ain't me and my brothers that collects that reward, you know it's a fact that somebody will. Ten thousand dollars is a pile of money for three outlaws and a bank robbin' lady."

The only change in Asa's expression was the narrowing of his eyes to mere slits. Drawhorn took note of this fact, and began flexing his gun hand to limber it up.

Asa said coldly, "My mother and sister are being held hostage by the Dolvens. I'm not going to let you kill them. This blood quest of yours stops right here."

"Well, ain't you the high-and-mighty shining example of humanity. Cain, you've shot down more men in cold blood than I've ever killed in fair gunfights. What is the number of men you've bushwhacked? Fifty, or is it maybe two hundred like some claim?"

Asa clucked his tongue. "The number will be one more if you don't take off that gun of yours nice and slow, then ride out of town."

"Hell, Cain, you know I ain't gonna do that. My brothers are coming a long way for this. It'd be a shame to disappoint them."

"Most likely your brothers have been killed by Indians like Sheriff Reed was. We found his body on the way here. He died hard."

Drawhorn gave a slight shrug and turned to step away from the bar and face Asa. "I never hankered to do business with any sheriff nohow. If my brothers weren't smart enough to stay alive, I'll go after the Dolvens without them." He shook his long hair away from the pearl-handled pistol that rode low on his hip. "I'm a gunman, Cain, not some slow-moving bounty hunter that only shoots unarmed men. You've riled me to the point that I'm gonna kill you on the count of three."

Sand Drawhorn gave a sinister grin and shouted merrily, *"Three!"* And grabbed for his gun.

Asa was taken aback for a split second, but it was time enough for the Drawhorn to clear leather and level his .44 square at Asa's heart and pull the trigger.

The dull click of a hammer striking a defective cartridge caused Drawhorn's eyes to widen just as Asa's pistol began spitting fire and three red blossoms bloomed on the gunman's chest. Sand Drawhorn stared in shocked bewilderment at Asa for a moment, then sagged to the floor, dead before he landed.

Moe Cash broke the heavy silence. "You'd best have that drink now, Mr. Cain. There ain't but blessed few folks live through what just happened to you. I swan, I never seen the like of Drawhorn's speed with a gun or your plain dumb luck."

Asa holstered the Whitney Eagle. He noticed his hand was trembling. "I should have expected him to cheat."

Timberline ambled over and presented her massive bosom to Asa's face. "Sugar, you're so lucky that li'l ole me's gonna take you into my tent for half price, only five dollars instead of the usual ten."

Moe shook his head as he came over to stare at the dead gunman. "Boys, I'll give four of you a free beer if you'll pack him outta here. Bloodstains are the very devil to clean up." He focused his gaze on Timberline. "Hon', you ain't got five dollars for it since you was sixteen and workin' in New Orleans. Charge the man a silver dollar and get on with makin' money. We're gonna need it to leave here."

To Asa's surprise, Timberline sighed and nodded at her husband in agreement. "Yes, dearie, I'll do as you say." She placed a heavy hand on Asa's shoulder. "You'll want a drink or two first, won't you, lover?"

To Asa's relief, the batwing doors swung wide open and in stepped Cemetery John accompanied by Emil Quackenbush. The marshal cast a glance first at the bloody corpse on the floor, then at Asa.

"I was sure hoping this was the way things would turn out, but hedging a bet ain't never a bad idea." Quackenbush patted his big double-barrel shotgun. "Drawhorn had a reputation for being faster than a snake strikin'. I reckon he finally run across someone quicker on the draw than he was."

Asa walked over to Drawhorn's body, bent down,

and picked up the gunman's pistol. "He beat me to the draw. If his gun hadn't misfired, I'd be the one laying dead on the floor."

Timberline ran and gave Asa a rib-crunching hug. "This is the luckiest man in Texas. With the town foldin' the way it is, I thought he would likely be the last man to get hisself buried in Canan. Asa and me's gonna have us some drinks, then we're going to go celebrate out in my tent. Maybe some of his good luck will be catchin'."

Asa escaped the towering whore's clutches and quickly retreated to Cemetery John's side. "We've got business to take care of," he said loudly.

"Oh, we've got plenty of time," Cemetery John said, obviously enjoying himself. "Things here look pretty much under control to me."

Asa rolled his eyes and shot Cemetery John a look that would curdle milk. He noticed Timberline had a determined smile on her painted face and was heading his way.

Before he could come up with a way out of the situation, Marshal Quackenbush hollered from the batwing doors, "You fellows had better get over here. There's riders coming into town. There's two of 'em, and both have long silver hair hanging out of their hats."

"They'll be Drawhorn's brothers for certain," Asa said, sending Timberline scurrying along with the rest of the crowd to the rear of the saloon once again.

Cemetery John cocked the hammers of his ten-gauge. He sidled up to the doors and peeked around. The two strangers were less than fifty feet away. Both men wore their pistols low, gunfighter-style. Lever-action Winchesters were prominently displayed in the crooks of their arms. He noticed their dark eyes were flicking back and forth as they slowly rode toward the saloon.

"Asa, I'd reckon that passel of Indians didn't do near as much damage as we'd hoped," Cemetery John said softly.

"I haven't been very good at reading signs of late," Asa said. "This is another situation I didn't count on."

Emil Quackenbush brushed Cemetery John aside as he strode through the doors. He stopped on the dry ashes of the burned boardwalk and smiled broadly at the oncoming duo. "Howdy, gents," he said happily. Then he flicked up the shotgun and fired first one barrel, then the other into the gunmen's chests. "Welcome to Canan, Texas."

"Tarnation, Asa!" Cemetery John exclaimed. "That marshal sure don't go beating around no bush. Those fellows was only slightly more surprised than I was when he went and shot 'em."

From the depth of the saloon someone shouted, "That lawman didn't even bother to ask who they were or give 'em any kind of chance."

Asa hollered back, "If they aren't the Drawhorn brothers, we'll sincerely apologize to them."

Cemetery John and Asa went out to where Quackenbush was bent over searching the pockets of the bloody corpses. The marshal held up a wanted poster and beamed. "By cracky, it was them. Those idiots even had flyers in their pockets advertising the value of their hides."

"I didn't expect you to just up and kill them like that," Asa said.

"Hell, man, neither did they. Those two were

seasoned gunmen. Those type don't play fair, but expect everybody else to. For what it's worth, if it hadn't been the Drawhorns, I'd be tolerable upset, but I'd rather be upset than leaking blood all over the street."

"You've got a decent reward coming," Cemetery John said.

"Nope, it's *we* that have reward money coming. The deal we made was a fair one. I just happened to be the first one to pull the trigger."

"And you sure did it quick too," Cemetery John said.

Marshal Quackenbush stood and looked about worriedly. "Darn if I know how we're gonna keep these two outlaws from spoiling mighty bad before we get back. Then they've got to be carted all the way to Wolf Springs for the reward to take."

Cemetery John eyed the corpses. "Wilburn Deevers is a friend of mine and ain't too picky. I'm thinking things would go a lot more pleasant for us if we pickled just their heads in a keg of whiskey. They'll keep for quite a spell that way, and the heads will still look like themselves good enough for the law to pay. As hot as it is and considering how far away Wolf Springs is, the rest of 'em would just be a lot of bother."

"Makes sense to me," Quackenbush said without batting an eye. "I'd reckon we oughtta drag 'em out back of the office first. Some folks might take offense to the procedure. That's where the bucksaw is anyway."

"I'll go buy the whiskey," Asa said quickly. "I'd rather deal with that big whore than go with you two."

Cemetery John grabbed up one of the dead

gunmen by his boots and began dragging him toward the marshal's office. "You're right, Emil," he said, "some folks are just plain squeamish."

TWENTY-SIX

Darkness was claiming the Staked Plains when Cemetery John and Emil Quackenbush leaned their long-handled shovels against the back of the marshal's office, walked around, and went inside.

"Dad-gum, that grave-digging is a heap of hard work," Quackenbush said, shifting his brawny shoulders up and down. "I reckon undertakers do earn their money after all."

Cemetery John took a long-nine cigar from his shirt pocket and fired it. "I've been trying to tell folks that for years. And those three graves weren't so bad as they could've been because two of 'em didn't need to be long as normal." He studied an oak barrel that was sitting on the floor across the room from where Asa sat at a desk playing solitaire by lantern light. "I'm hoping Deevers won't try to be cheap and not want to pay me to plant the rest of 'em. I'll still have to dig a hole."

Asa raked in his cards, then deftly shuffled and restacked them. He leaned back in the swivel chair and spun to face the others. "I want to leave for the Dolven ranch first thing in the morning. But there's a problem."

Emil walked over to the potbelly stove that never

put out enough heat in the winter, and put out way too much in the summer, grabbed the black coffeepot, and poured himself a cup. "I reckon we all know what the fly in your ointment is." He motioned with his head to Asa, then to Cemetery John. "Either of you want a cup? This pot should be better than the one we had before, looks like it has more body to it."

"I'll pass," Cemetery John answered quickly. He took a puff on his cigar, blew a smoke ring toward the ceiling, and said, "Asa, it's a fact that all the family you've got in the world is out there at the Dolven ranch. I know, an' Emil knows, your thinking has likely become muddled just a tad because of it."

Asa held up a brass .44 cartridge and twirled it between his fingers. "If this shell had fired, I would have been buried in one of those holes you men finished digging. I let Drawhorn fluster me and then sucker me into believing that he was going to count to three before he made his play. I told you earlier, I can't read signs anymore and that makes me dangerous to be around. Therefore, I don't want you two to go with me. All I'll likely do is get you both killed, and that's not right. This fight is mine and mine alone. I'll see it through without you."

Emil blew on his coffee, then took a sip and grinned. "Now this is *good* coffee, lots of taste to it." He looked at Asa and worried his lower lip with his teeth before he spoke. "Cemetery John thinks you're a fine person, and"—he motioned toward the oak keg—"with six hundred-odd dollars apiece worth of dead outlaws over there, I'd say you're sort of growing on me too."

Cemetery John's brow wrinkled in thought. "The bounty on those Drawhorns was two thousand dollars. We're splittin' even, and my figuring comes out at seven hundred fifty dollars each."

"Nope," the marshal said, "it all boils down to arithmetic. A person has to take an even number and divide it by an odd. This give you a fiction—or something like that. Dang, I reckon I should have paid more attention to studyin' stuff like that those three years I spent in school. Looks like it would've come in handy, because now I'm confused. I don't know, maybe it does come out to seven hundred and fifty apiece after all."

Cemetery John took another puff on his cigar. "The Dolvens pay twenty-five hundred dollars"— he grinned evilly at the whiskey keg—"per head. Now there's three of them Dolvens an' I count three of us. Dividing that ain't gonna be a strain for anybody's thinker. When we collect our reward money in Wolf Springs, we can let Sam Livermore, he's the banker there, figure out the difficult part. Ol' Sam supposedly went clear through the eighth grade, so the odds an' evens won't be a struggle for him to divide up."

Marshal Quackenbush took a healthy swig of coffee and turned toward Asa with a firm set to his jaw. "There's no doubt now that Cemetery John and me will have to go with you and kill them Dolvens. The ciphering will be one helluva lot easier that way."

Asa kept his gaze on the bullet that he still held. "I expected Cemetery John to be too hardheaded to listen to good sense." He set the bullet down and focused on Emil. "Marshal, you seem like a decent man. I have the reputation of being the deadliest bounty hunter in Texas, but I believe that may now be all ballyhoo. I've made every wrong call possible since Cemetery John and I left on this quest. If you do ride with us, don't expect me to watch your back, or you could wind up dead."

Emil grinned. "When we was digging those graves, your friend and me decided that the only way you'd ever live through meeting up with them Dolvens was if we were there to watch *your* back. There ain't no way around the fact that the reward money won't ever split up right if it goes any other way. Besides that, he says your ma is a right nice lady and your sister is too. Those ladies are in a passel of trouble, and I reckon I'd be pretty low-down if I didn't go along to help them out, even if there wasn't no reward money to try and figure up."

Asa dropped his gaze to the floor and fought hard to speak through the knot that had formed in his throat. "Thank you, Marshal," was all he could muster.

"Call me, Emil. There's no reason for anyone to think of me as a lawman nowadays. Canan's mostly burnt up, and it's just a matter of time until the town simply won't be here anymore. I'm sorry there's no hotel left for you to stay in. Bunking on the floor here is the best I can offer."

Cemetery John spoke up. "Asa had a mighty pleasing offer from that big whore to spend the night, but he up and turned her down. I swan, that woman is one tall drink of water."

"Timberline and that mouse of a barkeep she's married to come to Canan last year and built that saloon with their own two hands," Emil said, lost in thought. "Lots of folks think they're strange, but like everyone else out here, they're just doing what they have to do to get by. This is hard country, mighty hard." He looked forlornly at Cemetery John. "What do you suppose possessed them Indians to set fire to this town? We were doing pretty well up until then. The railroad was planning on building here and things were looking up for everyone. Now it's all gone."

Cemetery John coughed a puff of smoke from his throat. It took him a moment to regain his wind and reply. "Heathens are mighty difficult to figure out. When we was at Adobe Walls, them filthy savages went and poisoned the well by dumping dead bodies down it. A mighty pretty lady durn near died of the cholera because of it. I'd venture they'd have burnt that place down too if'n it had been made outta wood instead of dried mud."

Asa decided this topic of conversation had gone on too long for Cemetery John's comfort. He grabbed up the deck of cards and began shuffling them. "Fellows, we could spend the rest of the night talking about depredations Indians have done. I know I have had more than my share of grief because of them. However, there's no redskins about tonight and it's too early to turn in. How about playing a few hands of poker?"

Emil worried his lower lip, then said, "Boys, I hate to admit this, but I don't even have a whole dollar to my name to ante up with. The bank here in Canan was right alongside the Overland House hotel. I'd been saving my money there for two years. Reckon I should've blown it, 'cause it sure didn't keep once the place caught fire."

Cemetery John stared out the window at a rising

full moon, then reached into his pocket, took out a twenty-dollar gold piece, and plunked it down in front of Emil. "You can pay me back when we cash in on the Dolvens."

Asa eyed the greenish edge of the double eagle and frowned slightly, but said only, "Scoot up your chairs and let's play poker."

"Have you ever been to the Dolven ranch?" Asa asked Emil as the trio rode eastward along the bank of the Canadian River.

Quackenbush looked away from the fiery orb that had just risen to above the horizon, and blinked watery eyes at the bounty hunter. "Dang, but it's rough on the ole peepers having to face into the sun. There was a drummer came through Canan a while back selling spectacles. He had something called 'sun specs' that were made out of smoked glass to keep the glare down. They were only a dollar. Reckon I should've bought a set 'cause now I don't have either them sun specs or the dollar. They might've saved my peepers a heap of abuse—"

"We was just playin' a friendly game," Cemetery John interrupted. "Don't fret losin' that double eagle any. It's only money among friends."

"But now I owe you twenty dollars that I don't have," Emil lamented. "I know we've got plenty of reward money coming later on. It's just that I hate being in debt only slightly less than getting hung."

Asa shook his head and spoke up. "Emil, sometimes Cemetery John likes funning people a mite too much. That double eagle he loaned you was counterfeit as a government Indian treaty. No one could pass it off in sunlight without getting shot, it's so blame bad. You don't owe him a nickel."

Quackenbush turned and glared at Cemetery John. "You loaned me a counterfeit twenty dollars?"

"Like Asa said," Cemetery John replied quickly, recalling just how fast Emil could be on the trigger. "It was all in fun." He reached into his pocket, pulled out the coin, and handed it over. "Here, you keep it an' have fun with some of your friends. Just make sure they've got a right decent sense of humor, like you do. The thing could cause upset to serious-minded folk like bankers."

"Or small-town marshals," Quanckenbush said, eyeing the greenish edge of the double eagle. "I'd got a flyer on a couple of real deadly lowlifes posing as mining promoters who've been passing coins like this one. If I remember correct, they're traveling with a whore. That bunch has robbed stagecoaches all over the West. If a stage ain't handy, they'll rob or kill anyone they run across. How did you come by this, may I ask?"

"Oh, I've had it for years," Cemetery John said, puffing furiously on a cigar. "Bought it down in Mexico, just to tease my good friends with. I'd reckon we oughtta quit funnin' an' get back to Asa's question about the Dolven ranch."

Emil tucked the counterfeit coin away and turned to squint into the building sun. "I went out there twice before. Both times was before they were wanted. All I did was serve papers on Brock because he hadn't paid the mortgage. There was a rancher from over near Fort Worth that sold Brock that place and carried the note himself.

Right after I served Dolven with the final foreclosure papers, that fellow—I can't recall his name—dropped plumb out of sight. He never made the court appearance, so the Dolvens have never had to pay the place off." He cocked an eyebrow. "I just can't figure for the life of me what *could* of happened to that man."

Asa said, "Tell us about how the ranch is laid out. We can't simply go riding in there."

"I'd reckon that might be real fatal, real quick," Quackenbush said seriously. "That's why I haven't gone after them. Plenty hard to spend reward money when you're pushing up daisies. Those Dolvens are bad enough, but there's a couple running with them that's maybe even worse. Bull Grossman and Wyatt Klinkinbeard are their names. That gives them five guns against our three. At least Slim Dolven got himself killed a while back. Folks claim he was the best of all of them with a gun."

"I did the honors for Slim Dolven," Asa said. "That's probably why they attacked my home and kidnapped my family."

"All I heard up here was that he got killed. At that point a lawman uses the wanted poster to start a fire with and puts up another on the wall in its place. Texas being the way it is, having paper to build a fire for a pot of coffee is never a worry.

"But about the ranch itself. The place is built on a loop in the river. This gives quicksand and water on all sides except for the road that runs into the place."

"See," Cemetery John said heartily, turning to Asa, "there is such a thing as quicksand."

"Oh, yeah," Emil confirmed. "Men, horses, cattle, buffalo, and wagons have all been drawn under without a trace. And the Canadian River has the best-quality quicksand to be found."

Asa turned to Quackenbush. "You just described the Dolven ranch as being like a blasted fort. Even if we did cross the river, we'd be easy targets out there with no cover."

"I plain ain't gonna cross that quicksand-infested river no more," Cemetery John said firmly. "My luck's likely done run out when it comes to not getting sunk and drowned. I hate crossing even a draw with a trickle of water in it to the point of taking a chill."

"There's no choice but to ride straight in," Emil said. "The ranch buildings are only a couple of clapboard cabins and a shoddy barn. Bullets will go right through the sides of them. The way I figure it, we can charge in using nice thick and safe trees for protection, and pick those outlaws off while they're shooting at us."

Asa snapped, "There can't be any indiscriminate shooting. My family's there. I won't tolerate risking hitting one of them accidentally."

"I can understand your feelings," the marshal said with a nod, "but if you come up with a better idea, let us in on it, because we'll be there before noon."

Asa began to worry his lower lip with his teeth the way Quankenbush did. He said nothing more, and wished desperately that he had a better plan to attack the Dolven ranch than the marshal's. Riding silently east against a blazing sun, he had to admit to himself that, once again, he was at a loss to read the signs.

TWENTY-SEVEN

The crudely lettered sign nailed to a warped and weathered mesquite post where a lightly traveled road forked toward the south and the Canadian River read:

THIS IS THE DOLVEN ROAD
STAY ON THE OTHER ONE

"Friendly cusses, ain't they?" Cemetery John commented.

Quackenbush snorted. "I'd reckon it keeps down on drummers and stump preachers, but I doubt if the Comanche would pay it much mind."

"What bothers me," Asa said seriously while staring intently at the thicket of trees in the distance, "is the fact they've got a price on their heads big enough to send every bounty hunter and lawman in the West chasing after them, and here they don't ever bother to take down a sign advertising where they live. Nothing about any of this makes sense. It's like the Dolvens want us to find them, and that makes it worrisome."

Emil spat a wad of tobacco juice to splatter against the sign. "The biggest upset I have is the fact that two of 'em, Grossman and Klinkinbeard, ain't even worth the cost of the bullets it'll take to blow 'em to hell. Those things don't come cheap out there in the Texas Panhandle."

"You've got twenty whole dollars to spend," Cemetery John quipped as he reined his horse to face the same direction as Asa.

The bounty hunter took the brass spyglass out of a saddlebag, clicked it into focus, and studied the tree-shrouded hideout for a long while. Finally he forced the telescope closed and said with a snarl, "Nothing! There's not a single thing moving down there but an occasional bird. I don't even see a wisp of smoke from a chimney. People have to cook to eat, and I can't fathom why they wouldn't at least have a pot of coffee on. The place has every look of being deserted."

"We could just ride on down and say howdy," Emil said, then glared at Cemetery John. "That twenty-dollar gold piece would be the right amount to pay a certain rascal of an undertaker to bury me, if it turns out to be an ambush."

"I don't like it a'tall," Cemetery John said, ignoring the marshal's gibe. "We'll all be tombstone bait if five guns open up on us."

Asa scanned the area once again. The scowl remained etched on his face. "There's no one going any closer until it gets dark. At least that'll give us some cover. I suggest we ride on ahead for a spell and make camp. If anyone is down there looking back at us, they might think we're simply passing by. Right now we're only about a half mile away from that ranch house. Billy Dixon did considerable damage with a Sharps rifle from twice that far."

Cemetery John's eyes widened. "Well, let's not keep lollygaggin' out here in the open. Besides that, I've been hankering to fry up that slab of bacon Missus Olds give us."

Emil said, "My belly's rubbing on my backbone. A nice helping of bacon on a biscuit with grease drippin' out of it sounds great. And putting those Dolvens off till tonight seems like a mighty fine idea."

Asa took one last look at where the river made a protecting loop around the tree-covered ranch. He flicked the reins and led the way east. "Emil," he said seriously, "you might find it safer to ride down and see what the Dolvens are serving for dinner rather than eat what Cemetery's planning to fix us."

Cemetery John snorted. "First you complain about eating turnips and liver, now you're complaining about digestin' moldy bacon. I swan, Asa, you're the most persnickety person I ever run across in all my born days when it comes to food."

Emil Quackenbush, the ex-marshal of Canan, Texas, kept his silence. There were more important things to think about rather than listen to an undertaker and a bounty hunter bicker. Things like concentrating on how to live through the night.

The wan light of a rising half-moon outlined the trio far too well for comfort as they made their way on foot along the muddy bank of the Canadian.

"At least there's some scrawny trees growing about for cover," Cemetery John said as he moved the big shotgun close to his body to keep it from snagging on a branch. "These blasted Staked Plains don't cast a shadow that counts for much."

Asa, who was in the lead, stood straight behind a thick cottonwood tree and carefully poked his head out to survey the ranch house, which was now only a couple of hundred feet away. After a moment he turned to his companions. "I can't figure this. There's not even a lantern lit. If that place isn't deserted, the Dolvens are doing a right smart job of making it appear that way."

"I'm not going to complain any if the place is empty," Emil said. "Actually, I'm kinda surprised to still be alive, and I'm beginning to really enjoy the feeling."

Cemetery John knelt behind a bush and shook his head as he surveyed the house. "I'm glad there ain't too many folks think the way you do, Emil. If that happened, it'd play hob with my undertaking business." He shifted his gaze to Asa. "I'm saying there simply ain't nobody in there."

Asa clucked his tongue. "That's beginning to be my guess too. It might be wise for just one of us to charge the place and kick the door in. If it turns out they're expecting us, at least you two will—"

A rifle shot split the still air, and a window facing them shattered. Emil Quackenbush levered shell after shell into his Winchester and fired continuously into the house as he ran toward it and kicked in the door.

"That man has a tendency toward rashness," Cemetery John said.

"I agree," Asa said, stepping into the clear. "But

he's just as surprising to everyone else as he is to us."

"Come on up, ladies," Emil's voice boomed from the doorway. "It's safe, the bad men are all gone."

In a moment Asa had a coal-oil lamp lit, allowing them to inspect the house. Below an open window, the form of a large man lying in a bed shifted about when bathed in yellow light.

Cemetery John jumped back, cocked the hammers on his ten-gauge. As he did so, he pointed both barrels of the shotgun at the man. "You make one false move and I'll blow you plumb through that wall."

"You'd favor me if'n you did," a weak, halting voice said. "Dyin' can't be near so bad as waitin' for it, like I'm doin'."

Asa held the lantern high. The smell of rotting meat assaulted his senses when he stared down at the gray-faced man with hollow cheeks and rheumy eyes. Still, even when only a speck of life is left, a person can pull a trigger. Asa stood to one side and stripped off the single filthy sheet, sending up a horde of flies. The stench was nearly overpowering.

"Gangrene," the man gasped. "I seen enough of it durin' the war to know."

Asa nodded in agreement. "How long since it began?"

"Hell, I dunno. A few days. Brock an' me was choppin' firewood. Both of us drunk. I whacked my foot with an' axe."

Asa examined the black swollen flesh that engulfed the lower half of the man's body, and marveled that he was still alive. "Who are you? We'll need to know what to put on your marker."

"That won't matter none. . . ." The man shivered uncontrollably. It was a moment before he had the strength to speak again. "Ain't nobody left in my family that'll care. The ones that would are all kilt. But I'll favor you with my name if'n you'll promise to shoot me. My God, I can't take goin' slow like this."

Cemetery John and Emil came close. Asa set the flickering lamp on a washstand. He stared down at the dying man. "I'll end it for you, but first I need some information."

"Go to hell," the man wheezed. "You're the damn law."

"No, my name is Cain, Asa Cain, and *you* are the one heading for hell. It just might take you a few days more to get there."

The man coughed. *"Now,* you go an' show up. Brock an' his bunch waited an' waited for you, but you never came. I'll favor you with my name now. It's Wyatt Klinkinbeard. I reckon you've heard of me. Now you owe me a quick killin'."

"Not just yet," Asa said coldly. "First the information, then the bullet. Why did Dolven kidnap my mother and sister? Who was the man killed at the ranch when they attacked it?"

A wheezing laugh escaped the gunman's throat. "You're really believing Ol' Brock an' his boys went an' kidnapped your sister? Hell, I never thought you dumb enough to go for that. I wasn't at your place for all the fun. My friend, Bill Brown, got kilt by some pepperbelly, they said. Reckon that's who you was askin' about."

Asa let the insult slide. The man was asking to

be shot. There was nothing to gain by becoming overly angered. "The *truth*, damn you! Where's my family?"

Klinkinbeard had roused to the point of enjoying the pain he saw in Asa's face. "Pretty Jenny an' sweet Sadie. Those two like to do it better than a man. Link's married up that young sister of yours. Their bedsprings sure do squeak a lot. Reckon he'll pass her around once he gets tired of her."

"Where are they?"

Asa's hissing voice crashed into Wyatt's fevered brain. "Brock's dead set on killin' you, Cain. You shouldn't have messed around where you don't belong and kilt his boy for a bounty. Hell, we did everything we knew to draw you out here, but you son of a bitch, you never showed. Brock got all antsy an' took his gang to Wolf Springs."

In spite of the sultry night, Asa felt a chill trickle down his spine. "Why there? What's he planning?"

The gunman's taunting voice dwindled. "They're gonna rob the bank an' kill a sheriff that's your friend. Sadie said if you was still alive, that'd bring you fer sure."

"When did they leave? Tell me, God damn you!" Asa shouted.

"Closer," Wyatt gasped, "come closer. I'm gettin' terrible weak."

Asa bent over the prostrate man, only to have the gunman spit into his face. "That's for not showin' up, Cain. We'd have had you an' your friends kilt an' I'd be havin' fun in a whorehouse instead of lyin' here dyin'."

Emil Quackenbush pushed Asa aside. He

grabbed up the flickering lamp, unscrewed the brass wick holder, and allowed some coal oil to stream down onto the gunman's crotch. "There's more than one way for a fellow to have a hot time. Folks have told me that burning to death slow is the worst pain there is. If you don't answer my good friend's question, nice and truthful-like, I reckon I'll let you find out firsthand if that's true or not."

"You bastard!" Wyatt snarled.

Emil turned to Cemetery John. "Could I trouble you for a match?"

"All right, damn you to hell. Brock's gang left here yesterday mornin'. I hope you do kill him, bastard wouldn't even leave me my gun, said he was gonna sell it an' buy whiskey."

"Now that wasn't so difficult being nice, was it?" Emil turned to Asa. "While he's behaving himself would be the time to ask some more questions."

Asa eyed the outlaw through flickering light. "More time spent with the likes of him is a waste. I'll find out from my mother what really happened."

Wyatt Klinkinbeard rolled his rheumy eyes to Asa. "If you kill the Dolven gang, Cain, you'll have to kill her an' your whore sister. They're *all* ridin' together." He wheezed from the exertion. "Now you owe me that killin' you promised."

"*I* never promised you a damn thing." Emil dropped the burning lamp onto the bed. "Oops, I am *so* clumsy sometimes." He turned to his companions. "I think this would be a good time to leave this place." He grinned evilly. "And I wasn't even out the cost of a bullet."

As the trio made their way back to where the

horses were tied, they could hear Klinkinbeard's screams echoing across the plains long after they had lost sight of the blazing ranch house.

TWENTY-EIGHT

The red glow of a coming dawn was building on the eastern horizon as the three tired men rode side by side for the final few miles to Canan. Most of the long nighttime journey had been accomplished with only the rhythmic clopping of horses' hooves striking hard, dry earth to break the silence.

Cemetery John was burdened by the fact that his friend, Wilburn Deevers, was to be killed by the Dolvens when they robbed the Wolf Springs bank. He felt that somehow he had been duped into coming along on what had turned out to be a wild-goose chase, but no matter how hard he studied the situation, he could not figure out how or why. All that mattered at this time, however, was to get back to Wolf Springs before the Dolvens could organize and spring their deadly trap. Asa's mother and sister were a quandary that would have to be solved later. Having the marshal riding with them was an unexpected blessing. Emil could be somewhat rash at times, but all in all, he was a good man to have along.

"We can catch a few hours sleep in my office," Emil said. "Then we can get some fresh horses from Sage Taylor, who used to own the livery stable before it got burnt down. I reckon with no restaurants left standing or any store to buy provisions, we'll be forced to eat antelope rabbits or whatever we run across. Leastwise, what goes into the skillet won't be green."

"That bacon fried up mighty tasty," Cemetery John said with a snort. "Before we make Wolf Springs, you'll wish I'd brought along another slab of bacon."

Asa rode along in silence, listening to what had become normal bickering between his friend and Marshal Quackenbush. He was in a deep funk over what that dying outlaw had said about his family. None of it could be true, he knew. Some people are simply mean right up to the end. At least Emil had given Wyatt Klinkinbeard a decent send-off.

Out of the corner of Asa's eye he caught the gleam of something in the distance. Something quite large and bright was blazing against the retreating night. "Whatever was left of Canan looks to be burning."

"Damn it all!" Emil swore. "From the looks of things from here, that's my office and the Cash Bar goin' up in flames."

Cemetery John stood up in his stirrups to get a better look. "Reckon it's just your office, Emil. The bar seems fine."

"Ain't that our bad luck," Emil said, shaking his head. "If we hadn't left two thousand dollars worth of dead outlaw heads in there, that office would've still been standing a hundred years from now."

* * *

"Things burning up sure seems to be rather common hereabouts," Cemetery John commented as he puffed on a long-nine cigar and studied the smoldering remains of what had been Marshal Quackenbush's office. "Too bad the barbershop was so blame close to your place and caught fire. The only building left in Canan appears to be the Cash Bar."

Emil sighed and turned to face the saloon. His expression kept shifting between anger and sadness. "This hunt for the Dolvens has just got personal. It was a strong irritation when they cost me my reward money for the Drawhorn brothers. But when that Bull Grossman fellow killed Moe Cash and hurt Timberline like he done, that was the last straw."

"They're animals," Asa said. "Nothing but wild animals. I don't know what causes some people to turn mean, but I know the cure for it when they do." He patted the handle of his Whitney Eagle. "Rabid dogs and men like the Dolven gang have to be killed. I just wish there weren't so damn many out there like them."

"How is the lady—Timberline?" Cemetery John asked. "I reckon that's the only name I know her by."

The marshal turned to him. "Now that you brought up the matter, I can't say I've ever heard her called by anything else. Even Moe always called her Timberline." He sighed. "She's in bed resting. I think she'll be all right. Bull Grossman made a lot of bad bruises on her face and one eye's swole almost shut. I have a feeling that outlaw likely hurt her insides, but Timberline's too broken up over Moe bein' dead to complain any about herself."

Cemetery John motioned to the blanket-covered body that lay on blackened earth alongside the saloon. "Folks that were there tell me the little fella just went to protect his wife when that gunslinger hit her. He didn't even have a gun on him."

"We'll have to see he's buried quickly," Emil said. "The weather's too hot for him to keep without smellin' bad."

"From the looks of things, we'll have to do most of the digging." Cemetery John swept his arm around to indicate the ruined town. "Durn near everybody's gone, and I can't say I blame them any after the Dolven gang came through and bullied around what folks were here like they done."

"Those bastards are gonna pay for costing me my third of that two-thousand-dollar reward money," Emil Quackenbush fumed. "There ain't enough of those two heads left for even the devil to recognize. And I really have need of that seven hundred and fifty dollars nowadays."

Asa rolled his eyes toward the batwing doors of the saloon. "I need to talk with the lady, if she's able."

"Timberline's going to want us to go after the Dolvens for killing her husband. Whether or not she's fit won't matter much to her." Emil shrugged. "Let's go visit."

Four obviously drunken buffalo-hiders were the only customers inside the Cash Bar. One of them slammed down a shot of whiskey and staggered over to the marshal. "That plumb ain't right what that gunslinger done last night," the man's voice slurred. "Vern, Hank, Willie, an' me was there.

Not a one of us did nothin'. Hell, we ain't gunmen, but we shudda done somethin'."

The marshal shook his head sadly. "They would have killed you for sure. That Dolven bunch has no problem killing anyone, and they're damn good at it. You men have nothing to be sorry for."

The hider reached into his pocket and brought out a handful of silver coins that he handed to Emil. "This is all the money we got. Could you see to it that the lady Timberline gets it?"

"That's right decent of you men," Cemetery John said.

"Ain't no more'n right," the hider slurred. "We been drinkin' since last night without payin' for it."

"She's in the back room," the marshal said, motioning with his head. "They have their living quarters there."

The woman known as Timberline lay in a brass bed propped up high with feather pillows. There was a lone open window across from the foot of the bed. She kept her gaze focused on the charred remains of the town of Canan, ignoring the three men who she had invited in.

"Ma'am, uh, Missus Timberline." The marshal did not know how to approach the subject of the Dolvens. "I, uh, brought along Mr. Cain and his deputy . . . John. I reckon you remember them."

The lady remained silent as a stone.

Asa stepped close. He forced himself not to wince when he observed the patchwork of red and black bruises that covered her swollen face. There was no doubt in his mind that far worse damage was concealed beneath the white bedspread. "Ma'am, the Dolven gang killed some good friends of mine and kidnapped my mother and sister. I'm going to kill them for it. Now I'll be proud to kill them for what they did to your husband, too."

"Tell me what good that will do me, Mr. Cain." Her voice was emotionless, distant. Her gaze never faltered from the open window. "And while you're at it, tell me how many killings it takes to make up for my Moe's death and the end of my happiness."

"I can't do that, ma'am. I don't know the answer."

"I'm sorry, Mr. Cain." She rolled her head to face him. "I know you're just wanting to help. I'll tell you what I know. It was yesterday afternoon when they rode in. There were six of them, four men and two pretty women.

"The Dolvens have been through here before. They get meaner every time. Brock complained about having to ride cross-country and avoid the main roads to go anywhere now that the bounty's so big on them."

Cemetery John raised an eyebrow. "That explains why we didn't run square into each other. That would've been exciting."

Timberline continued in her monotone. "The trouble started when Brock found out that you, Mr. Cain, had been in town and just left that morning. That man's always been mean when he drinks, and nobody's ever seen him sober. This time he went crazy. He blamed the whole town of Canan for helping out his sworn enemy. That's when Old Man Dolven himself went down and set fire to the marshal's office. Then he told his men to help themselves to anything that caught their fancy, that the town owed it to him."

"And that included you," Emil said softly.

"Especially me. I would have done it. I didn't want them to kill anyone, and I knew they were building up to it. They were all drunk. Then that big fellow named Bull began hitting me. . . ."

Timberline choked back a racking sob. "Moe and me, we've been together for nearly twelve years. I wish Moe'd just let him slap me around. I've been beat up before, I would of healed. But he tried to protect me, and got killed for it."

"Ma'am," Asa said. "There's not one of us here that's not sorry for your terrible loss. I'm only afraid there may be other innocent folks gunned down by the Dolvens if we don't stop them. Can you remember anything that they might have said that will be of help?"

"Brock Dolven never shut up all the time I was there. He ranted about how much he hated you and how glad he was to have taken your family away from you for killing his son."

Asa sighed. "My mother, Jenny, and my sister, Sadie, are their prisoners."

Timberline blinked. "Those women didn't look to be anybody's prisoner. The young'un, she claimed to be married up with Brocks's boy, Link. They sure acted like they was still on their honeymoon. The older woman was with Brock, but mostly she sat by herself drinking whiskey. Come to think on it, she never even looked up from that whiskey bottle once, not even when Moe. . . ."

"Did they say where they were going?" Asa asked.

"Brock never tried to hide it any. That gang's

going to Wolf Springs to kill some sheriff friend of yours. He made it plain they're going to travel slow and lay over in Buffalo Gap."

Asa clenched his teeth and spun to face his friends. "We've got to be moving. This is the same story that outlaw told us. Brock Dolven is crazy enough to do just what he says. And there's only us to stop them."

Cemetery John said, "We rode all of last night. If you don't get some sleep, you'll doze off reaching for your gun."

"He's right," the marshal added. "We have to catch some sleep and eat something. Hell, it's cooler traveling at night anyway."

Timberline said, "There's a pot of beans on the cookstove out front. You can pitch your bedrolls on the floor. There's no other place left where you'll be out of the sun." She rolled her battered face to Cemetery John. "I would ask a favor of you."

"You just need to name it, ma'am."

"Folks say you're an undertaker. I want to give my Moe a good send-off, but I'm too stove up to do it. Would you see to it? I'll pay you. If we do the burying late today, you all can be on your way before dark."

Cemetery John let out a slight cough. "I'll take care of it, Missus Timberline, but I'm at a loss to where I'll find enough wood for a buryin' box. It's all pretty much got burnt up."

"Just wrap him up good in felt blankets. Ever preacher I run across always said it doesn't matter much what happens to the body once the good part's flown away, but I want to do right by Moe's remains."

"Yes, ma'am," Cemetery John said. "I'll see to him proper, but I'm not taking any pay."

Timberline nodded, and returned her gaze to the open window. After a few silent moments, the men went out and left her alone.

A fiery West Texas sun was dying bloodily in the west when Cemetery John patted the last shovelful of dry earth over Moe Cash's final resting place.

Timberline had somehow managed to get into a black dress and bonnet and make her way to the churchyard. The effort had tired her considerably, and she leaned heavily on the beefy Emil Quackenbush for support.

"I couldn't find a plank for a marker," Cemetery John said. "Even the ones that were already here got burned up when—them Indians set fire to the place."

"I know where he's buried. That's all I need." Timberline looked forlornly at the grave, then turned to the saloon. "That's strange, isn't it?"

"Ma'am?" Asa said.

"The fact that the saloon is the only building left standing. Moe and me built it ourselves. I'd venture we did a right fine job of it."

"Yes," Asa said. "I would say that's the truth." He gave her a worried glance. "Where will you be off to? I mean, once you're able to travel."

Timberline swept a glance over the motley few in attendance. There were no more than a dozen men. "These are my customers and the Cash Bar is my home. I know most folks are gonna move on, but this place was our dream, Moe and me. I plan to stay right here until I'm dead as my poor husband." She extended a hand toward the grave. "No matter what some folks thought about us, or the way we lived, I loved that man. I reckon that's reason enough to stay here with him."

Asa nodded to her, placed his hat on his head, and managed to choke out a hoarse, "Let's ride," to his companions.

In a short while the three men headed their horses south out of Canan, riding silently beneath the red canopy of a setting sun.

TWENTY-NINE

A few miles south of Canan, Emil Quackenbush broke the heavy silence. "That Timberline sure is a lady of convictions. There's a passel of Bible-thumpers out there who could learn a thing or two from her."

Cemetery John said, " 'Judge not, that ye not be judged' is a passage from the Good Book that I reckon must be the easiest one in there to miss. Leastwise, most folks manage to skip right over it with no problem."

Asa said, "When it comes time for Gabriel to blow his horn, I'm certain the majority of those sent to perdition will be downright shocked. A man who thinks he's got God's special favor is a man not to be trusted. I prefer to deal with—" He tensed and fixed his gaze on a small glowing blaze in the distant gathering shadows.

Cemetery John saw it the same time Asa did. He reined his horse to a stop, as did the others. "It's gotta be a campfire. And they likely had to pack in the wood. Dang near everything around here that could catch fire has already done been burnt."

"It could be the Dolvens," Asa cautioned. "I

would expect them to be further away, but it's what you *don't* expect that can kill you."

"There's where we cross the main stage road that runs from Fort Worth into New Mexico Territory," Emil said. "Some travelers have just made camp for the night is all. I swan, not everybody in West Texas is some bloodthirsty outlaw."

"In my experience," Asa said with a shrug, "it's a grand idea to treat them as if they were until you've known them and their entire family for a lot of years."

Emil eyed the distant campfire greedily. "I've been deprived of my coffee an' my supper. My guess is those nice folks yonder just might be in a sharing mood. I know I'm gonna ride over and check."

Cemetery John watched as the marshal spurred his horse and headed off by himself. He turned to Asa. "That man surely is a tad rash at times. The decision we need to make is whether or not it's wise to wait and see if somebody shoots him, or stay here and let him get first chance at anything to eat they might be offering."

Asa slid the Henry rifle from its scabbard and jacked the lever. "Let's follow that idiot and see what happens."

"I don't think the Dolvens will be traveling by wagon," Cemetery John said as they rode close to the camp. "Emil ain't gotten himself shot yet, and if my eyes don't deceive me, I think I see a woman in a dress."

Asa cautioned, "Remember, my mother and sister are with those outlaws."

"If I'm correct on the matter, that's why I came along with you in the first place. Wilburn thought my invaluable assistance might keep you alive. The way things are going, I could've stayed right there in Wolf Springs an' drank my hot chocolate and slept at night under—" A broad grin crossed his face. "Holy smoke, looky yonder, will wonders never cease?"

Asa surveyed the situation, lowered the hammer on his Henry, and returned it to its scabbard. He rode slowly into the camp and dismounted.

Billy Dixon greeted him with a smile and handshake. "Asa Cain, I never figgered on seein' you again, but it shore is a pleasure. Pick yourself out a soft rock to sit on and have a cup."

Asa looked across the flickering campfire at a surprisingly healthy Willow Olds. "Howdy, ma'am, good to see you up and about. You were a mighty sick lady for a while."

Willow smiled and poured a tin cup full of coffee from a blackened metal pot. "I owe the fact that I'm alive to you, Mr. Cain. Have some coffee and I'll fry up some bacon and heat a few biscuits. I'm quite sure you and your friends are starved." She glanced at Cemetery John, then turned to the marshal, who had yet to say a word. "And you, sir, I don't believe I've had the pleasure."

"My name, well, ma'am, my name's—Quackenbush—Emil Quackenbush. I'm, or rather I was, the marshal of Canan." He was so taken aback by the beautiful lady, he couldn't get his tongue to work correctly. "The town, ma'am, well, it got burnt right flat to the ground, all except the saloon, that is."

"Dang funny prairie fire," Billy Dixon said. "Looks like the thing got started not too far south of here."

"Indians set the whole country afire," Cemetery John said quickly. "Those savages do some right terrible things on occasion."

"When the war parties attacked Adobe Walls, they come in from further north." Dixon shrugged. "Oh, well, I sure piled some hurt on them redskins, didn't I, darlin'?"

"You certainly did, Billy," Willow cooed. She turned and faced Asa. "Billy and I are on our way East." She nodded toward the wagon. "Once Hibb is buried proper, we're going to be married."

Something caught in Emil's throat, and it took him several tries to clear it.

"By golly." Cemetery John slapped Billy Dixon on the shoulder. "I want to be the first one to congratulate you. Willow's the prettiest lady west of the Pecos."

"We're plannin' on living in that big city in Illinois called Chicago," Billy said. "Willow says there ain't no buffalo to speak of back there, but she wants us to open a tavern. I've been hankerin' for indoor work with no heavy lifting, so things should work out fine."

"I'm riding along with them as far as Fort Smith," George Maledon's unemotional voice intoned from beneath the wagon. "Judge Isaac Parker will hire me for a hangman. I can feel it in my bones."

Asa felt a cold shudder. He had put his guns away, and was enjoying a good cup of coffee and relaxing conversation among friends. All the while he had failed to notice the ominous George Maledon had been sitting underneath the wagon. He knew full well Maledon could have shot him through the heart and killed him before he even knew where the bullet had come from. Dumb luck, that was what the late Moe Cash had said. *Dumb luck.* Asa wondered deeply how long *any* kind of luck would last.

"George plain up an' saved our skins last night," Billy Dixon said. "We'd just made camp when these two fat old geezers came in acting nice and friendly-like. They pulled their guns on Willow an' me before we knew what was going on. George was sittin' where he is now, an' ventilated both of 'em good and proper." He cocked his head at Emil. "You say you're the marshal of Canan?"

"When there *was* a Canan, I was the law there."

"Would you take a gander at those two carcasses in the back of the wagon that're drawin' more flies than poor Hibb? I've got his box fairly well covered with salt, but there ain't none to spare, especially for worthless highwaymen. If'n there's no reward for 'em, I'll treat the buzzards."

Willow Olds went about cooking supper while the men lit a coal-oil lamp and walked to the wagon. Billy Dixon flipped back a canvas, sending a horde of flies buzzing off into the sultry night.

The open eyes of two nattily dressed, corpulent, gray-haired men stared up at the star-studded sky.

Cemetery John said, "It appears the brokerage firm of Mudgett and Woodhall is permanently out of business."

"You know these gents?" Billy Dixon asked him.

"Just a passing acquaintance." He pointed to the bullet hole in his hat. "I think I'm darn lucky those two couldn't shoot straight. They were a lot better at being actors. I really believed they were mining promoters. That's what they were passing themselves off as anyway."

"I swan," Dixon said. "You an' Asa can get into the darnedest scrapes." He grinned at the marshal. "But if these two had nothing at all to do with the gold-mining business, they've *got* to be wanted for something."

"Yep." Emil nodded and wrinkled his forehead in thought. "My flyers got burnt up along with my office and a new pair of handmade Mexican boots. I ain't certain on this, but if I recollect right, Mudgett pays three hundred, Woodhall ain't worth but a hundred. He was only wanted for skinnin' folks with counterfeit money. Mudgett did the shooting."

Billy Dixon chuckled, reached down, and grabbed up a handful of gold coins from an empty coffee can that was wedged between Woodhall's stiff legs. He laughed when he passed them around. "Twenty-dollar double eagles. The worst durn job of makin' money I ever saw. The blame things are even turning green. The biggest idiot in Texas would be too smart to be suckered into taking one of these for real."

Quackenbush studied one of the coins intently, then glared at Cemetery John, but said nothing.

"What of the whore who was traveling with them?" Asa asked. "Her name was Helen Pickman."

Billy and George both shook their heads.

"I saw no one other than these outlaws," Maledon said flatly. "I am glad she was not there. It would be undignified to shoot a woman. They deserve a decent hanging."

"Is she wanted for anything?" Dixon asked the marshal.

Emil shook his head, and turned to continue glaring at Cemetery John.

"Oh, well," Billy Dixon said happily. "For four hundred dollars, we'll put up with the stink and the flies." He flipped the wagon cover back into place. "Maledon's offered to split any bounty between us for givin' him a ride. The little darlin' an me can sure use that money." He motioned to the fire. "Let's go help rustle up some grub. I know my belly's rubbing on my backbone."

The three men rode south by moonlight beneath a jeweled Texas sky. It had been a sore temptation to spend the night with Billy Dixon's group, but when Asa mentioned the fact that they needed to be going, no one had voiced a word to the contrary.

"You know, Asa," Cemetery John said, keeping his eyes focused on the road looking for snakes. In his opinion diamondback rattlers loved to come out in the cool of night just to bite passing horses. "I'd say we're plenty lucky those two mining promoters, if that's what they really were, didn't shoot the both of us when they had the chance."

Dumb luck, Asa thought. *That's all I have keeping me alive these days.*

Emil Quackenbush shot a hard gaze at Cemetery John. "Those two outlaws must have bought that canful of counterfeit coins from the same place in Mexico where you got yours."

Asa ignored the marshal. "Mudgett and Woodhall were likely afraid of Indians after seeing what happened to that sheriff from Tascosa. The way I figure it, they thought a couple of extra guns were worth more to them than what money we had on us."

Cemetery John took a puff on his cigar. He had never smoked but a few long-nines before leaving on this trip. Nowadays, he was seldom without one. "Both of 'em sure looked harmless to me. They were simply not my idea of what killers look like. I even overlooked the fact that they missed my head by a few inches with a rifle ball." He glanced at Asa. "That whore's a mystery. I wonder what happened to her."

"We may never know," Asa said.

"If she was watching when her friends got filled full of holes by George Maledon," Cemetery John said, "we could start looking for her by checking out nuns that just recently got converted."

Emil spoke, his voice serious. "Asa, we're going to have to come up with a plan to take those Dolvens soon, or all three of us could catch a fatal dose of lead poisoning. I don't care to have that happen. Besides, if they kill us off, there won't be a soul left to help out those ladies. From what you told me, Governor Davis is determined to hang your mother. Our staying alive is likely all that stands in the way of that happening."

Cemetery John returned to keeping an eye out for rattlesnakes. "I was rather hoping we might come up with a better plan than simply riding up to the Dolvens and let 'em shoot us. For Wilburn Deevers' sake, I'd like to make our play before those outlaws get to Wolf Springs. He won't even know they're out to kill him until after he's plugged."

Asa kept his gaze on the black horizon. He realized he had been so filled with anger and concern for his family that he *hadn't* thought out what they would do once they caught up with the Dolven gang. Always before on a bounty hunt, he had carefully studied his prey from afar with a cold calculating eye. Emotions, he knew, had no place in a showdown. A man could not think objectively under those conditions. That was why a doctor never treated his own family. If Asa was going to get through this, he either had to place his feelings into a little-used room in his mind and slam the door closed, or turn the decision-making over to someone else. His judgment on the matter could be delayed no longer.

"I've mentioned before," Asa said, having difficulty keeping sadness from showing, "that I can't read sign like I used to. I love my mother and sister. And I hate the Dolvens with more of a raging hatred than any man should ever feel. Yet I'm the only one here who has years of experience at manhunts."

Emil nodded. "A small town marshal generally only shoots folks when they get to be a bother. Shucks, I reckon I've only done in six or eight." He cocked his head in thought. "Or maybe a few more than that. A couple of them managed to ride off after I put slugs in their hides, so I don't know if the bullets took or not."

"I prefer to get them already dead," Cemetery John said. "They're a lot less trouble that way."

"I think what you're saying"—Asa swallowed—"is that it's time for me to concentrate on killing the Dolvens and sort out my family problems later."

"That nail just got hit square on the head," Cemetery John said. "Emil and I will back your play when the time comes. It's just that we're getting plumb tuckered out. A person can't think good when they're tired out."

Emil said, "I agree with Cemetery John—surprisingly. When we come to any kind of decent place to camp, I say we stop, catch some sleep. When we're rested tomorrow, all of us'll work together and figure out a plan to make that twenty-five hundred dollars apiece." He smiled at Asa. "And keep those two little ladies safe at the same time."

"Then we've got ourselves a manhunt," Asa said. "I'll do my best to concentrate on killing the Dolvens. If I get off course, I expect you two to let me know."

"Oh, we will," Cemetery John said, watching a falling star burn itself out before hitting the ground. "We'll even shoot you, if that's what it takes to make you happy."

Asa acknowledged him with a stern nod, then returned to staring ahead into the bleakness.

Dumb luck, don't fail me now, kept repeating itself in his mind like a stuck player piano.

THIRTY

"A few hours of sleep sure does a body good," Cemetery John said while feeding wood to the crackling campfire. "And it's a real blessing to be in country where a person can find something to build a fire with. This pot of coffee will be boiling in no time."

Asa cast a nervous glance to the high sun, and fought back a nearly overpowering urge to pull out his pocket watch and check the time. He knew it must be mid-morning, but he didn't want the picture of his mother to stare back at him when he flipped open the cover.

Last night he had made a promise to his friends that he would force himself to slow down and formulate a plan to surprise the Dolven gang. In the brightness of day, after some refreshing sleep, he found it very hard to keep from saddling up and riding hard for Buffalo Gap, promise or not.

Emil came over packing a long-handled skillet along with a slab of very green bacon. "That sweet lady Missus Olds sure was nice to let us have some bacon and coffee. I reckon Billy Dixon's the luckiest man I ever met to be fixing to marry up with that pretty woman."

Cemetery John pulled a faggot from the fire, lit the stub of cigar between his lips, and frowned. "A couple of days ago, when I cooked up some of that same moldy bacon, you complained worse than a man getting lynched. I wouldn't suppose the fact that Willow Olds herself handed it to you made the difference?"

"Why, a little mold never hurts bacon any. I'll scrape off the hairy stuff with my knife. The rest will fry up and be right tasty." He grinned at Cemetery John. "I was simply funning with you before about green bacon. Like you did when you loaned me twenty counterfeit dollars to play poker with. I'm sure you recall doing that."

"Yep," Cemetery John said, turning his attention to the fire. "It aids a person's digestion to have a little fun once in a while. I'm glad you agree with that."

Asa grabbed up a stick and lifted the black metal coffeepot onto some blazing coals. A moment later the wonderful aroma of boiling coffee began floating in the still air.

Emil sliced off the thick pieces of bacon after making an attempt to remove at least some of the mold. He placed the strips into the skillet, and set it on two flat rocks that kept the pan just above the fire. The sweet smell of frying pork blended with the coffee.

Cemetery John set a dozen biscuits that Willow had baked only a couple of days ago on rocks next to the blaze to warm them. He smiled broadly when he used his knife to open a small tin of honey that would complete their morning feast.

The food was wolfed down with relish. Each man reserved one biscuit that had been sliced open, stuffed with bacon and hot grease, then wrapped in cloth.

Cemetery John, along with Asa, fired a cigar, while Emil whacked off a generous chuck of tobacco, which he poked into his mouth with obvious glee. There was no longer any cause to delay the conversation they each knew was coming.

"Last night"—the marshal wiped a trickle of tobacco away with the back of his hand—"we seemed to think we might be able to come up with a plan to kill the Dolvens along with Bull Grossman and rescue your kin while living to spend the bounty. I'm hankering to see if we can do it with the sun shining."

Asa took a puff on his cigar and leaned back. "What we do know is that Brock Dolven and his gang will be expecting us soon. It wasn't that far out to his ranch, and Brock likely didn't leave Klinkinbeard a gun because he wanted him to tell us what he did in case we showed up."

Emil gave an evil grin. "Old Man Dolven was sure right there. When we met that fellow, he was simply dying to be helpful."

A shadow of annoyance crossed Asa's face. "Brock let it be known that they were going to be in Buffalo Gap for a spell before heading on to Wolf Springs. There's a common truth to all outlaws, and that's that a person can't believe a single word they say."

"Then you're of a mind they're going straight to kill Wilburn." Cemetery John was obviously worried. "Dang, if that bunch rides hard, they'll get the job done before we can possibly make Wolf Springs."

Emil ran his fingers through his red beard.

"From what I've been told, Old Man Dolven is out for Asa's blood, not Sheriff Deevers'. That Brock is cunning as a weasel, and just as kind and considerate to boot. I've been through this country a few times, and know there's a stage stop with a sprout of a town built around it called Hackberry. It's about a day's ride from Buffalo Gap, which means we could be there by tonight."

"I'm betting on Dolven planning to ambush us out here in the middle of nowhere," said Asa. "That man's tolerable mean, but what he's got in mind to do to us can't abide an audience like he'd get in a town. Murder, especially the cold-blooded killing of two badge-wearing lawmen, will get him hung sooner or later. Even Brock can't be stupid enough not to know that. No," Asa decided, "it's almost certain they'll try to kill us where they stand a good chance of getting away with it."

"I'd really prefer it didn't come to that," Cemetery John said.

Asa studied the dying campfire. "This place called Hackberry. How many people live there, and is it on the road to Buffalo Gap?"

Emil spat a wad of tobacco juice at a passing tarantula. "I'd reckon the place is bigger than Canan these days. Thorn Hackberry runs the stage stop by himself. He ain't never took a bath in his entire life and is plumb proud of the fact, so he's not married. There's a general store and a saloon without any whores. Thinking on the matter, I recollect a livery stable and a few cabins rounded out the place. I'm guessing maybe a dozen folks call Hackberry home for some reason. Not a single female there to my recollection."

"The Dolven gang could kill every living soul

there," Asa said. "And most likely the Indians would catch the blame."

"Yep," Emil said, working up another wad of tobacco to spit at the spider, which had decided to hold its ground. "And to answer your question, Asa, Hackberry station is square in the middle of the road to Buffalo Gap."

Cemetery John grabbed the coffeepot, divided the dregs into three tin cups, and set it aside to cool. "It sounds reasonable that if we ride into Hackberry, we'll have more holes punched in our hides than the brokerage firm of Mudgett and Woodhall wound up suffering. I swan, that George Maledon sure don't value the cost of bullets. He put a good five slugs from each of those two guns he packs square into their tubby middles."

"We're also giving Brock Dolven sense enough to stage an ambush," Emil said. "It's possible he's not much smarter than a turkey."

"I'm betting he'll be there with his boys and that woman-beater Bull Grossman," Asa said firmly. "They'll be at the north end of town just waiting for us to ride in and let them shoot us to pieces. I feel for certain that this showdown will happen there."

"Then I'd say we circle the place and head in from the south, where they ain't looking for us." Cemetery John reached down to the huge tarantula and slid his hand underneath the spider. "And if'n we show up early in the morning, we might even get lucky and catch 'em in the outhouse. Folks plan on one thing, and then something different happens to throw them for a loop.

"Take this tarantula, for example." He held the huge spider to his face and stroked its back with his free hand. "They look mean, and most folks think they're deadly, but they're not. Even if a person does manage to provoke them to bite, it's not as painful as a red ant." He lowered the spider to the ground and gently brushed it from his hand.

The marshal eyed the tarantula skeptically. He was not at all convinced that anything that ugly could be harmless. "I say we play these cards. I also think it might be a great idea to tie the horses some distance away and sneak in on foot. There's maybe some big sagebrush that'll give us some cover. Danged if I ever paid any attention to that detail before. Generally, Hackberry is one of those places that don't leave much of an impression."

Cemetery John grabbed up the coffeepot as he stood. "If this fellow Thorn Hackberry's never took a bath, *that* would make an impression. Well, I'm for heading south of Hackberry and making an early camp. A solid night's sleep won't do us one whit of damage. I agree those Dolvens are most likely there, but killing outlaws is tiresome work. Starting the task well rested would be a good idea."

Asa nodded in agreement. "Let's saddle up and head out. I'm more than ready to ask those Dolvens a few questions before they're no longer in any condition to answer them."

"From the looks of all those buzzards, something has turned up dead." Emil Quackenbush pointed to a heavy spiral of black birds riding the torpid air currents of mid-afternoon. "Anyway, whatever it was appears to have been courteous enough to croak close to the road."

Asa squinted through the wavering heat waves rising from the monotonous drabness of the Staked Plains. "How much farther is the town of Hackberry?"

Emil chuckled. "Once you set eyes on the place, you'll never sully the word 'town' again by using it on Hackberry. I've done told you, Ole Thorn, who started the stage stop, is plumb proud of the fact that he's never had a bath for forty years. From that glorious beginning, the whole place sorta lost its appeal and went downhill. But to answer your question, it's a good hour's ride from here. Those buzzards ain't being drawn by Hackberry. Buzzards have better class than to circle that joint. Thorn's too gamy to even draw flies."

"Whatever it is," Cemetery John said, "we need to check it out even if it is a deer that died of old age. That gang we're chasing through here might have decided to leave us a message."

Asa winced, causing Cemetery John to realize he had said a lot more than was necessary.

Emil read the desperation in his friend's eyes, and said to Asa, "Take it easy. It's too blasted hot out here for us to go charging off. We'll be to where those vultures are dining soon enough. It might be a good idea to use that spyglass when we get closer. I know we have good plans to ambush the Dolvens in the morning. It would just be a touchy situation to find out they had the idea first."

Cemetery John pulled the big ten-gauge shotgun from its scabbard. "I suggest we ride well apart from each other. That way, if it turns out to be an ambush, maybe one of us will be lucky enough to only get shot a *few* times."

"That's what I admire about you," Emil said to Cemetery John. "You're always such a cheerful cuss."

Asa slid the brass telescope closed and turned to Cemetery John with a rare grin on his face. "You can relax, it's not the Dolvens. But I will venture that that whore who took such a liking to you not long ago will be right happy to see you again. Helen Pickman is standing alongside the road leaning on a stick of wood."

Emil asked, "This whore, she's the one who was with Mudgett and Woodhall?"

"One and the same," Asa said. "I don't think she's smart enough to be dangerous."

"If she took a fancy to Cemetery John," Emil said, "I'd say we're plumb safe to put our guns away and ride over and see what the lady's problem is."

"Well, howdy, boys." Helen gave a snaggle-tooth smile. "I'm sure glad to see you fellows. I ain't had a drink of water for so long I can't even whistle."

Asa hopped down and brought over a canteen. He noticed her left ankle was badly swollen. "What happened to your leg?"

She nodded toward a clump of greasewood where some vultures were circling. "That jughead horse of mine stepped in a gopher hole or somethin'. I got tossed off an' kinda landed wrong. That durn ankle of mine snapped like a broke twig. The thing hurts like the blazes." Helen took a huge drink of water. "I was beginning to think nobody was ever gonna come by an' help li'l ole me."

Emil rode the short distance over to the dead horse. "How did you get the saddle off, ma'am?" he yelled back. "I don't even see the gun you shot it with."

"I didn't shoot the horse," Helen said, shaking her head. "That was them bastards that come along an' stole my saddle, my gun, an' supplies. I thought for certain they was going to ravish me, then kill me. But one of the pretty ladies with 'em talked the old man who led the gang out of it. He snorted and said I was too ugly to warrant a killin', but then he went and shot my horse 'cause he couldn't stand to see it suffer. That was one mean bunch of *hombres* to even steal my water."

Asa paled. "The lady who saved you life, did anyone mention her name?"

"The old man with her was named Brock Dolven. When he talked to the lady, if I recollect correctly, he called her Jenny."

Cemetery John cocked his head at Emil. "See what I was telling you earlier? Traveling with Asa Cain is anything but boring."

THIRTY-ONE

"Hold on to her real tight," Asa said to Emil and Cemetery John, who had grabbed Helen Pickman's arms. "I'm going to have to set and splint this ankle or it'll never heal right. The lower leg bone feels broken. If a sharp piece of bone pokes through the skin, it could cause an infection. I can't allow that to happen."

"Do what you gotta," Helen said. "No matter how much you twist the thing around, it can't hurt any worse than it does now." She batted her green eyes at Asa. "Are you sure none of you nice fellows don't have any whiskey? I could use a swallow powerful bad right about now."

"Sorry," Asa said. "We don't have even a flask. All I can do is offer you a bullet to bite down on."

"If that's the best you can do, lover, set that blasted leg of mine, then we can get to someplace decent where there's a jug."

Asa nodded to his friends. He took the woman's foot in his hands and carefully moved it from side to side. Then, he gave a quick pull that elicited a loud scream of pain.

"That should have done it," Asa said. "I'll use some sticks of greasewood to splint her leg with, and tie them together"—he motioned to his horse—"with some of that rope in my saddlebags."

Emil shrugged his shoulders. "I'll go fetch it. The lady's plumb gone and passed out on us."

Asa glanced up to verify Helen Pickman had indeed lost consciousness. "It's better this way. When I cut her boot off she kicked me worse than a mule. After she comes to, there's nothing to be done but wait for the bones to knit."

"If you haven't noticed, it's getting late," Cemetery John said, gently lowering Helen to the earth. "If I'm correct in my arithmetic—and I'm darn well better at cipherin' than a certain marshal I won't name—I count three horses and four of us."

"There's no choice but to take her along with us." Asa turned to take the hemp rope Emil had brought. "I've been thinking. The outlaws we're after would expect us to stop and help this woman. I'm betting that's why Brock didn't argue when my mother spoke against them killing her. What I can't figure is why. I'm under the impression that the Dolvens are anxious to meet up with us—"

Asa's words died on his lips. A feeling of fear and dread trickled down his spine. On a small distant knoll to the east, sunlight glinting off steel had caught his eye. "Emil, I want you to go back to my horse and grab the Henry. Stay to the west and use the horse for a shield. We've got company about five hundred yards ahead."

Emil nodded, and strode off as if he hadn't a hurry in the world.

Cemetery John hunkered down, keeping himself close to the woman. "Dang it, Asa, I should have figured on something low-down like this happening. Shooting us while we're trying to help out a hurt woman sounds like something the Dolvens would go out of their way to do."

Asa turned to check Emil's progress. The marshal had slid the rifle from its scabbard, and was reaching for the ammunition in the saddlebag when a heavy slug of lead slammed into the horse's shoulder, nearly knocking the hapless animal on top of Quackenbush.

"Damn outlaws," Emil growled, diving to escape the falling horse. He landed on his knees, and was shuffling toward Asa when the distant rifle boomed once again. "I'm really beginning to hate this job."

Cemetery John turned to his roan in time to see a spray of crimson erupt from the horse's belly.

Another crack of the rifle, and Asa's Appaloosa lay kicking its life away in a clump of prickly pear cactus.

"They're not even aiming for us," Cemetery John said.

"We're too far away for them to be accurate," Asa said, scooting over to take the Henry from Emil. "It would be a miracle to hit one of us from that distance. A horse makes a bigger target."

"I sure wish Billy Dixon was here." Cemetery John grabbed up the ten-gauge that he thankfully had not returned to its scabbard. "He could knock off those darn horse killers without even having to squint."

Asa grabbed the rifle. "I'm going to make for

my horse when she quits kicking around. The telescope is in the left saddlebag. If we're just a tad lucky it won't be broken. There's also a little surprise in that bag for whoever's shooting at us, if I can just get to it."

Helen Pickman gave a pitiful groan and attempted to sit up.

"Well, this just keeps getting better and better," Cemetery John said as he threw an arm around the injured lady and brought her to the safety of low ground.

"Hold her still," Asa yelled. "I haven't immobilized that fractured fibula yet. If she thrashes around before I do, it could be bad."

"I thought it was her leg that got busted," Emil said.

Helen Pickman's eyes fluttered open. She looked up at Cemetery John, who was cradling her in his arms. "Lover," she mumbled, "my leg hurts too bad to do anything now. Come see me later, after I get some whiskey."

"Ma'am," Emil said, worming his way over. "The same bunch of outlaws that stole your water and supplies are out there taking potshots at us. While you were napping, they shot all of our horses. We're sort of pinned down here. It'd be right smart of you to lay still."

"I can do that—"

A slug of lead hammered into Emil's dead mount.

"The idiots are trying to kill a dead horse," the marshal yelled.

"No, that's not it at all," Cemetery John said while desperately looking around for a depression in the ground or anything that might offer more cover. "This is just what Billy Dixon did back at Adobe Walls, whoever is out there is simply sighting in his rifle before he starts sending bullets at us."

"They sure managed to put us afoot," Asa said. "That was a wise move on their part. I should have seen it coming."

"Don't go blaming yourself for this slipup," Emil said. "I reckon we all got caught in the outhouse, so to speak, instead of us catching the Dolvens there. Damn, I hate it when I run across thinkin' outlaws. Most of 'em are too dumb to pour sand out of their boots. Anyway, we're here together and bad luck's being plastered on us with a trowel."

"That horse of mine's quit kicking." Asa motioned to the Appaloosa lying against a mound of cactus. "At least the saddlebag I need is on the up side. There's no choice but to get cactus in my hide." He scooted over and handed the Henry to Emil. "Lay three shots—no more—at their position to cover me while I'm in the open."

The marshal jacked the lever on the rifle, aimed at the distant knoll, and fired.

"I expected you to wait!" Asa exclaimed.

Emil snorted. "Well, quit lollygagging."

Asa gave a scowl, then bolted into a crouch and ran for the horse, which was a solid hundred feet away. He felt a rush of air whistle by his ear, and saw the blast of dirt from the bullet striking the earth before he heard the report. The sniper had missed him by only a couple of feet.

Emil grinned, spat a wad of tobacco juice, and

sighted in on the puff of white smoke from the distant rifle. "Keep your head up, you polecat." He fired, jacked the lever, and sent another slug screaming across the plain. "I hope like heck I got lucky."

Ignoring the pain of dozens of sharp cactus spines, Asa flattened himself out alongside the horse. He knew there was no time to search through the saddlebag. Besides prickly pear cactus and a dead horse, there was not even a bush to offer cover for fifty feet in any direction. At least the greasewood was fairly thick where his companions were holed up. He took his knife and sliced away the strap holding the leather bag. When he turned to bolt and run back to his friends, another bullet slammed into the carcass of the Appaloosa, missing him by mere inches.

"You low-life scallywag," Emil yelled at the top of his lungs. Then he began firing the Henry at the sniper as fast as he could send the bullets flying.

Asa used the fusillade to dash to where Emil had taken shelter behind his own dead horse.

"Blast you," Asa growled, diving to the ground beside the marshal. "I told you to only shoot three rounds. We need to save our ammo!"

"Well, he got me mad." Emil stopped firing and sat down. He handed Asa the still-smoking Henry. "Folks shouldn't do that. I sorta have a quick temper."

"We never noticed." Asa jacked the Henry open. "At least there's one shell left. I suppose it would be a good idea to make it count."

"What are you waitin' for, the second coming?" Helen Pickman yelled from behind a clump of greasewood where Cemetery John had dragged her. "Kill those sons of guns so we can go get us some whiskey!"

Cemetery John hollered, "I think the lady really *needs* a drink. She's going to be grabbing at bugs that ain't there and seeing spooks right shortly. I've seen too many folks with the delirium tremens to be mistaken."

Asa took a deep breath. From inside the saddlebag he fished out the telescope along with a small leather pouch.

Emil Quackenbush eyed the bag. "You mentioned earlier that you had a surprise for who's all out there. I'd feel a lot better about things if you'd go and spring it on 'em."

Asa glared at the marshal. "I was planning to have more than one shell left to do it with. Three shots—I distinctly remember telling you not to shoot over three times at them."

Emil looked hurt. "Well, I was only trying to keep you from getting plugged. If you look at it like that, I done good. At least you're not bleeding from anywhere except where you stuck cactus in your own hide."

Very slowly and deliberately, Asa removed the brass telescope from its case and inspected it. "At least the thing's not been bent or broken." He slid the spyglass open and rested it on the carcass. Carefully, he stuck his head up to focus. A heavy-caliber slug whistled over the top of his head, urging him back down beside the marshal. "A few shells left in this rifle would have given whoever's shooting at us good reason to stay down for a few minutes."

"You like to complain more'n any man I ever

knowed." Emil reached into the pocket of his shirt. "Here, I had these in my hand when they shot my horse. I was so worked up, I reckon I plumb forgot about having 'em."

Asa stared unbelievingly at the dozen brass .44-caliber rimfire cartridges. "These will be a big help, Emil. I'm really glad you're getting over being upset."

The marshal ignored Asa's sarcasm, and watched with great interest as the bounty hunter shook open the leather pouch. He methodically laid the small metal brackets and screws out on the dry ground.

Quackenbush grinned broadly. "You've got a mount to put that spyglass on your rifle. I seen that done some by snipers during the war. It never seemed fair to me, to kill a man that way. But right now my thinking has come around. Shoot the bastard."

"Whooskey! I need a drink of *whooskey!*" Helen's squalling was beginning to sound more desperate.

Asa hollered, "Cemetery, don't let her thrash around any. I haven't gotten that leg of hers splinted yet."

"I'm doing my best. But this woman's strong enough to knock crap out of a marble statue. To top off the situation, she's getting the deliriums so blame bad, she don't know the difference between an ambush or a chamber pot."

Emil Quackenbush sighed and turned to Asa. "I'll loan you my knife to turn those little screws with. There's some folks out there that really need killin' and I'm of the opinion the quicker it's done, the better."

"Let's fasten this spyglass," Asa said, grabbing up the brackets. "Daylight's wasting."

A few minutes later, Asa was adjusting and focusing the telescope sight on a distant lone mesquite tree.

"I had an X engraved in the front lens," he said to Emil. "When I sighted it in at Adobe Walls, the bullet pulled about a foot to the left at five hundred yards. I'd estimate the sniper to be about that far away, wouldn't you?"

The marshal kept flat to the ground. "That's exactly how far away he is. You can trust me on this."

Asa slid the rifle along his body, opened the muzzle end, and inserted all twelve cartridges. "I sure hope we get lucky. And my mother's not there with them."

Emil said nothing. Asa stuck the Henry over the body of the horse, jacked the lever, and quickly sent four slugs flying. Using the cloud of smoke as a shield, he levered in a fresh cartridge, raised up, and pressed an eye to the end of the telescope.

"I can see him," Asa's voice was tense. "He's looking straight at me—"

The Henry boomed once again.

"Damn," Asa swore.

"Don't get discouraged," Emil said. "Try another shot or two."

"Oh, I hit the gunman dead center. What I don't see is another living soul moving about over there." Asa moved the telescope and scoured the barren landscape. "There's no doubt about it, there was only one gunman. I can see his horse tied to a mesquite tree."

"Whooskey!" Helen Pickman screamed at the top of her lungs, "I need whooskey!"

Emil sat up and craned his neck. "Let's go see who got killed an' grab that horse. I've a feeling it's gonna come in mighty handy."

THIRTY-TWO

Asa glared down at the blood-splattered corpse. "Blast it all, this isn't one of the Dolvens. It has to be Bull Grossman."

Emil nodded sadly. "And he's the only one of that gang who's worthless dead or alive. The son of a bitch killed my good horse, and now this. I am getting really upset at Brock Dolven."

"Whoooosky," Helen Pickman wailed. "The snakes are everywhere! Everywhere!"

Cemetery John had carried her along to keep her from crawling off. An idea lit up his eyes like the morning sun. He carefully set the injured woman leaning against a bush, and traipsed over to the dead outlaw's horse, which was munching away on a clump of dead-looking grass. A moment after pawing through a saddlebag, his goal was realized.

"I've got a full bottle of Old Gideon here," Cemetery John announced happily. "For a woman-beater, Bull Grossman had surprising good taste in whiskey. Reckon it don't matter, because even rot-gut will chase away that whore's spooks and make her become a lot easier to put up with."

"Give her a healthy slug," Asa said, walking

over. He turned to Emil. "If you'll cut a few grease-wood sticks about a couple of feet long, I'll finally get around to splinting that leg." He winced. "Then, I'm going to take the time to pick about a thousand cactus stickers out of my skin before it gets dark. Blast, these things hurt."

"Take it easy, ma'am." Cemetery John had to jerk the whiskey bottle away to keep her from drinking it dry. "We best save some for later."

"Snakes!" Helen wailed. "There's rattlers ever where I look. I need *whoooskey!*"

"Let's get that leg splinted before she does something to hurt it worse." Asa walked over and gingerly knelt by the yelling woman. "It'll take a while for it to work, but that whiskey will have her close to normal by later tonight. We're lucky that Bull Grossman was a drinking man." He turned to Emil. "Where's the rope?"

"I sorta forgot to bring it along. I'll go get it and whack off those sticks you need on the way back."

"In the meanwhile, I'll start us a nice big camp-fire," Cemetery John said with a humorless grin. "We've got a lengthy walk ahead of us tomorrow, but we can feast tonight. As long as a person has a hankering for roasted horsemeat, they can digest all they can hold."

"We're all mighty pleased to see you feeling bet-ter this morning, ma'am." Cemetery John was leading Bull Grossman's horse with Helen Pick-man sitting straight in the saddle. Earlier she had realized begging for more whiskey would be to no avail, so she had taken to brooding. "Suffering with the deliriums along with getting robbed and having your leg busted is piling on the agony."

Helen glanced at Asa and the marshal, who were walking ahead as they trekked along the dusty lonesome road. "I've kinda been battlin' both men and the bottle most of my life. Being a whore, men are always offering to buy me drinks. It don't cause no bother until the jug runs dry."

Cemetery John nodded, keeping his gaze on the horizon. "We'll be at a little town called Hackberry in a few hours. Those remaining outlaws you met are going to be there too, most likely. Once we're done killing them, I believe the marshal mentioned there was a saloon in town. I reckon that oughtta improve your spirits a tad."

"Don't go and tarry about the killing part. My constitution craves a couple of bottles a day to keep them damn spooks where they ain't a bother." Her tone softened. "I do want to thank you boys for taking care of li'l ole me. I'll give each one of you a free poke once things get settled down."

"You just concentrate on getting well, ma'am."

"I thought I was gonna be able to quit whoring when I run into Webster Mudgett an' his friend. They claimed to be rich, but I wound up paying for most of that slow trip to Colorado. Those two kept running into folks they said owed 'em money and shootin' 'em. I was beginning to wonder if they were being honest with me when I came walking back into camp and overheard 'em talking about killing li'l ole me. I grabbed my horse and rode away."

"That was good thinking, ma'am. Those two were simply robbers who got put out of commission by Judge Colt a couple of days ago. If you'd been along, I'm afraid folks might've thought you were involved and shot you too."

"Glad to here those scallywags got plugged. Good riddance to bad rubbish. Here I went an' trusted the likes of them. At least I'll get even with 'em and get paid well for puttin' up with crooks and liars."

"And how's that, ma'am? The last time I saw 'em they were plenty dead."

Helen Pickman's voice rang happy. "In my other boot, the one your friend didn't slice off, I got that certificate for five hundred shares of valuable gold minin' stock. It sure is pretty too, all engraved with gold and silver. It's gotta be worth a real big bunch of money when I cash it in."

Cemetery John had to swallow before answering. "Yes, ma'am, I'm sure it'll turn out to be more than what you're expecting."

Asa and Emil stopped, laid the saddles and gear they had been carrying on the ground, and waited for Cemetery John to catch up to them.

"Towns and water holes are generally scarce in West Texas," Emil wheezed. "But when a person's afoot, they seem downright rare. Hackberry's a good five miles from here, it's hotter than a stump preacher's threat, we're near out of water, and to trowel on some more torment, I've gone and lost the heel off my boot."

"I'm glad to hear you're beginning to appreciate the joys of being a bounty hunter." Asa stretched his back and looked ahead along the narrow ribbon of dirt that disappeared into the shimmering tawny horizon. "I thought someone would have been along by now. After all, this is a stage road."

Cemetery John said, "That Indian uprising likely slowed folks from moving around. But I did figure on maybe running into some cavalry. Right about now, I'd like anybody to come along that had some water to spare."

"And whiskey," Helen Pickman added quickly. "I'm gonna need some real soon."

"That too, ma'am," Cemetery John said, looking back at her. "We're all hoping for you to get another bottle."

"We can't just walk into Hackberry," Asa said. "My guess is when Bull Grossman didn't come riding back last night, the Dolvens are going to be expecting us to show up."

Emil grabbed up his canteen and shook it. "The nearest water is Hackberry. If we ration out what we have, we'll be darn thirsty come tomorrow, but I reckon there ain't much other choice unless—"

"Asa," Cemetery John called out, "take that spyglass of yours and check our back trail. If my eyes aren't deceiving me, there's a cloud of dust heading our way."

Last night, by the flickering light of the campfire, Asa had removed the telescope from the Henry rifle and stowed it into his saddlebag. By the time he had it out and ready to focus, everyone could make out a Concord stagecoach headed their way.

"Well, this day certainly is looking better," the marshal said. He cast a quick glance at the fiery sun, then sized up its position compared to the horizon. "Not only is the Wheeler and Hawkins

Line still in operation, ol' Homer's close to being on time."

Asa fixed the glass on the approaching stage. He immediately recognized the beanpole-thin driver as the man Cemetery John and he had met in Buffalo Gap. He also remembered the pretty blond girl with an arrow through her throat who had been leaning out an open window. The shotgun guard looked familiar. Asa could not place who the man was, but he had certainly met him before. This was of no matter. The stage would be up to their position within minutes. He slid the telescope closed and replaced it in his saddlebag.

"Hold up there, you damn mules," the skinny man yelled at the six mules pulling the coach, spraying the behinds of the closest pair with a shower of tobacco juice. "Hold up when I tell you or I'll trade you for horses."

The stage squeaked to a dusty stop alongside the assemblage. Homer Penbrook looked down from the driver's seat and surveyed Emil and Asa with a jaundiced eye. Then he fixed his gaze on Helen Pickman. "Howdy there, ma'am." He tipped his hat. "I surely never expected to find a lady of your quality travelin' along with such riff-raff."

"Good to see you again too," Emil Quackenbush grumbled while wearing a grin. "Homer, if you weren't so plug-ugly and dumber than a rock fence, I'd introduce you as my friend. It's just that I have a reputation to uphold."

"Don't need no formalities, Quacky." The driver motioned to the guard by his side. "I've done met Asa Cain an' Cemetery John back in Buffalo Gap. The shotgun guard here's a new hand. This is Reverend Jedediah Green. He may well be the first sky pilot you'll ever run across with a real job." He smiled at Helen. "Ma'am, my name's Homer Penbrook an' I'm at your service."

"*Quacky,*" Cemetery John chortled, his face alight. "They call you Quacky?"

"I've called him that for years," Homer said. "Chaffs his rear end somethin' fierce. I really enjoy spreadin' that about too."

"Those Indians surely missed a great opportunity for a scalp." The marshal's smile fled. "I reckon you noticed where that little ruckus happened yesterday."

"Buzzards were thicker than fleas on a jackrabbit. Four dead horses an' one feller with his eyeballs pecked out and most of his face eat off." The driver nodded at Helen. "Sorry about bein' so frank, ma'am. But I know the marshal won't figger out what I'm talking about if'n I beat around the bush any."

"You seem like such a sweet man," Helen said, peering inside the stage. "I don't see a solitary soul inside there."

"It's the Indians," Jedediah Green said. "That's why I got the job. The regular guard was afraid to come to this country anymore."

Homer Penbrook spat another wad of tobacco on a mule's behind. "Mail contracts the only reason we're runnin'. Passengers are too skeert to travel. I still figger on runnin' into some wild Injuns. They plumb burnt the whole town of Canan."

Cemetery John growled, "Those savages got their comeuppance in Adobe Walls. Billy Dixon used his Sharps rifle to blow Lame Bear and Moon

Fox right outta their moccasins from a mile away. That'll teach 'em to burn up a decent town."

"I heard it was from two miles away," Homer said, bringing out a twist of tobacco, whacking off a huge chunk, and poking it into his mouth. "No never mind 'cause we ain't runnin' there no more. Not much reason to stop in Canan anymore either. I'll miss seein' that Timberline. She was a real good whore." He nodded at Helen. "Excuse me, ma'am. I was just gonna say that Missus Timberline sorta filled us in last night on what was goin' on with that Dolven gang. It weren't no real surprise to run across y'all."

"I stayed with the stage while you went inside," Jedediah Green said, glaring daggers at Homer.

Asa stepped close and looked up at the guard. "I can't say I've ever known of a preacher doing your job."

"I can see no conflict, my good sir. Some souls simply need to be sent back to their maker sooner than others." He patted the huge eight-gauge shotgun. "If they mess with this stage, I'll send them straight to judgment without tarry."

Homer Penbrook looked over at Helen's splinted ankle. "You'd best ride with us, little lady. There's a real doc in Fort Worth. I'll be glad to take you along. No charge."

"If you've got some whiskey, lover," Helen cooed. "The trip will be a lot more pleasurable than usual. I guarantee it."

The Reverend Green had something lodge in his throat that took a long time to cough out.

"Mr. Penbrook," Asa said, "you mentioned that you were told of the Dolven gang and why we're after them."

"Timberline said you were after 'em for burnin' your ranch an' kidnappin' your ma an' sister. That sounds like a tolerable good reason to me. I hope you'll tell me that feller back there feedin' the buzzards was Bull Grossman. He really beat poor Timberline bad, not to mention killin' Moe like he done."

"That was Bull Grossman."

"He was the only one of the bunch that was worthless either dead or alive," Emil complained.

"Even sinners deserve to be buried," Jedediah Green stated.

Cemetery John snorted. "That outlaw shot all of our horses and then was fixing to plug us. This dirt up here's harder than the hubs of hell, even if a man was to have a pick and shovel, which we don't—"

Homer held up his hand. "The reverend needs a little time to get used to how we do things on the trail. He'll either learn or I'll shoot him." The driver spat more tobacco. "The choice is his."

"Mr. Penbrook," Asa began.

"Dad gum it, you're thick as a brick between the ears, bounty hunter. I've tol' you an' tol' you until I'm blue in the face, my name's Homer. Here I am with no passengers, a preacher—a teetotalin' preacher no less, an' now I get myself addressed like I'm some skunk of a politician."

Asa smiled. "Homer, the Dolvens planned on Bull Grossman killing us. We have every good reason to believe they're waiting for us in Hackberry. I'm certain my mother and sister will be there too. If you're willing to help us out, I'll pay you my share of the reward money. That will be twenty-five hundred dollars."

Homer Penbrook cocked his head in thought for several minutes. "Well, let me think. Wheeler an' Hawkins pays me fifty dollars a month. Now that comes to right about five hundred dollars a year. I reckon if this job takes less'n five years to do, I'll come out ahead."

Cemetery John kicked a pebble and watched it roll down the road. "I'll swan." He couldn't contain a laugh any longer. "Quacky and you must've gone to the same school."

Penbrook shrugged his shoulders. "Nope, can't say as we did." He looked over at Asa. "Well, spell out your plan, sonny boy. If it looks like I might live through it, count me in."

"What about me?" the reverend whined. "I've got the shotgun and I should get paid same as everyone else for killing outlaws."

"Reckon that's fair," Homer said. "The Good Book's real specific on that point. Ten percent'll be your cut, just like God ordered preachers to get paid. Now shut your tater trap an' let Asa Cain lay out his plan."

THIRTY-THREE

The Staked Plains were being baked by a merciless sun hanging high in a cloudless sky when the Wheeler and Hawkins Concord stagecoach groaned to a stop in front of the Hackberry station.

Homer Penbrook set the brake lever tight, locked it in place, and joined the shotgun guard in holding on to his hat with both hands and bending over with closed eyes to allow the zephyr-driven cloud of gray dust to blow past.

"Yer late as usual," the grating voice of Thorn Hackberry boomed through the maelstrom. "I ain't got yer mules even caught, let alone grained an' ready to harness."

The driver waited until the dirt had settled. He wiped his eyes and turned to the stationmaster. "You know, Thorn, I always enjoy stoppin' here. That warm friendly attitude of yours coupled with good service an' sweet hospitality makes me think that if you were a woman, I'd marry you."

Thorn Hackberry cocked his head in puzzlement. He couldn't decide if he had been insulted or complimented. Homer Penbrook always did that to him. He bit off a chew of tobacco to help himself think. Rivulets of brown tobacco juice trickled down his long gray beard to dry and join years of spittle, which had eventually hardened and caused his whiskers to take on the consistency of tree bark. He was supposedly the fattest man in West Texas. Most guessed his weight at over four hundred pounds. Aside from never bathing and being so heavy, Thorn was also noted for having the disposition of a grizzly bear with an aching tooth.

"It'll take me a spell to cut out six mules, grain 'em, an' harness 'em," Thorn grumbled. "Damn Wheeler an' Hawkins don't pay me near enough to put up with the crap of stagecoaches showin' up at all hours expectin' me to be Johnny-on-the-spot."

"Why, the whole darn stage line would go broke without you," Penbrook said, climbing down from the driver's seat, grinning happily. "For three whole years I've been telling every person who'd listen that if they wanted to know how a stage stop should be run, for 'em to go to Hackberry, Texas, and see how Thorn does the job."

Thorn snorted. "It'll still take me a good spell of time to get you on yer way."

"Why, that's fine," Penbrook said as Jedediah Green came to his side, packing the eight-gauge in the crook of his arm. "We're gonna rest up a spell. I need to wash some of this sand outta my craw. Come to think on the matter, I've never set foot inside the saloon here. Then my new guard an' me'll let you favor us with one of your delicious meals before we leave. There ain't a single hurry to cause you a dither."

"I'll get on it," Thorn said, "but I really don't think this is a good time to visit the saloon."

"Why would that be?" Homer asked pleasantly. "I hope it doesn't have anything to do with all those dead folks and horses we passed a few miles out. Those people were shot with regular lead bullets. Jedediah here an' me plumb relaxed when there weren't no arrows sticking out of any of 'em."

"We took it as a falling-out between thieves," Green said, "and none of our affair. The vultures had their faces pecked clean to the bone so we couldn't tell who it was."

"How many dead people did you find back there, driver?" a voice hissed from the shadows alongside the station.

Jedediah Green's knuckles grew white gripping his shotgun tight.

Homer kept his smile and turned to face the lanky, beardless man with silver hair spilling from underneath a black derby hat. The stranger wore two pistols, a rare sight. Both guns were worn low, and the tips of the holsters were tied tight with leather straps. From the easy way the man walked, holding his hands palm-open facing the ivory grips of the matching Colts, it was obvious he was an experienced gunman.

"There was five of 'em, friend," Homer said in an amiable tone. "Along with five horses. That feast sure drew in a passel of buzzards."

"I'm sure it did." The gunfighter fixed Homer and the guard with his unblinking gray eyes. "Name's Dolven, Brock Dolven. My boys and some friends are over at the saloon." He nodded at Thorn Hackberry, keeping the duo fixed in his gaze. "When that wagonful of lard told you fellows not to go to the saloon, he was referring to us being there. Weren't you, Fats?"

"I didn't mean nothin', Mr. Dolven, sir." Sweat beads formed on Thorn's brow. "I was simply tryin' to keep these folks from botherin' you's all."

"I'm *certain* that was your intent." Brock Dolven turned slightly to face the Reverend Green square on. "Guns make me nervous. If you'll take that shotgun you're so proud of and give it to me, using one hand only, there's a reasonable chance that you might live past the next ten seconds."

Green glared at the gunman and showed no sign of giving over his weapon. "Are you robbing this stage?"

"No," Brock said icily. "If what you told the stationmaster about finding those bodies checks out the way I expect it may, we'll be moving on. But you're down to three seconds on handing over that scattergun."

"Give it to him," Homer said quickly. "There ain't nothin' on that stage worth gettin' killed over. Even if he does decide to rob us."

The guard shuffled his feet nervously, then cleared his throat and held out the short-barreled eight-gauge to the gang leader.

"Smart man," Dolven said, grabbing onto the shotgun. "I wish Bull Grossman had been smart enough to kill Asa Cain without gettin' shot himself. I promised him he could have Jenny Cain if he took care of the matter. He was really looking forward to that. She is one pretty woman, but I'm getting powerful tired of her whining and complaining."

Homer Penbrook forced himself to keep a thin

smile. "We heard tell about the Dolven gang kid-nappin' that bounty hunter's ma an' little sister. I reckon that story ain't been made up."

"Kidnapped!" Brock Dolven shouted. "That's a damn lie. Sadie, Cain's sister, is the one who had the idea in the first place and invited *us*. She's real happy married to my boy, Link. Her ma ain't real content with how things are goin', but the young lady understands as soon as Asa's dead, her ma's gonna have to be killed. Sadie says it will be worth it to avenge what her brother done to my family."

Penbrook's leathery features paled. "Asa Cain's *sister* plotted with you to burn the family ranch, kill the hired help, and kidnap her own mother? I never heard of such a thing in all my born days!"

"Link's mighty convincing when he needs to be. That Sadie was really lonely. A little good loving was all that girl needed to persuade her to help us draw Asa Cain out so we could kill him for plug-gin' my boy, Slim, and taking his body in for a bounty. Then"—a vestige of a grin crossed the out-law's face—"that Sadie done started liking killing and being on the owlhoot. Damn, that girl's turned more vicious than a panther."

Jedediah Green sighed and stared square into the emotionless gray eyes of Brock Dolven. "And now that you've told us this, I expect you will kill us. I only ask you to allow me time to say a prayer."

"You're right about the killin' part. Wrong about me lettin' you yammer out a pile of religious nonsense." Brock Dolven whipped down the shot-gun, cocked the hammers, and fired both barrels into the reverend's chest, nearly blowing him in two.

"Don't kill me!" Thorn Hackberry yelled, backing away with his hands held palm out. "I ain't never gonna say nothin' about this to no one."

"Oh, I'm sure of that," Brock said calmly.

Focused on the terrified station owner, the outlaw failed to notice that the lid on the wooden trunk on the back of the stagecoach had cracked open a few inches. Cemetery John poked the twin barrels of his shotgun through the slot and pointed them at the side of Brock Dolven's head, which was only a scant dozen feet away.

Perhaps it was intuition that warned the gang leader. In the blink of an eye, he spun toward the stagecoach, drawing his guns at the same time.

Cemetery John had been expecting this. His shotgun spat fire, sending Brock Dolven flying back in a spray of crimson. The last act the outlaw did on this earth was to pull the triggers on his Colts. The bullets slammed harmlessly into the dusty street.

"Damn!" Cemetery John swore as he flung open the lid and jumped to the ground. "I don't reckon any of us figured on that son of a bitch bein' so quick to start shooting folks." He shook his head at the bloody remains of Jedediah Green. "I'm sure sorry about letting this happen."

Homer said, "There weren't no way anybody could've predicted what just happened. It's darn plain that those Dolvens ain't plannin' to leave anybody in Hackberry alive. Asa said they'd likely do somethin' like this, an' hope it'd be blamed on Indians. But Lord Almighty, just to kill good folks in cold blood's terrible."

Cemetery John motioned to the long low building with a weathered saloon sign over the front door. Before he could say anything, the lone front window blew open with the blast of a gun.

Thorn Hackberry gave out a yelp and grabbed at his left arm. "I've been hit!"

"Head for cover," Cemetery John hollered. He threw up the ten-gauge and fired the remaining shell of buckshot at the saloon as he dashed for the shelter of the stage station. A hail of rifle fire followed him and Homer Penbrook as they lunged through the door. To their amazement, Thorn Hackberry was not with them.

"That fool's dead," Cemetery John said when through the open door he saw the big man standing in the middle of the road, his hand clasped to a bloody arm. Thorn Hackberry stood still as a stone statue, except for blinking tears from his eyes and making mewing sounds like a small hurt kitten.

"He's gone into shock," Homer said. "Some folks you wouldn't believe will go plumb idiotic an' freeze up at the wrong time. Looks like Thorn's joined 'em in pickin' a bad time."

A rifle barked, and Thorn Hackberry's right ear exploded. Bright blood glistened in the sunlight as rivulets of crimson began streaming down his face and beard. Yet the huge man stood immobile, bawling now like a baby.

Raucous laughter came from the saloon. One of the voices belonged to a girl, a happy girl. "Come on, Link." She giggled. "Let me try a shot."

"I don't believe this." Cemetery John was incredulous. "That bunch in there's so drunked up they don't even know Brock's been killed."

Homer shuffled around to get a better look.

"That outlaw's layin' next to the boardwalk. If they weren't watchin' when it happened, there's no way anyone in there can see the body. I'd venture Brock shootin' folks ain't likely to draw quick attention from the likes of them."

An instant later, a slug of hot lead ripped a bloody gash alongside Thorn's chest. The big man did not seem to even notice.

"Thorn Hackberry," Homer yelled. "Get your carcass in here where it's safe. I'd reckon you'll get killed if you keep lettin' outlaws use you for target practice."

Cemetery John stared out the door and shook his head. "It ain't gonna work. That fellow's gonna stand right there until he's got more holes in him than a screen door."

"No, he's not," Homer Penbrook grabbed up a Winchester rifle that was leaning against a wall. He jacked the lever to assure himself it was loaded. "I've often thought I'd enjoy shootin' Hackberry. Now that it's come down to it, I don't feel very cheerful."

"Hold off a spell," Cemetery John said with a sigh. "We've got to give Asa and Emil time to sneak up from behind 'em like we'd planned. That damn Brock Dolven was just more bloodthirsty and quicker on the trigger than anyone had thought. Thorn Hackberry's drawing their attention and their fire. Those killers are plumb enjoying this."

Homer Penbrook lowered the hammer on the Winchester. "Reckon it don't matter whose slug kills him, but I've got another fret that just chilled my innards."

"What's that?"

"Asa Cain and Emil. They don't know that girl Sadie's out to kill them. If they make the mistake of trusting her for one second, they're dead."

"I've thought about that," Cemetery John said sadly. "I just don't know a single thing we can do to stop it from happening."

THIRTY-FOUR

"It sounds like all hell has busted loose up there." Asa Cain's voice was tight with tension. "I told Cemetery John to wait until we fired the first shots, damn it!"

"That shoot-out was probably started by the Dolvens, not Cemetery. You are always saying how much that gang likes killing folks. It shouldn't be unreasonable to think they might've started the fracas." Emil pursed his lips. "I only hope the hides getting perforated up there are the right ones."

Asa and the marshal were hunkered down in a low arroyo, about three hundred feet behind the town of Hackberry. Aside from a few spindly mesquite trees, the entire distance from their position to the long, low building that Emil knew to be the saloon was barren of any type of cover.

"Blasted goats," Emil growled. "I don't know why anyone with good sense would have 'em around. Those stinking things have eaten the whole area clean as a plague of locusts would."

"If anyone in that saloon is keeping an eye this way," Asa said through pinched lips, "we'll get cut down before we're halfway there. This isn't good."

He glanced at the high sun. "I knew we should have waited for nightfall."

Emil sighed. "Let's not get a burr under our blanket. The shootin' seems to have stopped. A little patience might save a goodly quantity of our skin."

Asa had started to answer when the crack of a rifle caused the words to wedge in his throat.

"Dag nab it, Asa, I wisht we could see who's shootin' at who without getting plugged in the process."

"If we go poking our heads up and charge the place, we'll likely be dead before we get an answer to that question."

Emil Quackenbush cocked his head in amazement. "Do you hear what I do?"

Asa was barely able to stop a gasp of surprise. Rafting on the wind was the giggling laughter of a girl, obviously enjoying herself immensely. "My God," he said, his voice strained and hollow like an echo from an empty tomb. "That's Sadie! I'd know that laugh of hers anywhere."

The marshal placed a heavy hand on Asa's shoulder and drew him lower. "If she's as happy as she sounds, there's no reason for us to provide the Dolvens with a couple of targets. I say we stay put and try to figger out what in the blue blazes is going on up there."

Asa breathed deeply a few times. "Okay, Emil. I know we can't do anything to help if we get ourselves shot. But let's figure out how to get into that building damn quickly."

"It is a puzzlement—" The marshal grew silent when, inside the saloon, someone began playing a piano. The rousing church melody of *"Rescue the*

Perishing" seemed a strange choice given the situation.

Cemetery John shrugged his shoulders. "Those drunken owlhoots ain't figured out that Brock's already in hell. They're making a party outta shooting that loco Thorn Hackberry to pieces."

"I've never knowed anyone gettin' killed to piano music before," Homer commented. "This might start a trend."

"C'mon, Link, honey." It was the girl's voice in the saloon again. "Take a try at his other ear. I'm betting you'll miss."

"Damn," Cemetery John said, looking out the door to where the trembling, bawling station keeper stood bloody in the dusty street. "That woman's got an icicle where her heart oughtta be. I've never seen the like."

A rifle boomed. Thorn Hackberry flew back and fell with a cloud of dust. The bullet had entered his eye. The fat man lay sprawled in the dirt, kicking his remaining seconds away.

"Oh, you've done gone and killed him, lover." Sadie's voice was mocking. "I wanted to do that." There was a moment of silence. "It's all right, Mama. You can quit playing now. The game's over."

The piano music faltered and grew silent, leaving only the sound of wind whistling around crude plank buildings and carrying away the acrid smell of burnt gunpowder.

Another voice bellowed over the batwing doors of the saloon. This time it was the coarse shout of a man. "Hey, Pa. C'mon in an' have another drink with us. We got the stage driver an' some nigger pinned down in the station house. We can kill 'em later on. They ain't going no place."

Cemetery John bristled. He kept low, shuffling on his hands and knees to the side of the doorway.

"Don't go do nothin' foolish," Homer hissed. "Getting riled is what they want you to do."

Cemetery John breathed deep, then turned to the driver. "Asa's had all the time he needs. That man's got a reputation for being the best bounty hunter in Texas. I'm gonna find out if he really is."

"Don't do noth—"

Homer was cut off when the undertaker shouted. "He ain't gonna answer, you drunken son of a bitch. This here buck nigger took time away from sayin' lawdy, lawdy an' keepin' my po' knees from knockin' to put a load of buckshot square in your pappy's ear. You'll see him again right soon—in hell."

A barrage of bullets began slamming through the clapboard siding, smashing windows and sending splinters flying.

Cemetery John dove behind the shelter of a thick counter that held a huge brass cash register, to join Homer Penbrook, who was already flat on the floor.

"My, but you do have a tendency to get easily upset," Homer said. "I reckon you never heard before that sayin' about sticks an' stones might break your bones, but words'll never hurt you. I venture that if Asa and Emil was plannin' on sneaking up on 'em from behind, this would be a grand time for 'em to do it. I'd say you done

went and got their full attention focused on killin'
us."

"Yep." Cemetery John was showered with broken glass and bits of flying cash register. "That's
what I thought would likely happen."

"Next time, give a little consideration to the
nice folks with you."

"I'll do that—if there *is* a next time."

"Sounds like a damn war going on up there,"
Emil said. "One minute they're playing a piano
and having a grand time. Then, before a body gets
settled down, they're shooting the whole town full
of holes. I simply can't figure what's happening.
But I *do* have a suspicion that Cemetery John is
behind it."

"I thought *you* were the rash one." Asa raised
up his head to study the cloud of white gun smoke
drifting skyward from the front of the saloon. "If
Cemetery John is trying to get their attention, I'd
say he's doing a bang-up job of it."

"We really should go help those chaps out.
They're liable to run out of ammo at the rate
they're burning it up."

The marshal came to his knees and focused on
the rear of the saloon. "There's a window on each
side of the door. I wonder if they were smart
enough to have locked it."

"I'm betting they didn't, but let's each head for
a window. Perhaps we can see what's going on before charging in the back door."

"Well . . ." Emil's red eyebrows drew together
as he said with a rasp of eagerness, "I don't reckon
either of us was planning on dying in bed."

The marshal bolted up and took off running in a zigzag manner toward the saloon, with Asa following a few scant feet behind.

Emil hunkered under the west window; Asa took position beneath the east. Not a single bullet had been fired at them. The shooting from the front of the building continued, but at a dwindling pace.

The marshal ventured a peek through the window. His eyes widened as he stood erect to gawk. After a moment, he dropped and rushed over to Asa.

"That's a storeroom," Emil panted. "But I can safely say we don't need to worry about the innocent folks of Hackberry."

"Why's that?"

"They're all likely in that room. I counted about eight or nine. Most had their throats cut. The Dolvens might've used an ax on a couple from the looks of things. They're a thrifty bunch, to conserve ammo like that. Also, knives don't make noise to upset folks who they don't want to know what's going on."

Asa clucked his tongue. "It ends for them right here. I'm going to kill those bastards for everything they've done to me and a lot of good people."

Emil motioned to the window above their heads. "Let's venture a look-see. It'd be a shame to accidentally hurt your family."

The duo moved into position on each side of the window. Keeping tight against the rough sawn boards, they slid upward then rolled their faces to the edge of the glass.

This window opened into the main part of the

building. They saw two slender men occasionally firing their rifles from the front window toward the stage station. Asa winced when a lovely young girl with blond hair laughed happily, grabbed a gun from one of the men, and fired at the depot until it was empty.

Along one wall, another lady sat at a piano staring at sheet music, ignoring the constant firing.

"What do you make of that girl shooting like she is?" Emil asked in a low voice.

"I can't explain it. But I sure as hell can tell you that's my sister, Sadie. My mother is at the piano. I'm sure she's the one we heard playing earlier. We've got to get them out of there."

"I count two gunmen. They look kinda young, so I'd reckon them to be Link and Nolan Dolven. What I want to know is, where the hell's Brock?"

Asa readied the Henry rifle he carried. "If you see him, kill him. Let's go!"

Emil was mildly surprised when the doorknob turned easily in his hand. He flung the door open, only to have Asa dash through ahead of him.

In less than a second, Asa had sent a slug of lead into the middle of Nolan Dolven's back. The outlaw was blown nearly through the window to drape over the sill. Asa jacked the lever and watched as Link Dolven spun to meet him with a snarl and a cocked Winchester in his hands.

Asa had years of practice with his Henry rifle, and Link Dolven was obviously drunk. Before the outlaw could take aim, the bounty hunter had leveled the Henry square at Link's forehead and pulled the trigger.

The back of the outlaw's head exploded in a spray of blood. He was slammed against the wall to slowly slide down it, leaving a stream of gore in his wake.

A stunned silence claimed the inside of the saloon. In less than a heartbeat two desperadoes had been stilled for all time. Asa jacked a fresh cartridge into the magazine, and joined the marshal in scanning for Brock Dolven or anyone who appeared to be a threat.

Emil Quackenbush nodded to Sadie, who was standing by the open window, the radiant sunlight accenting her face, which was a mask of rage and hate. "Don't worry, li'l lady, you're safe now. We've killed those bad men."

Sadie spun toward Asa, fixing him with a gaze of pure fury. Her ice-blue eyes sparkled with the cold fire of malevolence. "You bastard, Asa, you've killed the man I love. I never could have a life because of you." Sadie reached down and grabbed the Winchester from Link Dolven's bloody hands. "Now I'm going to enjoy killing *you.*"

Asa froze, dumbstruck at the turn of events. Slowly, Emil Quackenbush grasped the situation, but eternal seconds too late for him to swing the big shotgun he carried around in time to save Asa's life.

A deafening explosion shook the small building. Sadie Cain was slammed against the wall by a charge of buckshot to her chest. She looked about for a fleeting moment with pain-filled, uncomprehending eyes. Then, with a small groan, she collapsed to drape across the bloody corpse of her dead lover.

Asa's heart fell to the pit of his stomach when he saw his mother holding a smoking shotgun. He could not understand why he had not noticed the gun beforehand, nor seen his mother stand and grab it.

"Mom," Asa said, his voice breaking. "I'm so sorry."

Emil scanned for danger, but saw nothing. He swallowed, stepped over, and took the shotgun from Jenny Cain's hands. She did not resist, nor did her emotionless blue eyes move to acknowledge his presence.

"I'll put this away, ma'am," the marshal said calmly. "I don't think we'll have much need for it now." He edged to the window and hollered, "Cemetery John, are you fellows all right, and where's Brock Dolven?"

"Dolven's dead by the boardwalk," Cemetery John answered. "The reverend got himself killed by Brock. Homer and me's dodged enough lead to sink a ship, but we're fine. Is everyone okay in there?"

Emil Quackenbush took a long look at Jenny Cain. The lady had not moved an inch since he had taken the gun from her. He noticed sadly her once-lovely face, that was now a portrait of utter defeat. It was the portrait of a strong woman who had seen and suffered far too much. The only place left for her to retreat to had been a hiding place inside her own mind.

The marshal glanced down at the bleeding bodies of Sadie and the man she had called her husband. Then he looked at Asa, who stood staring uncomprehendingly at his mother. The bounty hunter's lower lip was trembling.

"We're alive, Cemetery John," the marshal shouted. "I can at least say we're alive."

THIRTY-FIVE

By late morning of the next day, the dead who would remain in Hackberry for all time had been interred in a shallow mass grave behind the saloon. There would be no marker. Of the nine bodies buried there, only Thorn Hackberry's name was known with any degree of certainty. Cemetery John commented that it would be an insult to put just one name on a marker, and carving took a lot of time, so to be fair, no headboard was inscribed.

Brock Dolven, along with his two sons, Link and Nolan, were draped and tied securely over horses. The reverend Jedediah Green resided in a pine coffin on top of the stagecoach. Homer Penbrook was of the belief the preacher had some kinfolk in Buffalo Gap, and insisted on taking his body at least that far. The fact that an unused coffin was found in the general store made the task an easy one.

Sadie Cain lay wrapped in wagon canvas scant feet from where she had fallen. No one, it seemed, wanted to ask the distraught bounty hunter what to do with his sister's body.

From a barn beside the livery a buggy had been

found, brought out, and harnessed. Jenny Cain sat beneath the shade of the black fringed top, staring complacently across the prairie. She had yet to utter a single word.

Emil Quackenbush came onto the porch of the saloon to join Cemetery John, who was smoking a cigar and watching Asa pack a few things onto the buggy.

"That whore and Homer are getting along in grand style," the marshal said. "Both of 'em can drink a quart of whiskey before noon."

Cemetery John nodded in agreement. "Yesterday, when we left her under that mesquite tree with a bottle, she was carryin' on a real intelligent conversation with a cactus when I came back to get her. I'd venture that any man who supplies her with liquor will have a faithful friend."

"Well, they're both working hard not to leave any whiskey behind for someone who don't appreciate it as much as they do."

Cemetery John took a long puff on his cigar and blew a smoke ring into the hot breeze. "That's a mighty terrible shame about Asa's ma having to kill his sister. I'd never have figured on any woman becoming evil enough to do what that Sadie went and done."

"I reckon Asa's not in tolerable better shape than his poor ma. That lady's not said a single word. I wonder if she'll ever get her mind back."

"I don't know." Cemetery John flicked ashes from his cigar. "Having to shoot her own daughter to save her son's life is a choice not too many women ever have to make, thank God. Something like that would be hard to get over. Damn hard."

The pair grew silent when Asa tossed his saddlebags into the back of the buggy and began walking toward them.

"It's going to be a mighty hot day," Asa said casually.

"Yep," Emil agreed. "Not a cloud in the sky."

Asa pulled a cigar from his pocket and was a long while lighting it. He took a puff and motioned toward his mother. "Governor Davis will have the law hang her if I take her to Wolf Springs. I doubt anything any of us would say or do could change that fact. I know in my heart Mom thought she was saving Sadie's life when she went along with the Dolvens. The problem is, there's no way to prove any of that." He glanced to the shattered window of the saloon. "Especially now."

"Where are you taking her?" Emil asked.

"There's a hospital in New York City I've read about. They have an alienist on staff there who has done remarkable things with victims of violence. Perhaps, in time, she can recover."

"Why an alienist?" Cemetery John asked. "Ain't an American doctor good enough?"

Asa's expression remained stoic. "In medicine the term alienist is used to describe a doctor who works with disorders of the mind. The belief is that mentally ill people become 'alienated' from their real selves. I only hope they can help my mother."

"Amen to that," Emil said. "She's been through hell."

Cemetery John cleared his throat. He wanted to present Asa with an idea he had, but wasn't sure how to begin. Finally he decided to simply come out with it. "There's a way to make the governor happy and keep the law from looking for your mother."

Asa cocked his head. "What are you talking about?"

"That sister of yours who started all this trouble can end it. We can take her back to Wolf Springs along with the Dolvens. She already looks a lot like your mother. After a few days draped over a horse in this heat, no one could ever tell the difference. Governor Davis pays out the bounty for her and the case is closed. The bad part of this is your ma'll never be able to come home."

Asa turned to watch a hawk sailing high in the cloudless azure sky. After a long while he said, "I hadn't thought of that. But it's a plan I can't see an alternative to. I can't risk losing my mother." He looked around at Cemetery John. "Thank you—" His voice trailed off.

"No problem, Asa. I'll tell Wilburn that you needed to take some time off. I reckon we also oughtta say that the Dolvens killed Sadie early on. There's no one but us that'll know any different. After all that's happened, nobody'll question you being gone for a spell."

"I can't take that reward money," Asa said, eyeing the hawk again.

"Ain't nobody going to want it," Cemetery John said. "But it's gotta be paid."

Marshal Quackenbush shook his head. "Damn, that would be a hard bounty. Killing a woman's something no man would want to own up to."

Asa didn't hesitate. "Tell Wilburn I shot her. If I keep being a bounty hunter the reputation won't damage me any. There's damn few outlaws who'd want to go up against a man who would kill his own mother."

"I'd reckon that's a fact," Emil said. "But we still need to know what to do with that reward."

"Tell Soak Malone to start keeping a jar under the counter of the Rara Avis." Asa's voice was firming with determination. "Cemetery, I want you to keep adding money to it until that bounty's spent. Fridley Newlin and a lot of busted up old cowboys can't afford a hot meal or a few drinks. See that it's done so at least some good will come out of all this pain."

"Yes, sir," Cemetery John said. "You can count on that happening. I reckon I'll dole it out slow, or Ole Fridley won't live past a hundred drinks."

Asa gave a heavyhearted look to the saloon window. "I think it's best if I take my mother away from this place right away. I don't want her to watch—"

"You get on your way," Cemetery John said. "And see to taking care of your mother. Emil and I will take care of what has to be done."

Asa blinked away some dirt from his eyes, climbed aboard the buggy, and sat alongside his mother. Without looking back, he flicked the reins and drove away.

Cemetery John and Emil Quakenbush stood in silence as the small buggy leading a horse became but a black dot against the wavering tawny grass of the Staked Plains.

"Life's mighty hard on a woman in Texas," Emil commented.

Cemetery John placed a hand on the marshal's shoulder. "And it's fairly rough on horses, dogs, and men too. Let's get to doing what we have to do. There's no reason to stay around here."

"Yeah," Emil said. "Anyplace is better than here."

After a while, Asa reached to the back of the jostling buggy and grabbed up a saddlebag. He knew full well it would take a lot of both medicine and luck to heal his mother's broken soul.

And there were more types of medicine than those practiced by learned doctors in the East.

Asa Cain reached inside the leather bag, grasped his trophy, and held it high against the fiery sun. Aloud, he shouted a prayer to the Great Spirit for his mother's swift recovery.

Sometimes the gods answered sacrifices swiftly, other times more slowly. For a magnificent sacrifice such as the one he held, perhaps even the great *Wakan* would take note and answer his fervent pleading.

His sacrifice was an honorable one. When he reached a river he would toss it into the flowing water and send it on its way to the Spirit World.

The greasy black scalp with a blaze of white through it glistened against the sunlight. Asa thought he could actually feel the medicine inside it. He only hoped there was enough to heal all of the wounds.

The prayers said, he replaced Lame Bear's scalp in the saddlebag and flicked the reins, heading east toward New York.

Western Adventures
From Pinnacle

Western Adventures
From F.M. Parker

William W. Johnstone
The *Mountain Man* Series

Call toll free **1-888-345-BOOK** to order by phone or use this coupon to order by mail.

Name_____

Address_____

City_____ State_____ Zip_____

Please send me the books that I checked above.

I am enclosing $_____

Plus postage and handling* $_____

Sales tax (in NY, TN, and DC) $_____

Total amount enclosed $_____

*Add $2.50 for the first book and $.50 for each additional book.

Send check or money order (no cash or CODs) to: **Kensington Publishing Corp., Dept. C.O., 850 Third Avenue, 16th Floor, New York, NY 10022**

Prices and numbers subject to change without notice.

All orders subject to availability.

Visit our website at **www.kensingtonbooks.com.**

Complete Your Collection
William W. Johnstone
The *Mountain Man* Series